Changeling Press, LLC

ChangelingPress.com

Owned by the Mob Duet
A Dixie Reapers Bad Boys Romance

Harley Wylde & Paige Warren

Owned by the Mob Duet
A Dixie Reapers Bad Boys Romance
Harley Wylde & Paige Warren

ISBN: 978-1-60521-849-6

Publisher:
Changeling Press LLC
315 N. Centre St.
Martinsburg, WV 25404
ChangelingPress.com

Printed in the U.S.A.

Editor: Crystal Esau
Cover Artist: Bryan Keller

The individual stories in this anthology have been previously released in E-Book format.

Table of Contents

Dedication

For all those who have suffered, who have waited in darkness, too scared to hope they might see the light again…

You are not alone.

Collateral Damage (Owned by the Mob 1)
Harley Wylde & Paige Warren

Cerys: Blind since birth, I've learned the hard way I can't rely on my father. When he gets in too deep with the wrong sort of people, I find myself the property of Viktor. I've heard whispers of the Mob and what they're capable of and know I should be terrified. It doesn't take much for me to fall for Viktor, seeing a side of him he seems to show only to me. His kisses make my knees weak, and just one touch makes me dream of forever. He makes me feel… special. Precious. Important. But what would a man like him want with collateral damage? He can have any woman he wants, and probably has. I don't see a happily-ever-after in our future, no matter how much I might want one.

Viktor: Death and destruction cling to me, blood and violence just a way of life. I didn't climb my way toward the top of the Bratva by being a saint. I may be gruff and dangerous, take what I want when I want, but when it comes to Cerys, I find that I can't be harsh with her. She's gentle. Sweet. An angel. My *myshka*. She's the light to my darkness. Now that I have her, I know that I can't let her go. I'll make her mine in every way possible. Only one problem. Artur Orlov. He wants me to marry his daughter, but I won't. I didn't count on him retaliating by taking my *myshka* from me. I'll get her back, and if she's been harmed in any way, I won't stop until every last man responsible has breathed their last.

Chapter One

Cerys

I could hear my heart thundering in my ears as I strained to listen to my father's conversation. The men had forced their way into our home, and I'd heard the crash of furniture. At first, I'd been terrified because I'd thought we were being robbed. Now I knew different. I'd known my father was in trouble, but I didn't realize how much. Money had been tight for a while, since Mom died several years ago. Things had been getting better, or so I'd thought. I never realized the reason we suddenly had money, or rather my father suddenly did, was because of some shady dealings he'd had with the wrong men. He'd claimed he'd been working, and I thought things were going well. Had he lied to me? Why did he always have to control me? Everything he did seemed to be designed for the express purpose of keeping me under his rule, and miserable.

"Please, Maksim. I just need more time," my father begged.

I didn't know a Maksim. The Russian accent of the men in our living room sent a shiver down my spine. In our neighborhood, the only Russians I knew were an elderly couple, or people who belonged to the mafia. I'd heard it called the Bratva, but it meant the same thing. The men sequestered with my father did horrible, evil things. Every last one of them had blood on their hands. I could only imagine what they'd ask of him, or the ultimatum they would give.

"You've had time," said a deep voice I assumed belonged to Maksim.

"You don't understand. I've moved as much product as I can, but I don't have enough connections. I can get them! I just need... a month? Yes, give me another month."

"*Nyet.*"

I heard the rustle of clothing and it sounded like something was being screwed onto something. I strained, needing to know what was happening. The door I hid behind was cracked open a bit, but it didn't do my sightless eyes a bit of good. I'd relied on my other senses from birth, but sometimes it wasn't enough.

"Nikolai, tie up the loose ends," the man said.

No! I knew what that meant. I now understood the sound I'd heard. A silencer. At least, that's what they were called in books and movies. They were going to shoot my father. Kill him. He might not be the best dad, but he was all I had. What would happen to me if he were gone? I shoved the door open and stumbled into the room.

"Don't!" I fell to my knees and pushed myself up, but I'd lost my bearings and as I stood, I stretched my arms out, feeling for any furniture or people. I didn't know how the room had changed after they'd barged in and started throwing things around. "Please. Don't kill him."

"And who is this?" Maksim asked.

"My daughter. Cerys. Don't hurt her. She's blind and can't recognize any of you. I beg of you. Let her go," my father said.

Now he was going to act like a loving parent? Maybe we should have invited these men over sooner. Not that they'd received an invitation now.

A hand grasped mine, rough and large. I was pulled against a firm chest and a tantalizing scent teased my nose. I couldn't help but lean in a little closer. It was stupid, and maybe the stress of the situation was skewing my logic, but I used my hands to explore the body holding me, inching up toward the man's face. My fingers scraped across a close-cropped beard and up to a strong nose. I didn't feel wrinkles, only firm smooth skin. I couldn't guess his age, other than he was likely under forty and over twenty.

"Who are you?" I asked.

The man gently grasped my hand and pulled it away from his face. I felt an odd sense of loss. Again, I wasn't reacting like a normal person. Not that I'd ever been considered normal, but this was out of the ordinary even for me.

"Viktor, you seem intrigued by the young woman," Maksim said. "Perhaps we can make a deal, Mr. Humes? Your daughter in exchange for the debt you owe."

"What!" I heard my father struggling. "No! You can't do this! Cerys is blind. Please, don't hurt her."

I wanted to snort and roll my eyes. The man had never given a damn whether or not I was hurt. He'd actually enjoyed moving pieces of furniture on occasion just to watch me trip over them. Then the bastard would laugh. I'd had to learn how to fend for myself after my mother died. If it weren't for the elderly couple down the street, I'd have never gotten as far in school as I did. After my mother died, Mrs. Popov had ensured that I continued with my education. I'd been a few months from graduating, when my father pulled me from school completely. Somehow, he'd gotten forms signed saying I was dropping out of the homeschool program, and out of school all together. He'd heard me tell Mrs. Popov about my excitement over graduation, and had decided to ruin it like everything else in my life.

The fact he was acting like a loving, concerned parent, made me wonder exactly what he was up to because I knew he'd never loved me. Not since he'd discovered I was blind. He wanted them to think I was important to him, and in a way, I was. Without me, the house would be completely trashed and he'd probably starve to death. The man would certainly never go fetch his own beer, that was for damn sure.

"Who said anything about hurting her?" Maksim said. "I doubt very much that Viktor plans to cause her any harm. In fact, he'll likely have her screaming in pleasure."

The men chuckled and the breath froze in my lungs. He couldn't mean what I thought he did. The man holding me tightened his grip around my waist and I felt the evidence of his arousal. My cheeks warmed and I stared at what I assumed was his chest. I'd never been with a man, never been kissed. Truthfully, I'd thought I would die a virgin, alone.

"She's barely eighteen!" I heard my father struggling again, and assumed they were holding him back.

I knew the only reason he was trying to talk them out of it was due to the fact he'd lose his servant. Me. Even though I couldn't see, I'd learned how to keep our home clean, and I managed to cook microwave meals. Each box was marked in a way that I knew what it was, and my father had me memorize the heat settings and cook time for each one. The lazy bastard couldn't even be bothered to pop a frozen lasagna in the microwave.

"Barely?" Maksim asked.

"Yes. She just turned eighteen two days ago. She's a child, Maksim!"

I felt someone run their hands down the length of my hair, then squeeze my ass. From the direction, I knew it wasn't Viktor. I squeaked and pressed closer to the man holding me. Someone laughed before harshly grabbing my breast. I whimpered and my hands fisted on the material of Viktor's shirt.

"Enough, Feliks." I could feel the rumble under my fingers and knew Viktor had spoken. His voice was deep and rich with a hint of roughness. "Touch her again and I'll remove your hands."

"You'll tire of her. Then I'll have a turn. We all will." The man laughed. I assumed it was Feliks and a shiver raked my spine. Was that my fate if I went with them? To be their whore?

"You can't do this," my father said. "Surely, you can't condone this, Maksim. You have daughters. What if someone took one of them?"

"I always pay my debts," Maksim said. "And no one would dare come for my family, unless they wanted to die. I'm sorry, Mr. Humes, but my terms are simple. Either you give your daughter to Viktor, or I'm afraid we'll have to use you as an example to others who owe us."

Someone laughed. "And then we'll take your daughter anyway."

Viktor's arm tightened around me again until I worried I wouldn't be able to breathe. I felt his body shift, then his lips brushed my ear.

"Do not fear, *myshka*."

Was he crazy? Of course, I was scared! I was terrified! They were threatening to kill my father, then... I shuddered. If those men got their hands on me, especially the one who had grabbed my ass, I had no doubt that I'd be brutalized repeatedly for their enjoyment. *Oh, God! I'm going to be sick!*

I shoved at Viktor and broke free just enough to turn and lose what little food I'd eaten earlier. I fell to my knees, tears leaking from my eyes as I heaved again. I hated that I cried whenever I got sick. As if puking my guts up wasn't humiliating enough.

"Maksim, control Feliks or I will," Viktor said. "There's no need to terrify the girl."

"She's all I have," my father begged. "Don't hurt her. She's innocent in all this. She didn't even know what I was doing."

Again with his lies. Oh, not about my lack of knowledge when it came to his dirty dealings. But all he had? He had never given a shit about me, and I knew he didn't now. All he cared about was having to take care of this place himself. If I was taken, he'd find a way to lure someone else here with some sob story. I almost felt sorry for whatever woman fell into his trap.

"Viktor will take good care of her," Maksim said. "I'd suggest you straighten up, Mr. Humes. Selling drugs and guns doesn't seem to be a good fit for you. Find a nice, safe job. One that doesn't end up with a gun to your head."

"Cerys."

"It's okay, Daddy." I swallowed hard, trying not to throw up again. Not over the loss of my scumbag father, but over the unknown fate that faced me now. "I'll go with Viktor."

"No, Cerys. It's too dangerous."

A spark of anger filled me. "Then you should have thought of that before you decided to break the law! We would have managed. Stop acting like you actually care. You've never cared!"

Hands gripped me and lifted. Before I could utter a word of protest, I was carried out of the only home I'd ever known. Viktor's scent washed over me, and I knew he was the one who had picked me up. For whatever reason, I felt like I was better off with him than my sperm donor. The man had never been a father to me, not in the true sense. I'd been more of a slave than a child.

"Your father cannot harm you anymore, *myshka*. I'll keep you safe," Viktor said.

At what price? Had the other man been right? Would Viktor tire of me and pass me on to someone else? Would I be little more than a whore now? This wasn't how I'd seen my life going. I'd been blind since birth and had led a solitary life. Other than my parents and a few neighbors, I didn't really know anyone. My mother had permitted me to attend school, but after her death. Mrs. Popov homeschooled me. They'd sheltered me as much as they could, but I had to wonder if they hadn't really been doing me a favor. Now I faced the unknown, and I wasn't the least bit prepared. I'd never really thought about what it would be like to leave my home, to live somewhere other than the only place I'd been my entire life.

Viktor held onto me even as he ducked down and sat in what I assumed was some sort of vehicle. Then I heard a door slam. He caressed my side with his hand and pressed a kiss to my temple. I didn't know why he was being so nice, or so gentle. Weren't members of Bratva known for their brutality? I'd heard horror stories around the neighborhood of what happened to young women who went out alone at night. Picked up by Maksim or his men, and never heard from again.

"What will happen to him?" I asked.

"He's been given a second chance. What he does with it is up to him."

"And... me?"

"You now belong to me, *myshka*. Do as I say and we'll get along fine."

Do as he said. I was too scared to ask exactly

what that would entail. I could still feel the proof of his arousal pressing against me. I wasn't stupid. I knew what happened between men and women. Theoretically anyway. I couldn't exactly watch porn, or read about sex except for the few romances I'd found in Braille. And who knew if any of that was factual? The audiobooks at the library didn't cover things like sex education, and there was a limited supply of Braille books at our local branch. None of them taught what to do when you found yourself in the midst of the Bratva. Not that my father had permitted trips to the library. Once my schooling ended, that had been taken from me too.

"My things. I don't have my clothes or shoes," I pointed out.

"Not to worry, *myshka*. I'll handle it."

Three more doors opened and shut, and then we started moving. I felt a breeze across my face and frowned.

"Did someone just wave a hand in front of my face? Or is the window open?" I asked.

"You really can't see?" someone asked.

"No, I really can't see. I've never been able to see. I was born this way." Why would I fake being blind?

"Then how did you know I put my hand in front of your face?" the man demanded, his tone suggesting I was lying.

"I felt the shift in the air," I said. "I'm blind. Not stupid."

Viktor laughed softly. "Leave her alone, Aleksi."

"We'll drop you off first, Viktor, so you can get your woman settled into her new home."

I sat quietly, trying to process everything. Home. I was going to Viktor's home, which meant he planned for me to live with him. Was he married? Would his wife be angry that he was bringing another woman into her house? No one had packed my things. What was I supposed to wear? He'd said he'd handle it, but what did that mean? I didn't even have a toothbrush, and I could really use one right now.

"Something wrong, *myshka*?" Viktor asked. He rubbed between my eyes. "You have a fierce look right now."

"I need a mint."

I heard some rustling, and then something was pressed into my hand. I lifted it to my nose and smelled spearmint. I popped it into my mouth, and hoped I hadn't just poisoned myself. It wasn't wise to eat something a stranger had given me, especially *these* strangers, but I couldn't stand the yucky taste in my mouth another moment. Not to mention my breath had to be grossing out Viktor and anyone else close enough to smell it.

"If you need anything for your new pet, get Ilya to pick it up for you. I wouldn't leave her alone just yet, until she knows what's expected."

I thought the voice belonged to Maksim, but I wasn't certain. I did know that I didn't like being called a pet. I was a woman, a human being, and I had rights and feelings. They were treating me like something they'd purchased at a store. Did things like this really happen? Weren't there laws in place to prevent something like this? I knew the police avoided my neighborhood, but had anyone seen these men carry me off? Would anyone care?

"Mrs. Popov," I murmured.

"What's what, *myshka*?" Viktor asked.

"Mrs. Popov will be worried if she discovers I'm gone. She knows what my father is like."

"Who is Mrs. Popov?" the man I believed was

Maksim asked.

"Mrs. and Mr. Popov live down the street. She homeschooled me after my mother died. Until my father made sure I wouldn't graduate."

"Look into it," the man told someone. "Assure them Cerys Humes will be taken care of and will come to no harm."

"I'll handle it." I thought that was Aleksi, the one who had waved his hand in front of my face. I hoped I would eventually be able to match the voices to the names with some amount of certainty. Assuming I was around that long. I still didn't know what Viktor planned to do with me.

The vehicle came to a stop and I heard the door nearest me open. Viktor gripped me tightly as he exited the car and I felt him step up onto the sidewalk. The car door slammed shut and I heard it pull away. Before Viktor could move, I reached up and placed my fingers on his jaw.

"What's it look like? Do you live in a house or an apartment?" I asked.

"I have the penthouse in a forty-story building of condominiums. There's a doorman, but I also have a private elevator that will only work with a certain code. Only my Bratva family have that code. You will be safe in my home, *myshka*."

"You keep calling me that, but I don't know what it means."

"It's a term of endearment in my country."

"Russia?"

"Yes. It means little mouse. My first impression of you was of someone small but fierce, regardless of the fear she felt. You were like a mouse, taunting a room full of cats, except without your sight you honestly didn't know what you were facing."

"Are all of you so very scary?" I asked.

"You would be wise to fear us."

"Even you?"

He growled softly and began moving. "Especially me, *myshka*. Especially me."

I didn't know what to make of that. Had I left one nightmare only to jump straight into another? Viktor seemed kind, or at least nicer than my father had ever been to me. Was it all a ploy? Maksim said I belonged to Viktor now. I didn't understand what was happening, or what was expected of me. Viktor had told me to obey him and all would be well. I only hoped he didn't ask me to do something I'd want to refuse. What would my punishment be in the hands of the Bratva? Would I survive? Or would I even want to?

It was quiet as we entered the building, but Viktor murmured something to someone. The doorman? I'd never felt sorry for myself for being blind, but there had never been a time I'd wished I could see more so than right now. I hated not knowing where I was, who I was with, where I was going. While my father had been cruel, at least I'd known what to expect from him. My stomach dropped and I felt a lurch. My grip on Viktor tightened.

"It's just the elevator, *myshka*. We'll be in your new home soon."

"Wh-where will I stay?" I licked my lips. "Will your wife be angry you're bringing me home?"

He snorted. "Not married, *myshka*. But if I were, she wouldn't have a say in the matter."

Right. So, he was no better than my father. I wondered how long before he insisted that I cook and clean for him. Would he be angry when he realized I'd never used an oven? I hoped he'd give me time to adjust to my surroundings before he demanded too much of me. Then again, I'd be lucky if that was all he asked. It hadn't escaped my notice he'd been hard the entire ride here. I might be a virgin, but I wasn't stupid.

"Why do you not have one of those canes? Or a dog?" he asked. "They're to assist people like you, aren't they?"

People like me? I wanted to take offense, but I couldn't. I understood what he meant. Someone blind was at a disadvantage without either of those items, at least in a strange place.

"My father got angry and broke my cane. There wasn't money for another."

"And the dog?"

"Too expensive. I'll be fine once I learn my way around your home. It might take me a little while to memorize the layout." I hesitated, not wanting the next part to sound like I was issuing a demand, which meant choosing my words wisely. "If you move the furniture, I'll have to relearn that particular room. Sometimes my father would move something just to watch me trip and fall."

Viktor growled, but before he could speak, the elevator came to a stop. There was a soft ding, and then the doors slid open with a soft *whoosh*. Viktor stepped out and I heard his shoes click against a hard floor. I couldn't tell from the sound if it was wood or tile. If he lived in a penthouse, depending on the location of the building, it could very well have marble floors for all I knew. I'd never lived in a place like this, or even visited. Even when my mother had been alive, we hadn't exactly been well off. We'd struggled a bit, but we'd been happy. Or at least I had been happy.

When Viktor released me, I wobbled a moment. He pressed down my shoulders and I sat, giving a sigh of relief when I realized there was a chair behind me. The cushions were soft as I sank down. I ran my hand over the seat. It felt like leather, but not the tough kind we'd had in our house. I had a feeling the piece of furniture under me cost more than everything inside my home.

"You never said where I'm staying," I reminded him. "And I won't have a change of clothes. It wouldn't have been any trouble to get my things."

"If they're like the clothing you have on now, I'm sure they're little more than rags."

I swallowed hard and bit my lip. It wasn't my fault I hadn't had money for nice things. I didn't even know if what I had on matched. My father had made sure everything I owned was monotone, but I didn't know for sure. It wouldn't surprise me if he'd dressed me in neon colors.

"*Myshka*, do you even know what you're wearing?" he asked.

"No."

He ran his hand down my leg and a shiver went through me from the heat of his touch. "These leggings are so thin I can see the color of your panties."

I gasped and pulled away, suddenly self-conscious. How could my father do that to me? How many times had I worn these out somewhere? Had the entire neighborhood seen my panties?

"Your shirt is see-through." He trailed his fingers across my collarbone. "And your bra is lace. There is little left to the imagination, *myshka*. Who purchased your clothing?"

"My father. He assured me everything would match regardless of what I picked out from my closet. I..." My cheeks flamed hot. "I didn't know. I've been out in these clothes. Men have seen me, I..."

I didn't understand why no one had told me, not even the Popovs. It made me wonder if my father had threatened them in some way. It seemed like the nasty sort of thing he'd do.

He cupped my cheek. "Easy. We'll get you proper clothes. No one will see so much of you ever again." I felt him lean in closer, the scent of him wrapping around me. "Except me, *myshka*. I plan to see all of you."

And that answered the question of exactly what I'd be doing here. Little more than a whore. Should I tell him I was a virgin? Would it matter to him? Was that the only reason he had for bringing me here?

I felt the rasp of his beard against my cheek a moment before his lips brushed mine. I tensed and wanted to run, but didn't know where to go. He reached up and cupped the back of my head, holding me still as he deepened the kiss. My first. He was the only man to ever place his lips against mine. And now I was terrified for a different reason... because I enjoyed his kiss a little too much. His tongue stroked mine, and I tried to mimic him. Could he tell I'd never done this before?

"Relax, Cerys. I demand your obedience in all things, but I won't be cruel to you."

Obedience. I was good at obeying. It was all I'd ever done.

"Give yourself to me, *myshka*."

"I'm scared, Viktor," I admitted.

"No one will harm you. Not while you're mine. I don't share. If I find out you've entertained another man, your punishment will be severe. But for as long as you're faithful and remain by my side, I will protect you."

Cheating on him had never crossed my mind.

Since I'd never been with a man before, I didn't think I'd be tempted by anyone else. And if I remained in his home, who exactly would I see? Well, figuratively speaking, since my entire world was nothing but darkness.

But if I was going to give myself to him, I needed some assurances. Did I need to worry about him giving me some sort of disease?

"What is it, *myshka*?" He rubbed a finger between my eyes. "You'll get frown lines if you worry so much."

"What if you give me something? If you're with other women, then --"

He pressed a finger to my lips. "As long as you're in my bed, I will not be with another woman. I haven't been intimate with anyone since the last time I was tested. I'm clean, *myshka*. Can you say the same?"

I nodded, knowing I was clean since I'd never slept with anyone. Something told me that was about to change.

Chapter Two

Viktor

The woman on my lap intrigued me. She was beautiful. Not stunning, or the type of gorgeous you see in magazines, and yet I couldn't look away. The moment I'd held her in my arms, I'd known that I wouldn't leave that house without her. Not only did a man like Eddie Humes not deserve a daughter as sweet as Cerys, but I refused to let him continue to abuse her. The way she'd snapped at him, and what little she'd said, was proof enough that Mr. Humes was a rotten man.

I'd killed, and I didn't feel the least bit sorry for my victims. It was all done by order of the Vor. I'd been born into the Bratva, had worked my way up the ranks when I'd become old enough, and had made a place for myself toward the top. Very little made me feel much of anything. I enjoyed the release of being with a woman, but I'd never wanted to hold onto one and not let go. Until now.

Cerys was unlike anyone I'd ever met. My little mouse. Her skin felt like silk as I stroked a hand down her arm. She didn't look a bit like her father, and it seemed she hadn't inherited his evil heart. She could prove me wrong. Just because she didn't have her sight didn't make her any less dangerous. In fact, she was more so. Who would ever suspect someone like Cerys of being deadly? I could see her swaying people to her side with those pretty eyes, lulling them into a false sense of security.

"Come, *myshka*. Time for bed," I said, lifting her and rising to my feet.

She clung to me and I carried her through the penthouse to the master suite. I'd considered giving her a room of her own, but the more I thought about it, the more I liked the idea of her in my bed. Not just when I wanted her, but all the time. If she truly was as sweet as she seemed, I had a feeling I'd want to keep her close. Perhaps some of her goodness would temper the monster I kept locked inside.

I eased her down next to the bed, then went to close the door. Several men had access to my home, and I was selfish enough not to want any of them to see Cerys, especially since I intended for her to be naked, or damn close to it. When I turned to face her again, she was fidgeting, her hands worrying at the hem of her shirt and her weight shifting foot to foot.

"What's wrong, *myshka*?"

"Why am I here? What's my purpose?" She licked her lips and looked away, her voice dropping to a near whisper. "Am I your whore now?"

My gut clenched at that word. I'd used whores before, and the Bratva owned several brothels, but Cerys wasn't a whore. She was… mine. My property in the eyes of the Bratva, but I didn't just want the use of her body. I desired her, and I planned to have her as often as I wanted, but there was something about her that called to me, made me want to protect her.

"You're not a whore, but if that's your way of asking if I plan to fuck you, the answer is yes. I thought I'd made that clear already."

She flinched a little.

"Would the idea repulse you less if you could see me?" I asked.

"I'm not repulsed by you, Viktor. I just don't know you." Her cheeks warmed. "I may not be able to see, but I could feel the muscles in your chest and arms. I felt the scruff on your jaw and know you have a beard. And since I didn't feel wrinkles, I'm assuming you're not all that old."

Perhaps she'd only ever had lovers she'd dated. No one-night stands for my sweet *myshka*. Despite the fact she seemed sheltered, the fact she knew her neighbors, even those farther down the street, and had attended school proved that she'd had ample opportunity to date boys. She'd mentioned being homeschooled at some point, but had that been before she was old enough to be interested in dating? As for the other, I was amazed she'd picked up that much just from touch.

"I'm twenty-eight, my hair is brown, and my eyes are gray. And yes, I'm in shape because I work out. What else do you want to know?"

She felt behind her, found the edge of the mattress, and sat. "What's your last name?"

"Petrov. Before you ask, my parents are no longer living. I grew up among the Bratva. My father was one of their soldiers, and after the death of both parents, I bounced from home to home. When I was old enough, I started doing jobs here and there for the Vor."

"Vor?" she asked.

"The head of the Bratva."

She nodded. "What do you do besides work?"

I ran my hand along my jaw and sighed. This wasn't the way I'd seen my night going. I'd expected her to be naked and begging by now. Instead, we were playing twenty questions, with me doing all the answering. However, if it set her at ease, then perhaps it would be worth it. I'd never taken an unwilling woman, and I didn't want to start now. Especially with this woman.

"I read, and I enjoy dancing."

"Dancing?"

"My mother taught me ballroom dancing when I was a little boy. After her death, I gave it up. Occasionally, I like to go out somewhere and dance. It reminds me of her. I'm not sure why she taught it to me. Maybe she was lonely, or perhaps it was her way of sharing a special moment. I'll never know."

I'd never shared that with anyone before, and I wasn't certain why I was doing so now. Cerys was my property, a pawn in the grand scheme of things, and nothing else. What did it matter if she liked me? I knew I could have her screaming my name within minutes, just like all the others I'd been with before. Yet, something held me back. I wanted her trust, and more than that, I wanted her respect. Not from fear, or because I could give her multiple orgasms. I'd never had a woman want to be with me just for me. For once, I wondered what that would be like. Other women had flocked to me for my looks or power. With Cerys, I knew if she came to like me, it wouldn't be for some bullshit reason. She seemed more real and down to earth than the other women in my past.

"I learned to read Braille when I was in school, but my father said we didn't have money for books at home. The city library had some, but I didn't have a way to get there after my mother died," she said. "My father wouldn't permit Mrs. Popov to take me."

"What types of books do you enjoy?" I asked, thinking that it wouldn't hurt to find a few for her. It would help pass the time when she was here alone.

"Paranormal books," she said. "I know werewolves and vampires aren't real, but I enjoy reading stories about them."

I pulled out my phone and sent a message to Ilya in hopes he could find a few books and have them delivered to my door by morning. I asked my *myshka* what size clothes and shoes she wore, but she wasn't certain. I checked the labels in the items she was wearing and sent a request for a few items of clothing as well as a decent pair of shoes. Ilya would no doubt hate searching for the items, but I knew he'd rise to the occasion.

I let my *myshka* talk a bit more, but her unease didn't seem to abate. There was only one way I knew to proceed. Slowly, I removed my shoes and clothing. When the buckle of my belt clinked as it hit the hardwood floor, she tensed and her eyes went wide.

"W-what are you doing?" she asked, her sightless eyes scanning the room.

"Getting ready for bed, *myshka*. You should as well."

If at all possible, she paled even more. I wondered about her fear over being intimate with me. Had her previous lovers hurt her?

"Perhaps a shower first?" I asked.

She nodded emphatically and stood so fast she almost toppled over. I smiled, realizing that she had no idea I would be joining her. Instead, I led her into the bathroom, started the water for her, then walked to the door, letting it close loudly. Not moving or daring to even breathe hard, I watched as her shoulders sagged. There was still a frightened look in her eyes, and it was obvious that I terrified her, but she seemed a little less scared than before. I'd lived on the fear I instilled in people for years, but with her I didn't like it. I didn't want her to be afraid of me.

Her hands were shaking as she removed her clothes, and I had to fight damn hard not to give away my presence just yet. My gaze skimmed over her body, taking in her curves, as well as the bruises along her abdomen, ribs, and back. Had her father done this to her? She stepped under the spray, and I contemplating leaving her to shower alone. Then the tears started. She sobbed quietly, but as she curled in on herself, I knew I had to do something.

I stepped into the shower and reached for her. My *myshka* didn't scream, and much to my surprise, she actually came into my arms willingly. Stroking her back, I murmured softly to her, hoping to ease her sorrow and fears. It had to be a big change for her, coming here after living with her family all her life.

"I'll keep you safe, *myshka*. Who hurt you? Where did the bruises come from?" I asked.

"My f-father. He sometimes gets angry with me."

He was a dead man. I didn't care if Maksim had given the man a pass or not. I wouldn't tolerate him abusing the sweet woman in my arms. He'd had something precious, a daughter, one who no doubt would have loved him if given the chance, and he'd thrown her away like garbage.

I tipped her head up, then slowly lowered mine and pressed my lips to hers. She stiffened a moment before melting against me.

"I will never hurt you, *myshka*. You're mine and I protect what's mine. That isn't to say you won't be punished if you disobey me, but I will never bruise your tender skin. Not on purpose." At least, I didn't have the intention of doing that. I'd need to keep myself in check with my *myshka*. She was a sweet girl, not like the women I'd been with previously.

She took a shuddering breath and I kissed her again, this time prolonging it a little. As she softened toward me even more, I knew that she would give me anything I wanted, just like the others had. Deepening the kiss, I backed her against the marbled wall. The press of her curves made me even harder. Gripping her thigh, I lifted it over my hip, then reached for the other side until I had her legs wrapped around my waist. The head of my cock slid through her slick folds. As my lips devoured hers, I reached between us to rub her clit, loving the little moans and soft sounds she made. I could feel her getting hotter and wetter. Her nipples were hard little points and I pinched one, eliciting a cry from my sweet *myshka*.

"Already so wet for me," I murmured, then drove deep and hard into her tight sheath. Too tight I realized a moment later as she cried out in pain.

I stared down into her eyes and realized why she'd been so nervous and scared.

"Why didn't you tell me?" I demanded. "Did you think me such a monster that I wouldn't have taken better care if I'd known you were a virgin?"

"I didn't think it would matter. You were going to take me regardless. I just…" She took a sharp breath as I withdrew, then slowly eased back inside her. "I didn't realize it would hurt so much."

"I would have prepared you better, *myshka*, if I'd known. I didn't want to hurt you. When I'm inside you, I only want you to feel pleasure."

I kissed her softly as I slowly stroked in and out of her. Soon, she began to relax again, and her soft whimpers changed from signs of her pain to pleasure. I tried to hold back, wanting it to be good for her, especially since I'd already fucked things up. A woman shouldn't look back on her first time with regret. Reaching between our bodies, I rubbed her clit. It only took a few swipes before she was coming, her pussy milking me dry. I grunted as I slammed into her three more times, filling her with my cum.

It was only after that I realized what I'd just done.

"You were innocent." The ramifications of that sank into my sex-addled brain. "You're not on birth control, are you?"

She shook her head, looking scared once more.

I cupped her cheek. "Easy, *myshka*. I should have asked before I came inside you bare. I only asked if you were clean, which you were, and you told me the truth of that. Once I was inside your tight little pussy, I was too far gone to think about such things as birth control."

"It takes more than once, right?" she asked.

I hesitated. No, it really didn't, and more than that, I liked the idea of her swollen with my child. I wasn't getting younger, and being a family man could actually help with my position in the Bratva, help me rise further. Suddenly, I wanted to take her over and over, filling her with my cum until she carried my child. And it wasn't just to increase my power and position in the Bratva. I truly wanted to see her belly round, my child secure in her womb, wanted to raise a family with her. Her innocence drew me in, and knowing I was the only man to ever take her? It made me feel possessive of my *myshka*. There was just one small issue. Artur Orlov. Or more accurately, the fact the man expected me to marry his spoiled daughter, Tania. I'd not so much agreed as I just hadn't disagreed. It could pose a problem.

"Viktor? It's all right, isn't it?" Cerys asked softly. "W-what happens if I'm pregnant?"

"Then we have a baby, *myshka*."

I eased from her body, not missing the wince on her face. I helped her wash, then cleaned myself off quickly. Stepping out onto the bathmat, I reached for the two fluffy towels hanging nearby and wrapped one around my waist before drying off Cerys. I lifted her into my arms and carried her back to the bedroom, then settled her on the bed, drawing the sheet over her. I could tell that being naked bothered her, and while I wanted to look at her curves as much as possible, I didn't want things to become more awkward between us right now.

There would be time later to show her what I liked and expected of her. Having her shy away from my touch wouldn't expedite things. I needed her to be comfortable here, with me. Cerys wasn't like the other women I'd had. They'd known the score, knew to give in to my demands, and how to suck a cock. My little *myshka* was far too innocent for all that.

I finished drying myself before I slipped under the sheet and pulled her against my chest. She came willingly, even curled against me trustingly. It warmed my heart, a heart I hadn't even realized I still had. The Bratva had done their best to burn the humanity out of me, making me a killing machine, taking orders without question. But for my *myshka*, I had a feeling I just might be willing to buck the authority I'd followed all my life.

Sleep never came for me, though she slumbered in my arms. As the sun began peeking through the window, I rose from bed and quickly showered and dressed, putting on a crisp suit so I could get my day going. Looking outside my front door, I saw the bags on the ground and pulled them in the penthouse. One contained four Braille books, which I placed on the coffee table. The other held two outfits, two stretchy bras, and a package of plain panties. They weren't anywhere near good enough for Cerys, but they would do for now. I'd take her shopping when I concluded my business today.

I carried the clothing into the bedroom and set it

on top of the dresser, making sure the outfits would match regardless of which shirt or pants she selected. Never again would she wear something sheer out in public, or anything that didn't match. I'd never permit that to happen. Enough people had laughed at her, or stared at her body without her even knowing it. Which reminded me about the first errand I needed to handle this morning.

Brushing Cerys' hair back from her face, I kissed her cheek. "Morning, *myshka*."

Her eyes slowly opened. "Morning."

"You have clothing on the dresser and it will match regardless of which pieces you decide to wear. There are books in the living room on the table in front of the sofa. My kitchen is rather bare at the moment, but I will have breakfast delivered within a half hour and lunch a few hours later. There's bottled water in the refrigerator door and a carton of juice on the shelf. The glasses are in the cabinet to the right of the sink."

"You're leaving?" she asked, sitting up and clutching the sheet to her chest.

"Yes, Cerys. I have business to conduct this morning, but I'll be home as soon as I'm able. Until then, try to amuse yourself. No one will enter my quarters without permission. You're safe, *myshka*." I caressed her cheek before kissing her. Her tongue timidly stroked mine and it took everything I had to pull away and not get back into the bed with her. "I'll see you soon. There's a landline. The bar that separates the kitchen from the rest of the suite has a portable phone against the wall. If you pick it up and press one, it will call the downstairs main desk." I hesitated, wondering if she'd know where the one was located. "Press the top left button. Call them if you need something and they'll get in touch with me. I'll let them know about your presence in my home."

She chewed her lower lip and I reached out to tug it free of her teeth.

"Will you be in danger?" she asked. "On your errands."

I fought a smile. No one had ever cared if I would be in danger. It was… pleasant. I could get used to coming home to her, having someone waiting.

"No, *myshka*. Many have tried to kill me over the years and none have succeeded. I'll return to you."

She nodded and I pressed a kiss to her forehead before leaving, before I was too tempted to stay. Checking to make sure I had everything I needed, I took the elevator to the bottom floor and stopped at the main desk. Speaking briefly to the security staff on duty, I let them know about Cerys and her condition, with the express orders to call me should she need anything. I also made sure that only those I trusted the most would be permitted upstairs. The last thing I wanted was for someone to scare her, or think they could take liberties, like Feliks. Until I could get the elevator code changed, I'd need to take extra measures for my *myshka* to stay safe.

The doorman arranged for my car to be pulled to the front of the building, then I decided to pay a little visit to Eddie Humes. I sent a message to Maksim to let him know my whereabouts and then ignored his call. I knew he'd try to talk me out of it, but he hadn't seen the marks on her body, or heard everything she'd shared with me. There was no way I would let the man get away with the abuse he'd put his daughter through. Now that she was mine, that meant she was mine to protect, and I would exact vengeance on any who had harmed her.

At the Humes residence, I didn't bother

knocking, just kicked in the door and marched inside. Eddie was sprawled in a chair, half dressed, a mostly empty bottle of cheap liquor dangling from his fingers. He didn't flinch at my presence, didn't show any signs that he was apprehensive as to why I would be here.

"Bringing her back?" he asked, sneering a little. "Now that you've sampled the goods, I'll need to be compensated of course. Probably should have put her to use before now. Bet she'd have brought in a pretty penny. Enjoy that tight little cunt of hers?"

His words only built the fury inside me. It was boiling over, flowing like lava through my veins. He'd signed his death sentence when he'd hurt Cerys, but now, hearing the vile words spilling from his mouth, it only made me want to hurt him more. The fact he could prostitute his daughter sickened me. Yes, the Bratva owned brothels, but if I ever had a daughter, she would be sacred and treated like a fucking princess. This sorry excuse for a man didn't deserve to keep breathing.

I removed my jacket, draping it over a wood-backed chair, then slipped the brass knuckles from my pocket and slid them over my fingers. Eddie watched, but didn't utter another word. Everything that came out of his mouth would likely just enrage me further. Not that I planned to hold back. I wanted to make him bleed. To cry. To beg. I wanted him to be afraid, like his daughter was afraid when he attacked her. Cerys was mine now, and I protected what belonged to me.

"Your daughter has bruises covering her body. Some were new, some were old. Her clothes were see-through, which she didn't realize, allowing anyone to see her nipples and the color of her panties. She told me what you've done to her over the years since her mother died," I said.

He waved a hand. "Ramblings of a blind woman. You really going to believe some stupid cunt you don't know over me? Was she that good of a fuck?"

"Yes, I do believe her over you." I hauled my arm back and punched him as hard as I could, hearing his cheekbone shatter on impact. I'd never enjoyed my job as much as right then. Hearing his bones break, feeling the skin give under my fists, made my pulse race. Smiling, I whaled on him, breaking every bone I could, and making his blood soak into the disgusting carpet. Despite his show of bravery, I could see the fear in his eyes, the knowledge that I could easily take his life.

My hands were slick with his blood as I pounded on him some more. Ribs, stomach, his face. Anything I could reach, I tried to break. I wanted him in agony.

"Stop! Please." Blood bubbled from his lips and I could hear the rattle in his lungs. I'd likely punctured one with a broken rib, but it still wasn't enough. "I'll do anything…"

"You tormented her. Humiliated her. Treated her like unwanted trash." I landed three more blows, not wanting to stop until he was dead. "She's mine now. She'll be protected, and treated like something precious."

When I was finished, there wasn't much left of Eddie Humes, nothing recognizable at any rate. He was still breathing -- for now. I'd done my best to break every single one of his ribs, and I'd shattered most of the bones in his face. He was in pain, probably more than he'd ever felt before. I only wished I could let him heal for a few days, then start again.

"You don't deserve a daughter like Cerys. You'll never hurt her again," I said, spitting on him. "I'll let you live, but leave this town and don't come back. I see you anywhere near her, hear that you've contacted her, and I'll finish what I started. Are we clear?"

He nodded and groaned as he lay on the floor bleeding.

He disgusted me. I unzipped my pants and pissed on his face, hoping he felt even half as degraded as Cerys had when I'd told her about her clothing. The look in her eyes the moment she'd realized men had been staring at her body for years wasn't one I would forget anytime soon. I tucked my dick away, zipped up, and went to the kitchen to wash his blood from my hands.

I began searching for anything Cerys might need, like her social security card or birth certificate. I doubted she had any other identification since she couldn't drive and hadn't been in school recently. I found the documents I wanted, as well as a purse in what looked to be her room. I opened the wallet and saw that she had a picture ID that I hoped would suffice if she needed to prove her identity to anyone, even though it looked like something someone had made at home. Something Mrs. Popov had arranged perhaps?

On my way out, I picked up my jacket and held it away from the blood covering me. I kept a change of shirts in my car for such occasions and pulled one from the trunk, then changed quickly before driving away from the house. I'd worn black pants so any blood spatter wouldn't show. Using a towel in the trunk, I rubbed off a few drops on my shoes. No one on the street so much as looked at me despite the blood spatter, and I knew that the police wouldn't be called. Not only were they not welcome in this part of town, but I was well-known and there wasn't a single man or woman in this neighborhood who would dare call the police and report my actions. Not unless they wanted the full weight of the Bratva to come down on them, their families, and anyone else they cared about.

A glance at the time told me I'd been busy far longer than I'd thought and I hadn't had a chance to call in food for Cerys. Before I could reach for the phone, Maksim's name lit up on my phone as I pulled away. I answered, knowing he would be pissed that I'd gone against his orders. Not that he'd so much said that Humes was free and clear of the Bratva, but it had been implied that he was getting a second chance. Until I'd learned all that I had last night.

I wasn't afraid of Maksim. We both knew his time in power was limited. He wasn't the true ruler of this area, and while I mostly deferred to him right now, there were some things I needed to handle my way.

"What the fuck are you doing?" Maksim asked.

"Getting vengeance for Cerys. Humes is still alive. For now. Not sure if he'll remain that way without some medical attention."

Maksim was quiet a moment. "This girl is different, isn't she? You've never wanted to keep one in your home before, and I could tell you were taken with her right away. And I damn sure haven't seen you lose it and want to beat the shit out of someone for hurting a woman."

"She's… different," I agreed. "I'm not letting her go, Maksim. She's mine. I know Feliks thinks I'll tire of her and he'll have a chance to hurt her, but I won't let it happen."

Maksim cursed in Russian before sighing heavily. "This is going to be a problem with Artur, and you know it."

I was worried about the same thing. When Artur

wanted something, he generally got it. The fact I had a woman in my house wouldn't go over well. Especially since I had no plans to get rid of Cerys.

"I never made him any promises, or his daughter."

"But she changes things, doesn't she? This girl. You won't put her to the side and marry Tania like you should. Tania was raised in the Bratva and won't care if you're faithful. You could still keep the girl elsewhere."

"*Nyet*. Cerys belongs in my home, in my bed, and that's where she's staying." I paused and thought about the situation. I might not know why Cerys seemed important to me, why I felt the need to hold onto her, but I couldn't deny that I wanted her as more than a side piece. Knowing I'd been her first had changed things. I'd wanted her before that, but now... she was mine. And only mine. "Cerys wouldn't be the other woman. Tania would be, and my *myshka* doesn't deserve that."

"I'll see what I can do about Artur, but this may not end the way you want," Maksim warned. "Asking him to take a step back could backfire. I hope you're ready for that."

"It's going to end with Cerys right where she belongs and Tania far the fuck away from me. There isn't a damn thing Artur could say that would change my mind."

The line was silent for over a minute. I checked but the call was still connected.

"Maksim?"

"I'm here. But if you're serious about keeping this Cerys by your side, and you want to avoid any possibility of having to marry Tania, then there's only one way this can go."

"And what's that?" I asked.

"You'll have to marry Cerys."

Oddly, the thought didn't bother me. Marriage in my world was usually a power play. You married someone who could help advance your position, had a few kids, and found pleasure on the side. With Cerys, it would merely give me a stronger ownership of her and I'd have all the pleasure I wanted at home. I'd never been faithful to a woman in my life, but something told me if anyone could change that, it would be Cerys. As long as she was in my bed, I didn't see me wanting another woman. I'd promised her I wouldn't be with anyone else as long as we were together. If I married her, then that would mean being faithful indefinitely.

"I'll make the arrangements. Something quick seems to be the best option," I said.

"Take your woman to Las Vegas. You haven't had a day off for as long as I can remember. You could be married as early as tonight. I'll have the jet waiting for you in two hours."

"Thank you, Maksim. It will give me enough time to take Cerys shopping before we go to the airport."

When I reached the penthouse, I was assured that Cerys hadn't called down for anything. I hoped that meant she was handling her new life well. I took the elevator up and let myself into my suite. The absence of sound had never bothered me, but knowing that Cerys should be inside somewhere had all my instincts screaming that something was wrong. Pulling the gun from my holster, I checked room by room, stopping when I found Cerys still in the bed, curled up sleeping.

I sank onto the mattress next to her and ran my

fingers through her hair. Cerys murmured in her sleep and snuggled farther into the pillow. It was obvious she was exhausted and I had to wonder if this was her first day off since her mom had died. If her father had been as cruel as she'd said, and I'd seen the proof, then I didn't doubt that he'd tried to get as much out of her as he could.

"*Myshka*, it's time to get up."

I trailed my fingers across her cheek and she began to stir. Slowly, her eyes opened and she stiffened, her body tensing and her pulse fluttering in her throat.

"Easy, Cerys. It's just me. I need you to wake up so we can prepare for a trip."

"Trip?" she asked. "I've never been anywhere before. Where are we going?"

"Las Vegas." I curled my hand around hers and tugged her upright. "We're going to get married there. Tonight."

Her lips parted and she sucked in a breath before drawing away from me and leaning against the headboard. I could tell my words were unexpected, and I knew I needed to clarify the situation. I didn't need her thinking I'd fallen in love with her, or that this was some sort of fairy tale.

"There's a man who wishes me to marry his daughter. Maksim is concerned that Artur might force the situation, unless I'm already married. Since I refuse to give you up, he suggested a trip to Vegas for us to be married."

"Marry you?" she asked.

My jaw tightened at what I was sure was about to be a refusal. She didn't realize this wasn't a request. She would go to Las Vegas and she would marry me. It wasn't negotiable.

"Yes, *myshka*. I know you don't have anything to pack, but you can wear one of your new outfits. We'll stop by a few stores before heading to the airport and pick up enough to last you a few days, then we can buy more when we return. As my wife, you'll be expected to dress a certain way."

If possible, her back became even more rigid, and I wondered if she was about to start a fight between us. Not that it mattered. She'd do as I said, or I'd show her what happened when she disobeyed.

"I'm not asking, *myshka*. You'll go with me to Vegas, and you'll marry me."

Her chin tipped down and her hair slid across her face, blocking her from my view.

"Because you own me," she said softly.

"Yes."

She gave a slight nod and swung her legs over the side of the bed. Without another word, she stood and went into the bathroom where she washed her face. I kept a stash of toothbrushes in the drawer and told her where to find them. She slid it open, felt around, then pulled one out. She opened the new toothbrush to clean her teeth. When she was finished, she went to the dresser and pulled on some clothes, then stood at the foot of the bed. Waiting.

"You have some new shoes. They'll do for now," I said, then pulled them from the sack and slipped them onto her feet. "I need only a moment to pack a bag, and then we'll leave."

She stood stiffly, no emotion on her face. It was almost like looking at a statue.

"I'll wait in the living room, unless you need my help."

"No, *myshka*. You may go into the other room."

She turned and walked out, and I had this

sinking feeling. Something was wrong. She was listening, doing as I said, but the spark inside her seemed to have faded. There wasn't time to worry over it. I quickly packed, then escorted her down to my car. Once we were in Vegas and she was legally my wife, then I'd figure out what was bothering her. Until then, I'd let her work through whatever it was, give her time to realize this was the best thing for her. As my wife, she'd be protected, not just by me but by Maksim and the others as well.

Chapter Three

Cerys

Getting to leave town should have been exciting. I'd never been anywhere before. Being told that I would marry Viktor because he owned me, however, put a damper on my excitement. If he'd asked me to marry him because he wanted to spend the rest of his life with me, then I'd have gladly said yes. Viktor didn't ask. He demanded, and it was the least romantic thing I'd ever heard, and I'd had some pretty vile things said behind my back plenty of times.

Buying new clothes hadn't been as fun as I'd thought it would be. Not that I'd ever shopped for my own things, but I'd dreamed of what it would be like. The shop was packed, the hum of voices and people constantly knocking into me annoying at the least. It sounded as if a dozen people or more were in here with us. If this experience would be the norm, I think I'd prefer buying stuff online or just letting Viktor pick out something for me. It seemed he would have control over my every move anyway. If it didn't matter what I wanted, then I didn't understand why I needed to be here.

"Mr. Petrov!" said an excited female voice. "It's so good to see you again."

Again? He'd told me this was a women's clothing store. Just how often did he buy clothes here? Even though he'd declared I would marry him, he hadn't said a word about being faithful during our marriage. Now that things had changed, I didn't know if he still intended to be with only me. I was starting to wonder just how many other women were in Viktor's life, and rethinking him not using a condom. If he refused to use one, I'd have to find a way to get tested often, just in case. I knew denying him wouldn't do me any good. The Viktor I was observing today was different from the man who had taken me from my father's house. No, I couldn't see him, but his words, tone of voice, and actions were different than before. He was harder, colder. I didn't like this one, and I didn't know if I could trust him.

"Mary, we need at least a week of casual clothes, two cocktail dresses, two formal dresses, and all the underthings, shoes, and purses to match," Viktor said.

"Of course, Mr. Petrov," the woman said, and I could hear the simper in her voice. I tried not to sneer at her. She was fawning over a man who was clearly standing here with another woman, but as she flirted with Viktor I realized she didn't care. Or maybe she had no need to worry. Perhaps she already shared his bed.

"I don't feel well," I murmured.

I didn't wait for Viktor's permission, nor stay to discover if he'd even heard me. I walked away and managed to find the front door and step out onto the sidewalk. Leaning against the building, I focused on breathing. My stomach was churning and I seriously worried I might throw up. Maybe staying with my father would have been a better option, not that I'd been asked. Viktor had taken me as if I were no more than a possession. At least with my father, I knew exactly what to expect. He was nasty to me all the time. With Viktor, I felt off balance. One moment he was kind, and the next... the next he was cold and unfeeling.

I felt his presence before he gripped my arm.

"Never leave my side," he said, his voice low and deadly.

"I think I need to sit down," I said.

I pushed away from the wall, breaking from his hold, and my knees buckled. His arm went around my waist as he steadied me. My throat convulsed as I fought not to embarrass him further by throwing up all over the sidewalk. With a whimper, I broke free and rushed away from him, not knowing or caring where I was going. I could hear him advancing on me, his steps forceful and angry, but when I felt the edge of the building, I slipped around the corner before the contents of my stomach came up. Tears flooded my eyes, only making things worse.

His hand pressed against my back, his scent wrapping around me.

"I'm sorry," I said softly, wiping the moisture off my cheeks. "I didn't mean to embarrass you."

"*Myshka*, if you're sick, you need to tell me. Don't run off. You could have been hurt."

"I don't want to shop right now, Viktor. Could you just pick out some things for me and let me wait in the car?"

"Of course." I felt his arm slide around my waist, then he began leading me back in the direction we'd come. I heard the car door open and he helped me inside, leaning across to start the engine. I felt the breeze from the vents and took in a shaky breath. "I'll only be a few moments, *myshka*."

I tipped my head back and shut my eyes, wishing I could shut out my new life just as easily. I'd thought perhaps being Viktor's property would be better than being with my father, but I was starting to have my doubts. Anyone else might have been honored to be his wife, but I knew he wasn't marrying me for the right reasons, and it hurt.

True to his word, he returned what felt like five minutes later, opening and shutting the trunk. I assumed he'd purchased whatever he thought I needed, and then he slid into the car and I felt it pull back into traffic. The drive to the airport was quiet. Once we reached the airstrip, Viktor mentioned we were traveling on a private jet and led me to some stairs. I had a bit of trouble climbing them, the incline steep and my legs not so steady. Once I was seated and buckled, Viktor went back to ignoring me, speaking in Russian to whoever else was on board with us. He didn't even bother to introduce me to anyone, but then what had I expected? It wasn't like I was an important part of his life.

I pretended to sleep the entire flight to Las Vegas, not caring that I was hungry or thirsty. I just wanted to get the flight over with, as well as our farce of a wedding. The future was looking rather bleak, but I didn't fool myself into thinking I had a choice or any control over my fate. Thanks to my father, I belonged to Viktor, and I had a feeling that's how it would stay until I died or he grew tired of me.

"We're in Vegas, *myshka*," Viktor said near my ear. I lifted my head and stretched my arms over my head.

He unbuckled my lap belt and helped me stand, then assisted me down the steps to the ground below. To anyone else, he might seem like a caring man, worried over his fiancée. If only that were true. A driver greeted us, and Viktor helped me into the waiting car, then we were leaving the airport. I heard Viktor ask about procuring a marriage license, and my stomach started knotting again. I knew that I didn't have to say yes when the wedding officiant asked me to repeat the vows, but what would happen if I said no? Viktor didn't seem to be the type of man someone should cross.

Getting the license was simple enough with only an hour wait. While it was being prepared, Viktor took me to a hotel and got a suite for us, then had our things taken upstairs.

"*Myshka*, there's an errand I need to handle before we get married. Please stay in the suite and don't try to wander. I don't want you to get hurt or lost," he said, then brushed a kiss against my forehead before leaving.

Was this to be my life from now on? I wished I had a friend to call, someone to confide in. But I didn't. No friends, no family, no phone even if I did have either. It was just me, and as much as I hated what my life with Viktor might be like, I knew I didn't have anywhere else to go. I didn't own anything and had no way of earning money. My father had ensured that I wouldn't have options.

I didn't know how long I sat in silence, alone with only my thoughts for company. When the door opened again, I waited but didn't hear anything other than soft footsteps. My brow furrowed when something felt wrong. Viktor would have called out a greeting by now, wouldn't he? And the scent was wrong. Whoever had come in didn't smell like Viktor. Their cologne was stronger, and far more bitter.

"Who's there?" I called out.

Nothing. Silence. Total and complete silence. My unease intensified, but there was nothing I could do. Having never been here, I didn't know the layout of the suite much less the entire hotel. By bringing me here, then leaving immediately, Viktor had left me vulnerable. I could hear someone rummaging through the drawers in the other room, and I stayed still, my heart pounding and a chill seeping into me. If they didn't find what they wanted, would they hurt me?

"Please, just take whatever you want and go," I said.

Then wondered if that had been wise. What if they decided they wanted me? Would Viktor even search for me if I went missing? Would he care that I'd been abducted? Even worse, if he did care, I worried that he'd only be concerned that someone had dared to take his property. I was no more important to him than his gun or his clothes. Just a possession and nothing more.

Something cold and metal pressed against my temple and I gasped when I realized it was a gun.

"Not a word to anyone, bitch, or I'll be back. Heard you can't see, so I know you can't identify me, but I don't need anyone poking around and checking to see who accessed the room. This time I'm only leaving with the cash, but you say one thing to anyone and I'll take compensation out of your ass instead. Understood?"

I nodded frantically.

The gun was suddenly gone and I heard the whisper of his steps across the carpeted floor, then the door opening and closing. The moment all was quiet again, I broke. Sobs wracked my body as the tears flowed and I started shaking. Viktor found me that way a while later, not that I understood a word he said since it was in Russian. Then he switched to English and I couldn't help but laugh a little.

"I didn't realize being my wife would be so terrible for you," he muttered as he paced in front of me.

"Is that what you think?" I asked, wiping my face. "That I'm crying because you're forcing me to marry you? All men are the same."

I heard him stop and it seemed like the air

dropped a few degrees.

"What's what supposed to mean?" he demanded.

"Everything is always about you, isn't it? You wanted me, so you took me. You decided you'd marry me, so here we are. So, of course, if I'm crying, it must be over you." I took a shaky breath. "Go check our things. I believe something of yours is missing."

He stalked off only to return moments later.

"Where's the money, Cerys?"

"Do I look like I took your precious money?" I snarled and stood, nearly toppling back to the couch when my legs wouldn't hold me. "I didn't take a damn thing from you, Viktor. Maybe whoever broke in here should have taken me instead. Would that have been better? At least then you'd have your money. Women are easily replaceable, right?"

It was quiet again. Too quiet.

"What do you mean someone broke in?" he asked softly, his tone deadly.

"He said if I told anyone that he'd come back for me. He said…" I stopped and licked my lips, starting to wish I'd kept silent. "He said that if I told anyone he'd come back and take the compensation from my ass."

His arms went around me and he rested his cheek against the top of my head. "I'm sorry, *myshka*. I knew you were unhappy and thought you'd decided to get back at me. This suite is supposed to be safe. If I'd thought someone might come in and hurt you, I'd have never left you alone."

I noticed he didn't say that I wasn't replaceable.

"Is the marriage license ready?" I asked. Might as well face my fate head-on. Viktor had mentioned getting some of my things from my old house, including my fake ID. It must have been better than I'd realized because we hadn't had an issue applying for the license. Either that, or they just didn't look that closely in Las Vegas.

"Yes. I picked it up while I was out. I'll lay out a dress on the bed for you and change into a fresh suit, then we'll head to the nearest chapel. While you get ready, I'll deal with the hotel and their lack of security."

I nodded and held out my hands, trying to feel my way to the bedroom. Viktor grasped my hand and led the way, stopping and pressing my hand to what felt like the bed. There was some rustling and the bed slightly shifted, as if something had been set down on it. I moved my hand along the covers and felt the silky material of what I assumed was a dress, then found a bra and panties. My cheeks warmed, but Viktor had already seen me naked.

I heard him speaking to someone, but his voice was low enough I couldn't make out the words. The harshness of his tone made me think he'd called the hotel front desk to complain about the missing money. Would I have to speak with someone? The police? I didn't know how much was missing. I'd left out the part about the gun. Maybe I should have told him.

Removing my clothes, I listened as he ended his call and changed out of his suit. When I had the dress on, I realized I couldn't reach the zipper in back. The heat of Viktor's body pressed against me and he kissed my bare shoulder.

"You're beautiful, *myshka*. I'll be the envy of every man who sees you."

He zipped the dress, then placed his hands on my shoulders, just holding them there a moment. I felt the caress of his palms down my arms, then he moved away only to return. There was a *snick* like a box had opened, and then I felt the coolness of something around my throat.

"This necklace is the first of many beautiful things I intend to purchase for you, *myshka*. I thought something as special as our wedding deserved a gift."

I reached up and felt the piece of jewelry, my fingers running along what felt like a never-ending strand of stones. "Can you describe it to me?"

"It's a diamond choker, but the stones are cut and set in a floral pattern."

Diamonds. I should be thrilled. Instead, they were just as cold as my life was becoming. A loveless marriage. Nothing more than property. I felt another piece of my heart shatter.

"Thank you, Viktor. I'm sure it's stunning."

The whiskers on his chin rubbed against my cheek. "Only the best for my wife."

"I'm not your wife yet," I said.

"Then we should go remedy that." He kissed the side of my neck. "And then we'll celebrate by having a wedding dinner and a proper wedding night. I promise, no pain this time, *myshka*. Had I known you were an innocent, I'd have made sure you enjoyed it more, that you were prepared."

There wasn't much I could say to that. It had hurt, but he'd also made it better after he'd known. I'd hoped that next time would be even more pleasurable, and that maybe one day he'd come to care for me. But after only twenty-four hours with Viktor, I was starting to wonder if I'd been wrong about him from the start. I'd thought he was different from the others who had come to my father's home that night. Now I wasn't so sure.

We left the hotel and walked the short distance to

whatever chapel he'd found. I only half paid attention to what was happening, my thoughts focused on what this moment meant. I doubted that being married to Viktor would be anything like the books my mother and Mrs. Popov had read to me, where the families went on outings together, had quaint family holiday traditions, and everyone gave hugs freely. Being in his world was going to keep me in a cold, dark place, and I wasn't looking forward to it.

When he'd claimed me, I'd known he would tire of me eventually. I'd been scared of what would happen when that time came, but there'd been the slight chance I'd get to have a somewhat normal life in the future. Now that didn't seem as likely. I didn't know whether or not Viktor believed in divorce. Would he stay married to me, but live separately when he grew bored?

"Ready, *myshka*?" Viktor asked.

"Yes, Viktor."

He drew my hand through the crook of his arm and led me down what I assumed was the chapel aisle. The wedding was simple, and very fast. We said our vows, exchanged rings that I hadn't even realized Viktor had purchased, and then he kissed me. The way his lips pressed to mine it felt more like a promise, but a promise of what? For that brief moment, Viktor seemed warm and tender, his kiss sweet and soft. But I'd fallen for that version of him once already, and I wouldn't be tricked again.

The ring he'd placed on my finger felt heavy and was no doubt as ostentatious as the necklace felt. After Viktor's description of the choker he'd given me at the hotel, I was certain it had cost a small fortune. Probably more money than my family had ever had in my entire lifetime. It saddened me that my mother had lived in poverty, and that if she were alive now and I had met Viktor, perhaps he could have helped improved her life in some way. I'd have done anything for my mother, even live in a loveless marriage and pretend to be happy.

Viktor led me out of the chapel. His arm was around my waist as we walked down the busy sidewalk. I didn't know what time it was, but the heat was nearly too much to bear despite the fact I didn't feel the sun on my face, and the crowd was making me nervous. I'd never done well around large groups of people. It wouldn't take much for me to trip over someone, or for them to push me just hard enough I'd fall. I could smell food when we came to a stop and assumed it was the restaurant he'd mentioned. I heard the door open and Viktor escorted me inside.

"Mr. Petrov, your table is ready," said a woman with a sickly sweet voice.

"Thank you."

I bumped into a few chairs along the way, apologizing as I walked, but when we reached our table, Viktor pulled out a chair for me. He brushed a kiss against my cheek before taking his own seat, and while I wanted that kiss to be a real sign of affection, I worried it was all for show. Was this my life now? I felt cold inside, all the way down to my bones. All I'd ever dreamed about was having a happy life, maybe finding someone who would love me. Now it all seemed impossible.

There was a slight breeze and I heard something lightly land on the table in front of me. A menu most likely, not that I would be able to read it. My first time eating out wasn't going quite the way I'd hoped it might. I didn't even pay attention as the waitress flirted with Viktor, and gave her recommendations for the drinks and meals available. When she hinted that she'd be open to showing him around Vegas when she got off work, I nearly stood up and walked away, but I was worried I'd fall since I didn't know the layout. Instead, I dropped my gaze to where I assumed the table was and wished the night would just end.

"*Myshka*," Viktor said softly. "What's wrong?"

"Nothing." I forced a smile.

"Don't lie to me. I have very few rules I expect you to follow. Don't lie. Don't cheat. Don't disobey me. Now tell me what's bothering you. You've been acting differently since before we left home."

"It's nothing, Viktor. I know my place and what's expected of me."

I felt his fingers brush my hand, then he grasped mine. "Cerys, I can't promise you love because I don't remember ever feeling such an emotion. Just as I've asked you not to lie to me, I won't lie to you either. I may be incapable of ever loving someone. However, I plan to be faithful to you, and I will protect you, care for you. You're my wife now, *myshka*."

"You've never known love?" I asked softly, feeling horrified that even as a child he didn't know someone cared that much about him.

"I'm sure my parents loved me, in their way, but I don't remember much. No hugs or kisses from either of them. Neither of them showed their emotions well, unless it was anger. The bit of dancing I did with my mother was about the only time she focused on me."

I tightened my hand around his, knowing in that moment that I would find a way to show him the affection he'd missed out on all his life. It was sad that he'd never felt loved. Even though my father had been a monster, at least my mother had showered me with love. It didn't seem that Viktor had that same experience with his family, and my heart ached for him.

"You look sad, *myshka*."

"Every child should know they're loved. I know it doesn't happen that way, but it should. I hate that there are parents in the world who abuse their kids, or just withhold affection, when there are so many couples or even single men and women who can't have children and would love them with all their hearts. Doesn't seem fair."

There were footsteps drawing near, and I didn't even know what was on the menu. But Viktor seemed like the type to order for me without even asking my likes or dislikes. When the footsteps stopped by the table, there was a sickeningly sweet voice of the waitress. She was too close for comfort. I extracted my hand from Viktor's, trying to ignore the woman's blatant flirting. Part of me wanted to tell her to back off, that he was mine, but I didn't know if I had that right. Yes, we were married, but it wasn't like we had a conventional marriage. Viktor might claim to be faithful, but it didn't mean he wanted me to snarl at every woman who spoke to him. I somehow doubted he'd like his wife to be territorial.

"She likes you," I said as I heard the woman walk away again.

"And you'd be all right if I took you back to the hotel, then met up with her? Maybe stayed the night and fucked her until morning?" he asked.

I hesitated. He gave a humorless laugh.

"That's what I thought, *myshka*."

"It's not my place to make demands of you, Viktor. I'm yours. Just another possession like your watch or your favorite suit. I don't have a say in anything you do. If you want to be with her, I don't have the right to stand in your way."

I heard his chair scrape across the floor, then felt him kneeling next to me. His touch was light as he grasped my chin and turned my face toward him.

"Cerys, you're my wife. You have every right to ask me to be faithful, which I've already promised. If you're ignoring her inappropriate behavior because you feel it's not your place to say anything, then you're wrong. I don't want you to call me out in front of my men, my family, but if there's a woman encroaching on your territory, then you have every right to say something."

I licked my lips and thought about what I wanted to say.

"Viktor, I know you didn't really want to marry me. I was just a better alternative to the woman you were promised to. I understand that, and I'm honestly not expecting this to be anything like a real marriage."

My heart felt heavy as I said the words, but they were true. He'd made it clear that this wouldn't be my fairytale ending. We were married, and I'd share his bed, but I had no say in anything. We weren't equals. He didn't care for me. By his own admission, he possibly never would.

"Is that what you think?" he asked. "That you were just a better option?"

"Isn't that what you said before we left to fly here?"

He was quiet a moment. "That wasn't the way I intended you to take it. The reason Maksim suggested I marry you is that I refused to give you up. He asked if I would move you elsewhere if I married Tania, and I said no. I told him your place was in my home and in my bed. He said that sounded more like a wife."

While what he was saying did sound less

mercenary than what I'd believed, it still wasn't all that promising for a happy life. For either of us. Although, I wondered if Viktor had ever known joy of any kind. True happiness, not just whatever he felt when he made money or took a woman to bed.

"You could have anyone."

"Yes, *myshka*, and I've been far from celibate over the years. But the only woman I want is you. I didn't marry you because I didn't see another option, or because you were convenient. I married you because I wanted a way to keep you with me, to tie you tighter to my side." He kissed my hand. "I'm a possessive man, *myshka*. You're mine and I wanted to ensure that would always be so."

My heart warmed at his words. No, they weren't a declaration of his undying love, but if what he said was true, then he really did want me with him. It was more than just him owning me. He leaned in closer and pressed his lips to mine in a brief kiss.

"We'll eat and return to our room, *myshka*. Then I'll prove to you that our marriage was anything but one of convenience."

His words sent a thrill through me, and I suddenly couldn't wait to finish our meal. Maybe being married to Viktor wouldn't be so bad. Now that I understood better, I didn't feel quite so lonely or worried. If he truly wanted me, then my future was secure and I didn't need to fear being passed off to someone else, or left to rot while he amused himself elsewhere.

Now if I could just show him what it was like to be loved, and hopefully earn his love in return.

Chapter Four

Viktor

It bothered me that my wife had thought I only wanted to marry her to avoid being with Tania, that she was simply there and convenient. We'd barely known one another twenty-four hours so I could understand her reasoning, but the pull I'd felt toward her from the moment she'd burst into the room last night was unlike anything I'd experienced before. Yes, in a sense she was my property, but she'd been more than that even before I'd taken her home. I'd just had this deep knowing that she belonged to me.

She deserved more than I could give her, but I was too selfish to let her go. I wanted her to carry my children, to remain by my side. I'd give her everything I could, but it would never be my love. I honestly didn't think I was capable of such an emotion. Even if I couldn't give her my heart, I'd still pull the moon from the sky if I could and hand it to her. After everything she'd suffered, I wanted to treat her like a queen. And that included defending her.

The waitress at the restaurant had not only lost her tip from me due to her nonstop flirting, but I'd also had a word with the manager about her unprofessionalism. There was being nice and accommodating to your customers, but she'd blatantly been trying to get into my pants with my wife right across from me. We'd both been wearing our new wedding bands, and the twit hadn't seemed to care. Seeing the look on Cerys' face, then hearing her tell me she had no say in whether or not I slept with another woman, had pissed me off.

I hadn't expected her to throw a fit, or even tell the waitress to back off, but knowing that she would just accept me being unfaithful to her had hurt. Never once in all my life had I ever wanted to be with only one woman. Maybe my reputation preceded me and she was basing her assumptions off rumors. Most likely correct rumors, but it didn't make my job any easier, trying to get her to trust me.

The elevator slowly rose to our floor in the hotel. She stood quietly, her hand in the crook of my arm. My words at the restaurant had surprised her, that much had been clear, and I hoped that we'd be able to move forward. I hadn't missed the way her cheeks flushed when I'd spoken of having a wedding night with her. Even though I hadn't been as gentle as I should have for her first time, it seemed I hadn't scared her. She wanted me, and that alone was enough to make me hard. Then again, just looking at her got that reaction from me.

I checked the messages on my phone, seeing the hotel had found my missing money and the man responsible was in the custody of the police. As it had been a hotel employee, caught on camera no less, our room was being comped as well as anything else we needed during our stay. I'd have enjoyed dealing with the man on my own, but I didn't have the right connections here. This wasn't my town.

When we got out on our floor and I opened the door to the suite, I'd barely cleared the doorway before Cerys launched herself at me. I caught her, completely surprised by her behavior, then her lips were on mine and I didn't give a shit about anything else. I barely remembered to make sure the door was shut all the way before I shrugged my jacket off and started unbuttoning my shirt. I drew away long enough to divest myself of my clothes and help her remove her dress.

"Not that I'm complaining," I said, "but what brought this on?"

Her cheeks flushed a bright pink and she ducked her head, taking a step back. Reaching for her, I drew her close to my body.

"*Myshka*, I like this side of you." I ground my cock against her. "Feel how hard it makes me knowing that you desire me?"

"All of this is new," she said. "I've never been so much as kissed by anyone but you, and now I'm your wife. I thought you were just playing with me, keeping me until you grew bored and would, then pass me off to someone else. But hearing what you said at the restaurant, it… you made it sound like I'm more than just a plaything for you."

I kissed her, softly at first, then harder. I never wanted her to question how I felt about her, how much I wanted her. My desire for her burned in my veins, heating me from the inside out, until I thought I'd go insane if I couldn't be inside her soon. With a few deft movements, I popped the clasp on her bra and pulled it off her, then pushed her panties over her hips and down her thighs.

"Bedroom," she murmured.

"*Nyet*. Here. Now."

I turned her and moved closer to the sofa, bending her over the arm. She braced her waist on the cushion, her ass sticking out. It was too much of a temptation and I brought my palm down with a loud *crack*, leaving a pink handprint behind. She jerked and gave a squeak of protest, but she didn't try to get away. In fact… I slid my fingers along the lips of her pussy and found her incredibly wet. Inserting two into her tight sheath, I pumped them in and out as I spanked her twice more. Her pussy clenched down and I couldn't contain my smile. My little *myshka* enjoyed being spanked while she was getting fucked. I'd have to remember that.

Easing my fingers from her pussy, I used her cream to tease the tight ring of muscle between her ass cheeks. Her entire body went tense until I started working my cock inside her. By the time she'd taken all of it, I'd worked one of my fingers into her ass up to the first knuckle. A few more slaps to her ass had her skin turning a nice red that made my dick even harder.

"You like that, *myshka*? You like getting spanked?"

"I-I…"

Smack!

She yelped and nodded. "Y-yes, Viktor. I like it."

I took her hard and deep, my cock working her pussy while I finger fucked her ass. My hips slammed against her with every thrust and the moment she started coming I knew I wouldn't last much longer. Cerys felt incredible. Hot. Wet. Tight. I worked a second finger inside her ass, knowing that one day soon I'd take her there too, fill her with my cock, my cum. Just the thought of doing that was enough to trigger my orgasm. I came long and hard, filling her up, but I wasn't ready for it to be over yet. I kept thrusting my fingers and reached around with my other hand to play with her clit. I rubbed, pinched, and tugged on the engorged nub until she came again. A groan slipped past my lips as my cock jerked and more cum shot into her.

"Fuck, *myshka*. My beautiful, perfect wife." I kissed the back of her neck, then along her shoulders. Slowly, I removed my fingers, not missing the hiss of her breath. It likely stung since she'd never had someone touch her there before. "I have another rule."

"What rule?" she asked.

"You're not permitted to shower after I fuck you, unless I tell you otherwise." I withdrew from her pussy and watched as my cum slid down her thighs. Hottest thing I'd ever seen. No matter how many times I watched my essence leak out of her, I'd never grow tired of it. I reached down and rubbed my cum into her skin. "Anyone who dared to look at your naked body would know you belong to someone. They'd see my release on your skin, smell my scent on you."

"Viktor." She tipped her head back, her eyes sliding shut. The flush riding her cheeks wasn't just from her orgasm. She liked the things I was saying to her. My naughty little wife.

"Come, *myshka*. We'll rest a bit, but I'll want you again soon. Tomorrow you'll be very, very sore."

Taking a step back, I helped her stand, only to turn her toward me, then push her to her knees. She gasped and reached up to grab onto my thighs, steadying herself. I hadn't meant to scare her, or move too quickly. There were times I forgot she couldn't see. Gripping my cock, I painted her lips with our mingled spent passion. Her tongue flicked out to lick it off and I knew exactly what I wanted her to do.

"Open, *myshka*."

She parted her lips and I thrust inside. If the taste of us bothered her, she didn't show it. Fisting her hair, I dragged her down the length of my cock until she gagged. Again and again I thrust into her mouth, making her take all of me, even as her eyes teared and she struggled to take a breath. In time, she'd learn how to suck me properly, but until then, I'd enjoy teaching her.

"Relax your throat, *myshka*. Take me deep."

She struggled at first, but gradually figured out

how to breathe while I fucked her mouth, the head of my cock sliding to the back of her throat. Her nails bit into my thighs as I stroked in and out of her mouth faster, harder.

"I'm going to come, *myshka*. Swallow it. All of it."

Spurt after spurt filled her mouth, and she had a hard time doing as I'd commanded. When I pulled out, my cum coated her lips and dribbled from the corners of her mouth.

"Lick your mouth clean, Cerys. I said to swallow all of it."

A shudder raked her small frame, but I saw the way her nipples hardened and knew she enjoyed my demands. She licked every drop from her lips, then stayed on her knees, waiting. Such a good girl. I'd have to reward her later.

I reached down and lifted her into my arms, then carried her into the bedroom. After I laid her down, I went to the bathroom to clean up before sliding into bed next to her, drawing the sheet over us. Cerys cuddled against me, and I held her close. There was a contented smile on her lips, and the glow she wore made her look genuinely happy. I hoped that was the case. As I watched her sleep, I realized that perhaps my wife wasn't the only one who was happy. It was a foreign feeling, but it was one that I wanted to hold onto a while longer. Forever sounded good.

She snuggled closer and draped her thigh across mine. The wet heat of her pussy made my cock hard again. It would be easy to roll over and slip inside. I traced the line of her nose, the curve of her cheek. My *myshka* was beautiful, kind, and the sort of woman I should have never brought home with me. And yet I couldn't let her go. I needed her gentle touch, her innocence. Such things were foreign to me, but I liked the way I felt when I was in her presence.

I brushed my lips over hers and she sighed, arching toward me. It was all the encouragement I needed. Rolling so that she lay under me on her belly, I reached for her wrists and placed them above her head. Glancing around, I saw my tie from earlier in the day and grabbed it, using it to secure her to the bed. Lifting her hips, I smacked my hand against her pussy, making her cry out.

"Viktor!"

"This is mine, is it not?" I smacked her again. And again.

"Yes! Yes, I'm yours."

"I'm going to fuck this pretty pussy, then I want your ass, *myshka*."

Her body shuddered as I worked my way inside her. She was still tight, and I groaned at how incredible she felt. A soft gasp slipped from her as she opened her eyes, unseeing yet looking over her shoulder and meeting my gaze just the same.

"Need you, *myshka*."

"Then take me," she said, holding still and giving herself to me completely.

I stroked in and out of her slow and deep. The slide of my cock inside her tight pussy was the best thing I'd ever felt. I kissed her shoulder and down her back, tasting her as I made her mine. Would it always be like this? Being with a woman had never felt special before. It had been a quick release, or a business transaction. Nothing more. With Cerys, it felt as if we were truly joined.

As she came apart beneath me, I realized that I wasn't fucking her. It wasn't just sex. I was making love with my wife, something I'd never done. Slow and easy had never been important to me. I wanted her to enjoy every moment in my bed -- our bed -- and I loved the soft sounds she made.

"I love to watch you come," I said, and a flush spread across her cheeks. So adorable. Even now, she was embarrassed by my words. Such a good girl. "Love to feel you squeeze my cock and coat me with your cream."

"Viktor!"

I traced her shoulder with my nose. "Love how tight and wet you are."

I gripped her thigh and shifted her, letting me slide in deeper. Stroking into her harder, I didn't hold back anymore. I took her like a man possessed, and my sweet Cerys jerked at her bonds and begged for more. The hot gush of her release was nearly enough to make me come, but I wasn't done with her yet. Not by far. She lay panting, a dazed expression on her face.

My hands shook from the effort it took to not ride her hard and deep, but I was worried I might hurt her. My control was slipping and if I weren't careful she'd get a glimpse of the beast inside me. Spanking her was one thing, even tying her up, but she was nowhere near ready for what I craved. I slid in balls-deep, and tried to keep things slow and steady. When she shifted her knees and tilted her hips at a slightly different angle, then squeezed my cock, I nearly saw stars.

"Cerys. *Myshka*. I can't... I..."

"I won't break," she said, turning her head toward me.

Her words seem to snap what little control I had right then. I watched her for any signs of distress as I slammed into her again and again. My hand cracked against her ass, leaving a red handprint, but it only seemed to make her wetter.

"Offer me that ass," I told her, my voice deeper and rougher.

She pressed her shoulders to the bed and I gripped her hip. The only sounds in the room were our bodies slapping together, her soft gasps and whimpers, and my grunts and groans. The air smelled of sex and it only spurred me on. My hips snapped forward again, driving in harder, and as she screamed out her release I finally let go. My balls drew up and pumped her full of cum, not stopping even after the last drop had been drained from me. It wasn't until my cock twitched and became overly sensitive that I finally pulled out and released her.

Her wrists were slightly red from being tied and I released her. The handprint on her ass remained, and it looked like she might have slight bruising on her hip from how tightly I'd gripped her. I wasn't sorry, though. I liked seeing those marks on her, knowing they made her mine every bit as much as her ring, if not more so.

Cerys collapsed onto her side and I curled myself around her, drawing her tight against me. She wiggled closer and made a contented humming noise. I breathed in her scent and kissed the side of her neck. My sweet wife. I might not have planned to get married so soon, or to a stranger, but I had a feeling that things would go well between us.

"Rest, *myshka*. I plan to take you again soon."

She giggled softly. "Are you trying to get me pregnant right away?"

I growled and nipped at her ear. "Yes. I'm going to fill you with my cum until you carry my kid, and even then I won't stop. But next time, I have something else in mind. You've given me your mouth and your virgin pussy." I reached between us and slid my fingers down the crack of her ass. "I want this too."

"Such a caveman," she murmured, but I could hear the smile in her voice.

Perhaps I was. I wouldn't apologize for it.

I'd always been demanding in bed, and had typically taken what I wanted -- with the woman all too eager to give it to me -- but with Cerys it was different. I didn't want to scare her, and yet when I was inside her all I could think about was possessing her in every way possible. My marks on her body, my cum filling her, seeing her pregnant with my baby, and knowing that I would be the only man to ever touch her. She was the first virgin I'd ever been with -- would be the only one for that matter.

After she'd rested a bit, and my cock was hard and ready to go again, I had her back on her knees. I used the hotel provided lube that came with the honeymoon suite and worked my fingers into her ass while I pinched and teased her clit. I could see the strain in her body, but she didn't deny me. I needed this, needed to own every part of her.

"It might hurt the first time, *myshka*. But you'll get used to it the more we do this," I said as I placed the head of my cock against her tight hole.

I spread her ass open wide and slowly worked the head of my cock past the ring of muscle. She squeaked and whimpered, her body tightening. I murmured to her in Russian, trying to soothe her as I slid in deeper. When I was fully seated, I held her close and leaned back, holding her on my lap.

"Get your knees under you good, *myshka*. You're going to ride me."

"Wh-what?" she asked, giving me a startled look.

"Ride me." I helped raise and lower her a few times, showing her what I wanted. The position gave me the perfect opportunity to work her pussy and play with her nipples.

As I got her close to her climax, my little *myshka* nearly went wild. She rode me like she'd done it a hundred times, and when she came, it pulled my cum from my balls. My cock jerked and twitched as I loaded her full of cum. Holding her to me, I refused to release her just yet. Being inside her was the best feeling in the world, and her ass was even tighter than her pussy.

I was still hard, could easily go again. I lifted and lowered her, trying to gauge how much pain she was in. I had no doubt she'd be hurting after me taking her ass for the first time. As I worked her clit, she relaxed against me. I circled, pinched, and smacked her clit. It didn't take long before she was coming again. While she rode her high, I rocked her forward and took her ass again, driving in deep, taking what I wanted, what I needed. I filled her up a second time, then eased from her body. She was swollen and pink, but seeing my cum leak from her made me smile.

Yeah, I was a sadistic fuck, but I'd now claimed every part of my wife. I'd taken her virgin pussy, her virgin mouth, and her virgin ass. She was mine, and no one would ever take her from me. If anyone dared, I'd make them regret it.

Cerys slept, curled against me, and I felt a contentment I had never known before meeting her. My angel. My light. Marrying her was the right decision. Now I'd never have to let her go.

Chapter Five

Viktor

The next morning my phone showed no less than ten text messages and several voicemails, all demanding my immediate return. As much as I wanted to have a true honeymoon with Cerys, it seemed it would have to wait. Even a call to Maksim hadn't yielded more details, other than we had an issue, or rather I did. I had to wonder if had something to do with Cerys, or perhaps the way I'd handled her father.

I showered, dressed, then packed my bag before calling down for room service. While I waited for breakfast to arrive, I woke Cerys. She gave me a sleepy smile, reaching up to brush her fingers along my beard. It amazed me that without her sight she could brush her fingers through my beard on the first try every time.

"Morning," she said. "What time is it?"

"Early, but there's a complication at home I need to handle. I'm afraid our trip is being cut short. Breakfast will be here shortly if you'd like to shower and dress. After we eat, we'll have to go straight to the airport and fly home. The jet is being fueled and should be ready when we arrive."

I helped her out of the bed and started the shower while she picked out her clothes. Seeing her hold a white shirt and a red bra made me smile, and I realized that perhaps I hadn't thought out her wardrobe as well as I'd assumed I had. I took the bra from her and swapped it for one that wouldn't show through her shirt, brushed a kiss against her temple, then left her to get ready. If I remained in the room with her, I'd end up joining her in the shower, and then we'd be delayed in getting home. Truthfully, it was tempting to take another day with my new wife, but I knew there would be hell to pay if I did.

Maksim treated me like family, and I wouldn't abuse his trust just to have more time with my wife. By the time Cerys stepped out of the bedroom, fully dressed, our food was ready and waiting. I lifted the dome from the various dishes and told her what was available, letting her have first choice. Once her plate was made, I helped myself and sat next to her at the small table.

"What's going to happen when we go home?" she asked.

"I'll sort out the problem. There's nothing for you to fear, *myshka*."

She ate a few more bites, then turned her face toward me. "Viktor, what do you expect me to do all day every day? As your wife, will I have responsibilities? I don't know anything about living in your world, or what being the wife of someone like you would even entail."

Someone like me? I knew what she meant, but first and foremost, I was just a man. And like most men, what I wanted was for my wife to be naked in my bed. And happy. I wanted her to be happy. If that meant she didn't do the same things a typical Bratva wife would do, then so be it. I knew she would have limitations, though I intended to help in any way I could. While she'd gotten ready, I'd used my phone to search online for a cane. After purchasing it, I arranged for Ilya to pick it up, then deliver it to my condo. I didn't like the idea of Cerys bumping into things or possibly falling.

"Most work with various charities; they shop and spend time with other Bratva wives, handle any staff around the house, and make sure things run smoothly at home." I reached for her hand. "But I don't expect all of that from you."

"Because I'm blind?"

I smiled at the slight bite to her tone. It seemed she didn't like being considered incapable. I didn't doubt that she could do many things on her own, but I also knew how the other wives would react to her. It would take time for them to get to know her, and appreciate her the way I did. Tossing her into their mix immediately would be like feeding her to a bunch of sharks. They could be vicious and would feel threatened by her. As one of the more prominent members of the Bratva, I held a higher ranking than a lot of their husbands, which put Cerys above those wives. They wouldn't like it.

"No. Because I want you to be happy, and I don't think those types of things would be something you'd enjoy. I don't have a staff at home, although I should probably hire someone to help you with the cooking and cleaning. I know you took care of that for your father, but you're not a maid, Cerys. You're my wife."

Her lips twitched as if she fought off a smile. "Most wives, those who aren't married to men who can afford something like a penthouse suite, handle the cooking and cleaning for their families. You wouldn't be asking me to do something other women don't handle every day."

I didn't respond right away, wanting to be careful with my words. We'd already had one miscommunication that had upset her greatly and I didn't want to have another. I knew it was likely we'd struggle from time to time as we adjusted to one another, but I'd prefer to temper my words and avoid it if I could. I hadn't liked her being distant and looking like a beaten puppy.

"What do you enjoy?" I asked. "If you could do anything, what would make you happiest?"

Her lips pursed and her brow furrowed. "No one's ever asked me that before."

I gave her time to think about her answer, wanting to honestly know what she wanted or needed in order to be happy with me, with her new life. If it was within my power to give it to her, I would.

"I want to make a difference in someone's life," she said. "I know I'm not the only person who has had to fight against a disability, and I was struggling until you came along. If there's a way to help other people like me, then that's what I want to do. Everyone deserves a chance to make something of themselves or find happiness."

It wasn't what I'd expected her to say. I'd thought she'd ask for more books, or something that I could purchase for her. Perhaps even more time together, but helping others? While I knew most of the Bratva wives helped with charities, I didn't think they actually cared about any of the causes. It was mostly for show. Cerys, however, just wanted to help someone. It proved that she was different from anyone I'd ever known before, that she was sweet and good. I only hoped that being with me didn't destroy that part of her. The life I led was violent and bloody. I didn't want any part of it to touch her, but there was always a risk something would happen.

"I'll see if I can come up with a way for you to do that, *myshka*. I just need to handle the situation at home first." And handle it I would, by any means necessary if the problem was Artur.

Within the hour we were loaded onto the jet and heading back home. Cerys dozed with her head on my shoulder, but I knew I needed to get my mind back on business and be a little less focused on my new wife. She was tempting, and I would have loved to introduce her to the Mile High Club, but it would have to wait. I couldn't afford to be careless or sloppy. It wasn't just my life at stake anymore. I knew my enemies wouldn't hesitate to use Cerys against me. There was also the chance she could be pregnant already. I'd refused to use to protection with her, wanting to see her swell with our child.

If Artur wouldn't back down, I'd have to come up with another arrangement, one that didn't include making his daughter a part of my life in any capacity. At one point, it wouldn't have bothered me. Women in my world were to be used and discarded in whatever way might be advantageous to the men. It never had been a problem for me in the past, but if anyone tried to take Cerys from me, I'd put them six feet under. I only hoped my attachment to her didn't come across as a weakness. The weak didn't last long in the Bratva.

The flight was uneventful and soon I felt the wheels touching down. I roused Cerys, smiling as she stretched like a contented cat.

"We're here, *myshka*. Time to go home."

She nodded and stood, nearly falling. I reached up and steadied her, rising to my feet. Someone would handle our bags so I lifted her into my arms and carried her down the steps and to my car. After I settled her on the passenger seat and buckled her, I shut the door and strode around the hood. I popped the trunk so our bags could be placed inside, and once it was closed again, I slid into the car and started the engine.

By the time I parked the car outside my building and handed the keys to the valet, Cerys seemed more awake. She reached for my hand as we entered the building and rode the elevator to our floor.

"Home, sweet home," she murmured as I opened the door and ushered her inside.

I looked around at the place I'd called mine for the past several years. The modern furniture and floor-to-ceiling windows had been perfect for my life up to this point. If Cerys and I had children, would they feel welcome in this space? My childhood had been far from perfect, and Cerys' hadn't been any better. I wanted our children to be happy and to have the things we hadn't.

However, the security my building provided was still a perk of living here. If we did move, then I'd need a place similar to Maksim's home. Children needed room to run and explore. The penthouse didn't provide much of an opportunity for that. The bulletproof glass had been a big selling point when I'd purchased the place. A man in my position couldn't be too careful. Snipers could hit me even this far up in the air, especially from another rooftop. But I didn't want my kids to feel like they were in a prison, nor did I want Cerys to feel that way.

"You're quiet," she said.

"Just thinking it might be time for a change."

"What sort of change?" she asked.

"A house with a yard. I fully plan to get you pregnant. Preferably more than once. If I'd had a sibling, then maybe things would have been different when I lost my parents. If you'd had one, maybe your father wouldn't have gotten away with his cruelty."

She nodded, a wistful smile on her face. "Never really thought I'd have children. I'm not sure I'm capable of caring for one. I can't see to find them. What if my blindness put them in danger?"

I pressed a kiss to her temple.

"You'll have all the help you need, *myshka*. I'll hire the best of nannies to ensure that you aren't taking care of our children alone. And of course I'll help when I'm home."

She fidgeted a little, shifting from foot to foot, before leaning into me. I held her, enjoying the feel of her. Perhaps she was already making me too soft, but as long as I only showed that side to her, then it shouldn't be an issue. If the Bratva thought I was weakening, then my life, and Cerys' life, would be in danger. I couldn't let that happen. We'd have to talk soon about the way I would act in public versus here in our home. She needed to know it wasn't anything she'd done, and that it didn't mean I liked her any less. But I had an image to uphold, one that would keep her safe.

"Maybe we can discuss it more later. Right now, I just want to get used to being married," she said.

"Of course, *myshka*."

My phone rang and I knew if I didn't answer Maksim it would only anger him. Stepping out of the room, I accepted the call and placed the phone to my ear.

"Yes, Maksim?"

"I heard you're home. I need you to come to my place, but I wouldn't advise bringing your wife. She's not tough enough to handle herself in this world."

"That's part of what I like about her," I admitted. "She's soft and sweet."

He made a grunting noise and I heard the creak of his leather chair.

"Just get here, Viktor. I'll ask Ilya to stand guard outside your home. He's already headed in your direction. That way someone is close if Cerys needs something, and he's extra protection in conjunction with what your building offers."

I hesitated. Leave Cerys? If there was something going on, if an issue had arisen that could be potentially dangerous to my wife, I didn't want to leave her vulnerable.

"How close is Ilya? I don't want to leave her alone for long."

"He'll be there in ten minutes, maybe less. Leave now, Viktor. This can't wait."

I disconnected the call and ran a hand through my hair. I didn't want to disobey and anger Maksim, but I didn't like the idea of leaving Cerys alone either. Making my way back into the living room, I found her curled up on the sofa with a book in her lap. Her fingers slid across the Braille and there was a soft smile on her face.

"Good story?" I asked.

"It's a romance. Of course it's good."

I leaned down and pressed a kiss to her cheek. "I need to go somewhere for a bit. Maksim is sending Ilya to stand outside the penthouse. If you need anything, just let him know. Hopefully, I won't be gone long."

She reached up and tugged on my beard until she was able to press her lips to mine. I didn't know how she managed to do that without seeing. "Be careful, Viktor."

"Yes, *myshka*. I have something important to live for now."

I withdrew from her and left before I talked myself out of it. As I was getting into my car downstairs, I saw Ilya enter the building. It didn't stop the unease that was filling me, but there wasn't much I could do. Going against Maksim's orders wouldn't bode well.

The drive outside town took longer than I'd have liked, but traffic was a bitch. As I pulled up to the gates of Maksim's mansion, a guard waved me through. I stopped in the circular drive not far from the door and eyed the other vehicles present. It seemed we had company, and the fact Maksim hadn't disclosed any details to me made warning bells go off in my head. I checked my weapons before entering the premises, nodding to the butler who opened the door.

"They're in the great room, Mr. Petrov," the butler said.

I knew the layout of Maksim's home as well as my own and quickly made my way to the great room. It shouldn't have surprised me to see Artur present, but the fact Vadim Ivanov was here, as well as Gavriil Alexeev didn't give me a good feeling. Some of the most dangerous men in the Bratva were watching me, but I didn't let them see their presence bothered me.

"Maksim, I apologize if I kept you waiting."

"Do you often ignore a call from your brigadier?" Vadim asked.

"*Nyet*. However, he's a *temporary* brigadier, and I was out of town. Getting here took a bit longer than a drive across town," I said, stopping to pour myself a shot of vodka.

"Artur has asked us to be here for a special occasion," Gavriil said. "A match between yourself and his daughter, Tania."

I tried to seem calm and cool, when I felt anything but. Heat worked its way through me as my temper spiked. It didn't surprise me he'd try such an underhanded thing as to bring the top muscle with him. But it wouldn't work. I wasn't going to cower, wouldn't bow to him or anyone else.

"I never made such a promise to Artur, or to

Tania," I said.

"You're not getting any younger, Viktor. It's time to set up your nursery," Artur said. "My Tania knows how to be a proper wife for you, and the Orlov bloodlines are strong, as are yours. It would be a perfect match."

I downed my drink, then set the glass aside. My gaze met Maksim's and I saw his quick glance at Vadim, as well as the fear he was trying to hide. It seemed he hadn't conveyed to the Vor that I was now off the market and had, in fact, been out of town getting married. I wasn't certain how this would play out. As a Brigadier, I was technically of higher ranking than Maksim. One bad move a few months ago had changed things a bit. While Vadim hadn't stripped my ranking, he'd put Maksim in authority over me for a probationary period, which was nearly over. Or had been. Once Vadim found out I'd gotten married without discussing it with him, I might very well be at the bottom of the list, assuming he didn't kill me for insubordination.

"I'm sorry, but I'm unable to make such a match," I said.

The tension in the room built until it was a tangible thing. My body tensed in preparation for a fight, if one should start. I knew that Artur wouldn't take this well, had known it before I'd even married my *myshka*.

"And why is that?" Artur asked, his face going red with anger.

I faced him and the others, holding each gaze for a few moments. I could see Maksim from the corner of my eye, the tremor in his hand as he shoved it into his pants pocket. He was close to losing it, and I needed him to hold things together a bit longer.

"Because I'm already married," I said.

Vadim arched an eyebrow, but didn't say anything. With a nod of his head, I followed him out of the room, not stopping until we were far enough no one else would hear.

"You didn't think I would like to meet your wife-to-be? Or know that you'd been seeing someone?" Vadim asked.

To anyone else, it would seem like fatherly concern. I knew better. He wondered what I was hiding, why I'd married in secret. In my world, such a thing just wasn't done.

"I'm sorry, but it happened rather suddenly. I took her as payment for a debt, but when I realized that I didn't want to set her aside in order to take a wife, I decided to marry her. We flew to Vegas yesterday and were married last night."

Vadim sighed and cracked his neck. His hands flexed and I eyed the scars across them, knowing he'd earned them as he'd fought his way to the top. Despite our closeness over the years, I knew he wouldn't hesitate to put me in my place. Physically, if necessary.

"Viktor, if I'd known you were getting married, I could have put a stop to this nonsense with Artur before now. Instead, you have me looking like an idiot in there because I had no idea you'd taken a wife. I'd given him my support to request the match. This is bad, Viktor."

I tried to school my features. It had never occurred to me that Vadim would side with me, that he would give his blessing over my match with Cerys. She didn't have any connections to help me or the Bratva.

"I'll take whatever punishment you feel is necessary." I hesitated only a moment. "But if my penalty is death, I ask that you make sure Cerys is cared for and has all her needs met. I want her safe."

Vadim leaned against the wall and folded his arms over his chest. "Tell me about your wife."

"She's blind and was horribly abused by her father. He got too far into debt with us and when we went to collect payment or make an example of him, Cerys came tumbling into the room begging us to stop."

His lips twitched as if he fought back a smile. I wondered what he'd think of my wife. It would be good to have an ally, someone who would watch over her if anything should ever happen to me. Vadim was the closest thing I'd had to a parent since mine had perished.

"Any pictures?" Vadim asked.

I pulled my phone from my pocket and showed him the few I'd taken of her during our trip in Las Vegas. Most were cameos I'd taken when she was otherwise occupied. There was a soft smile on his face as he studied each one, then handed the phone back to me.

"She's beautiful, Viktor. I can understand why you're so taken with her. I'll see what I can do to smooth Artur's feathers."

The tightness in my chest eased and I breathed a little easier.

"Thank you, Vadim."

When we re-entered the room, it was to find Artur missing. Maksim looked uneasy as he explained Artur had left to make a call. The fact he'd left while the Vor was present made me think something was incredibly wrong. With someone as powerful as Vadim in attendance, it was considered an insult to walk out. Unless that call was a matter of life and death, then it should have waited, so that begged the question what was Artur up to?

Minutes ticked by. After twenty minutes, Gavriil left the room only to return a short while later with the news that Artur was gone. His car was missing from the driveway, and he couldn't be located inside the mansion, and no one had seen him wandering the grounds. Vadim's expression was grim as he stared at me.

"Does Artur know where you live?" Vadim asked.

Everything inside me went tight and hard at the same time. A cold chill went down my spine as his words bounced around in my mind. Home. Where Cerys was waiting for me.

"Yes, he's had papers delivered there previously."

"Who's watching over your wife?" he asked.

"Ilya," Maksim said. "I sent him over there before I spoke with Viktor. I knew he'd want his wife protected."

Vadim paced to the window, then turned around. The harshness of his features in that moment reminded me why he was the Vor. No one fucked over Vadim and lived to tell the tale. And those deaths were never easy.

"Get Ilya on the phone and tell him to watch for Artur. I have a feeling the man is going after your wife," Vadim said. "He's just started a war he has no hope of winning."

Maksim nodded and began dialing. I pulled my keys from my pocket and started for the front door, but Maksim's voice stopped me.

"He's not answering."

I froze and turned my head his way. "Excuse me?"

"Ilya. He's not answering his phone. He always answers."

"I'll ride with you," Vadim said. "Maksim, stay here in case Artur returns. Do whatever is necessary to detain him. Gavriil, use your sources to try and locate Artur. If he has Viktor's wife, ensure she's safe."

Without another word, Vadim strode from the room and I followed. He hadn't even closed the car door all the way before I pressed the pedal to the floor and shot forward. I broke every speed limit between Maksim's house and my penthouse. A few turns were so sharp and fast that the back end of the car fishtailed. The smell of burned rubber filled my nose as I slammed on the brakes outside my building and rushed inside, not even stopping to shut off the car.

The guards at the desk were slumped forward. I didn't dare take the time to check on them. The elevator took us to the penthouse and when I stepped off onto my floor, I saw Ilya on the ground, blood pooling under him. While Vadim knelt to check for a pulse, I shoved open the broken door to my home and went inside, gun drawn.

Cerys' book was dumped on the floor, the table knocked over and broken. Droplets of blood dotted the carpet leading to the bedroom. My heart thundered as I pushed the door open. The bedding had been ripped away. Blood smeared across the mattress, five long lines as if a trail had been left by bloody fingers. Small, delicate ones. My wife's! I checked the rest of the area including the bathroom, but Cerys wasn't here, and neither were any clues.

Vadim came up behind me and squeezed my shoulder.

"We'll get her back," he promised. "I'll put out the word. Artur will have nowhere to run and no place to hide."

Yes, but what would he do to my wife until then? What had he already done? I looked at the blood again and knew that I would make him pay for hurting her. I'd make him scream, beg. It wouldn't do any good. Once I found him, I'd have him taken to the lair. And then I'd deal with him once and for all. No one fucked me over, and no one had better *ever* think they could hurt my wife. I'd use Artur to send a message, one that people would remember for a lifetime.

I only hoped my sweet *myshka* would understand. She hadn't seen the darkness in me, had never witnessed the monster I held inside. I'd hoped she never would.

Chapter Six

Cerys

"Artur! What are you doing here?" I heard Ilya ask out in the hall.

The next sound was his cry of pain and the sounds of flesh meeting flesh. Was someone hitting him? I stood, unsure where to go or what to do. I didn't think I could find the phone fast enough to call for help. I felt my way around the side of the couch and moved in the direction of the bedroom. If I could get there, then maybe I could lock myself inside.

The front door splintered and slammed against the wall. My body locked up tight. I heard the thunder of steps rushing toward me, but I couldn't see the man called Artur. He hit me full force, knocking me off my feet. The air left my lungs as I smashed into the hard floor, leaving me dazed and gasping.

"So you're Viktor's little whore."

His fist met my cheek and I cried out as pain exploded through my head. He hit me three more times before I got my wits about me enough to start fighting him off. I twisted and tried to knock him off, but he was able to easily dodge my blows. He grabbed a handful of my hair and banged my head against the floor three times. My ears were ringing and I had a hard time staying alert.

Artur dragged me to my feet, then tossed me in the air. I landed hard on what I thought was the coffee table, and it broke beneath me. A piece of it jabbed into my side, breaking the skin and blood flowed freely. I didn't know how deep it was, but I nearly passed out from the pain. Artur pulled me off the broken table and slapped me around some more before tossing me back on the floor.

I finally managed to break free and ran for what I hoped was the bedroom. My knees hit the side of the mattress and I tried to crawl across it to put more space between us, but his hand wrapped around my ankle. He dragged me against the mattress, then pressed against my ass. I twisted and tried to kick at him, but it only made him laugh and grind his hard cock against me. Shock filled me and I went still.

"I like it when they fight. Maybe I should just have my fill of you, then leave you for Viktor to find. Once he sees my cum running out of you, he won't want you anymore." His grip tightened on me to the point of pain. "You'd like that, wouldn't you? Dirty little whore like you wants to be used, don't you?"

"Not a whore," I mumbled.

He knocked me to the floor and kicked me several times, landed a few more punches, then pulled at my clothes. His hands squeezed my breasts until I screamed out in pain. It only seemed to turn him on more and I made myself be still and quiet, hoping he'd lost interest. It seemed to work because he tossed me over his shoulder and took me down the elevator. I didn't know why the men at the front desk didn't stop him, but he carried me out of the building and tossed me into a small, hard space. When a lid slammed, I realized I was in a trunk.

I must have blacked out. When I came to, the pain in my head and side was sharp. The car was in motion and I didn't know how long I'd been locked in here. Every bump in the road had me wanting to cry out, but I bit my lip to stifle the sound. I didn't want to give the evil man the satisfaction of knowing I was hurting.

I touched every part of the interior, hoping for a way to get out. The carpeted trunk didn't yield any hidden latches or any other way to open the lid and escape. Then again, as fast as the car was moving, I'd likely kill myself if I jumped out right now. But it didn't mean I couldn't try once it stopped. I exhausted myself, trying to find a way out, and I fought not to cry. Where was Viktor? Did he know yet that I was missing?

I didn't know where we were going, or why he'd taken me. If Ilya had known him, did he work for the Bratva like Viktor? His name sounded familiar, but I was too nervous and scared to figure out where I'd heard it. The rocking motion of the car was making my stomach flip and flop. Every sharp turn sent me hurtling into one of the sides. I'd slammed my head more than once, but I knew he didn't care. The man who had taken me seemed to get off on pain. My pain.

When the car came to a stop and didn't move again, my heart started beating harder. What would he do to me? Where had he taken me? I heard the pop of the trunk opening and smelled the outside air. Rough hands jerked me from inside the small space and I was dragged along. I tripped and fell, but Artur only gripped my hair and started pulling, not caring if I got to my feet or not. I could feel the concrete or sidewalk scrape against my skin, breaking it open. My hip slammed into some steps and I cried out as he hauled me up and through a door.

With a hard shove, he sent me sprawling across a wood floor.

"Who is that?" a woman asked.

"That is your betrothed's wife," Artur said.

There was a moment of silence. "Viktor is married?"

"Yes, but never fear, my pet. He'll marry you, just like I promised. The daughter of Artur Orlov is a much better choice than this piece of gutter trash. Who knows where he found her? Fucking bitch is defective anyway. Can't see."

Wait. What? All this was because the man wanted Viktor to marry his daughter? We were already married! I didn't see Viktor willingly signing divorce papers. Especially not if I could possibly be pregnant already. *Oh, God*! I wanted to press a hand to my belly, but the last thing I needed to do was alert them to a possible kink in their plan. I hoped that the beating I'd gotten today hadn't hurt my baby, if there was one.

I remembered him speaking of a man who wanted Viktor to marry his daughter. I just hadn't realized it was *this* man. Maybe fear had addled my brains a bit.

I curled in on myself, hoping to give them less of a target if either of them got violent. Artur seemed to enjoy inflicting pain. A hand gripped my hair and jerked my head back. I stifled a scream as my neck was wrenched. The cloying scent of perfume stung my nose.

"You took my Viktor from me? How? You're nothing compared to me."

I kept silent, but it might have been a mistake. She slammed her foot down on my hip, a sharp heel from a dress shoe stabbing into me hard enough I could feel the skin break. She jammed the heel into my calf next, then one of them kicked me in the face. Blow after blow left me dazed and hurting so much I didn't even want to breathe. When they finished, I was lifted and carried back outside, then down the sidewalk. I must have blacked out because when I came to it was to the jolt of my body hitting the ground and slamming into something metal that smelled bad. A dumpster?

Had they left me in an alley?

"Be a good girl and die," Artur said. The man sounded like he was stark raving mad! How did he think he would get away with this? Did he honestly think Viktor would just let him kill me and there wouldn't be repercussions? "You're nothing. A plaything. Viktor won't even miss you once my daughter is in his bed. She's been well-versed in how to please a man."

Bile rose in my throat as I wondered if he'd been the one to teach her. The tone of his voice when he spoke of her was… more that of a lover than a parent. The thought made my stomach turn. I heard his steps move away from me, and then I couldn't hear them at all. I felt the ground around me, and hoped I wasn't about to put my hand on a used needle. Depending on the part of town where he'd taken me, anything was possible. I slowly crawled in what I hoped was the direction of the street. I didn't make it very far before the pain was too much and I collapsed onto my side.

I hurt everywhere. Even breathing was difficult. I didn't hear a single sound, which frightened me even more. No cars. No people walking by. I struggled to crawl a little farther, hoping I'd find a street, or someone who might at least help me. My hands found the curb and I wanted to cry in both relief and frustration because I still didn't hear a single car going by.

Trying to find a door and knocking on it could be dangerous depending on my location. Then again, so was lying by the street. I made it to my feet and nearly passed out from the pain. Hands outstretched, I walked forward and found the brick surface of a building. Banging my hand on the door, I waited but no one answered. I tried again. And again. Then I moved on. After four more doors and no one answering, I didn't know if they were fearful of Artur, or if I'd been dropped in a deserted area. Certain areas I'd been told were boarded up and abandoned. Was that where I was?

How would Viktor ever find me here?

Then I heard it. Footsteps. I tensed, not knowing if it was Artur returning to finish the job of killing me, or if it was someone else who would hurt me. The heavy tread and confidence of the person's walk made me think it was a man. I knew there was evil in the world, and it would be foolish to think a stranger wouldn't be dangerous.

I pressed my back to the brick and hoped that something worse wasn't about to happen to me. The footsteps halted directly in front of me, and I smelled cigarette smoke. He must have blown it directly into my face because I coughed and my sightless eyes burned. Or he was just smoking something strong.

"You look lost, love," he said with what I thought was an Irish accent.

"Help. Please."

I reached out, my hand patting at his chest before curling into the material of his shirt.

"Your husband do that?"

I shook my head, then wished I hadn't. I nearly collapsed, only the building holding me up.

"I was taken from our home. The man who took me did this."

My sightless gaze scanned the area, as I listened for any other sounds of life. I heard him put the cigarette out with his foot, then a hand gently took my arm. I went with him, hoping it wasn't a mistake.

"Come on, love. Let's get you cleaned up and I'll get a look at the damage that fucker did. Then you can decide if you want me to call your man."

Did he not believe me when I said that Viktor hadn't done this?

"What's your name? I'm Mac," he said. "Well, it's technically Ian MacKenzie."

So not Irish, then. Likely Scottish. I'd never really spoken to anyone from either place before, but I enjoyed the sound of his voice. It set me at ease, and I hoped it wasn't a mistake to let down my guard.

"Cerys," I said. "Cerys Petrov."

His steps faltered, then he grunted and kept moving, gently tugging me along with him. I wondered if he recognized my last name and might know Viktor? If I was anywhere near my old neighborhood it was possible. The Bratva had a heavy influence there. When I stumbled a few times, Mac stopped and gently lifted me into his arms.

"Easy, love. Just going to carry you the rest of the way."

I lost all sense of time, but eventually Mac stopped and I heard a door open. He carried me inside and down what seemed to be a hall or vast empty room, judging the echo of his steps. When he set me down on a cool, padded table, I was confused.

"Where am I?" I asked.

"At the Southside Clinic," he said.

I'd heard of it, and knew it wasn't far from my old home. Less than a mile in fact. I just didn't know why we were here. Yes, I was in rough shape, but I just wanted Viktor. I had no doubt he'd see that I was taken care of once I was back at his side. While he might not love me, I knew that he did want me, enough so that he'd married me to ensure no one would take me from him.

That hadn't worked out the way he'd planned.

Artur hadn't cared about our marriage. Instead of just trying to make me disappear or pay me to leave, he'd wanted me dead. I didn't think Viktor had considered that when he'd married me, or he'd thought he could protect me better. If he'd known Artur would come for me, I was certain he'd have asked more men to stay with me. Ilya had called to me through the door to let me know he was standing watch, but I knew Viktor had others who could have helped.

"Love, I need to see what I'm working with. Going to clean off the blood on your face and we'll go from there. All right?"

I nodded, then regretted the action. I swayed and nearly threw up. Whatever he used to wash away the blood was slightly rough, but the water was warm. I thought he might be using some sort of soap. It had an antiseptic smell to it and burned. It wouldn't surprise me if I were bleeding in several places, possibly more than that. Artur hadn't held back in his attack. He'd wanted me to hurt, to stop breathing.

My heart ached. Why was there such evil in the world? What purpose did men like Artur serve?

"I don't think any of the lacerations on your face need sutures. I'm going to glue two of them shut. The rest will heal with time," Mac said.

I didn't know how much time passed before he'd finished with my face. I could feel the tension as everything went quiet. My body was screaming in pain, and it would make sense that he would need to see the rest. For whatever reason, he wasn't asking, or demanding that I remove any clothing.

"Mac? Are you still here?"

"So, I was right. You're blind."

"Yes," I said softly. Should I not have let him know that? I knew it made me even more vulnerable.

In my current state I was at a disadvantage anyway.

"Christ," Mac muttered. "I need to call your husband, love. Swear to me he didn't do this?"

"Viktor would never hurt me like this," I said. "It was Artur. I think he said his last name was Orlov, or something like that."

Maybe. I'd had so many names thrown at me since the day the Bratva burst into our home. I couldn't have picked any of them out by their voice, except for Viktor. It was almost too much for me to handle. I could feel my body starting to shake, and I worried I'd finally met the breaking point. I'd handled everything my father dished out over the years, but now someone wanted me dead.

"Definitely calling Mr. Petrov," Mac muttered. "Wait here, love. I'm going down the hall to my office. No one's here but us. You're safe."

"Office?"

"It's technically Dr. Ian MacKenzie," he said. "But just call me Mac."

My lips parted and I blinked a few times. Doctor? At least I now understood why we were at the clinic, and why he seemed to know how to patch me up. For a moment, I'd worried he might have broken in.

"I mean it, Cerys. Don't move from that spot."

I nodded and placed my hands in my lap, trying not to wince as the motion made pain shoot through me. I could hear his steps, then a door opening and shutting. Minutes passed, and still Mac didn't return. Listening intently, I tried to pick up any sounds at all. Voices. Footsteps. I didn't hear a single sound in the entire building. Unease pricked at me. What was taking Mac so long? Why hadn't he returned?

He'd said to stay put. Not knowing the layout of

the room much less the building, that seemed like good advice. Unless something had happened to Mac and Artur was after me again. What if he'd been watching and waiting? What if someone knew I was here and had told Artur? I didn't want Mac to get hurt because he'd tried to help me. I didn't think a doctor would have the skills to deal with someone like the Russian. Mac saved lives, but Artur took them.

Click. My body went tight. What was that?

Something cold and hard was pressed to my temple.

"Couldn't die, could you?" Artur asked. "Stupid bitch. All you had to do was lie in that alley until you breathed your last, or someone came along to finish what I started."

"Why?" I asked. "What do you get from this? Where's Mac? What did you do to him?"

He gave a humorless laugh. "That poor excuse for a doctor is taking a nap thanks to some drugs, and a few kicks to some important places once he was down. As for what I get? Everything. Viktor is younger than me. Weaker. With my daughter by his side, I'll hold sway over him. She'll do whatever I tell her, and get Viktor to fall in line."

Power? This was all about power? I'd known that most people cared about things like that, or money, but neither really mattered to me. All I'd ever wanted was to be loved and happy. With Viktor, I doubted I'd ever have love, but he'd made me feel safe.

"He'll never listen to her," I said.

"Of course he will. My daughter knows how to work that pussy of hers. Taught her everything she knows. She'll have him eating out of her hand in no time. And once he's under her spell, then I'll pull the strings."

Bile rose in my throat. That was the second time he'd inferred he knew personally about his daughter's sexual expertise. It nauseated me, and I felt sorry for her. To have suffered at this man's hands. Yes, she'd attacked me, but having Artur for a father had likely warped her. Granted, living with my dad hadn't turned me into a monster, but then he hadn't tried to touch me sexually.

"You disgust me," I said. "I feel sorry for your daughter."

Probably not the best thing to say. The gun was removed from my head, only for his fist to slam into my cheek. I felt one of my cuts break open, and I wanted to cry from the pain that exploded across my face.

"It's just you and me," Artur said. "Took care of that doctor. He should have never stopped to help you."

The cold barrel of his gun pressed under my chin, then he slid it down my throat and farther still. He brushed it down between my breasts and kept going. I whimpered and tried to move away from him, but he quickly grabbed my arm, holding me still.

"This time, I'm going to finish the job. But first, maybe I should see why Viktor thought you were good enough to marry."

He released me, only to rip my shirt in half. The cool air of the room ghosted over my skin and I screamed as I tried to fight him off. As I tipped over the back of the padded table and landed on the hard floor, the breath was knocked from my lungs and I lay stunned. I heard something slam hard -- maybe the door into the wall? -- then a roar of rage.

"Maybe the good doc isn't as weak as I'd thought," Artur said. "Can't stop a bullet, though, can you, doctor?"

A sinister laugh filled the air before the gun went off. Not once, but twice. I heard a scream and only realized as my throat grew sore that it was me. I'd gotten that man killed! If I'd stayed in that alley, then Mac would have never found me. I sobbed and curled into a ball on the floor. With every tear that fell, I lost a little more hope. Viktor wasn't coming, and now Mac was most likely dead.

I just wanted it all to be over. I needed it to end before someone else got hurt.

Chapter Seven
Viktor

Vadim had called on every contact he had in the area, even those outside the Bratva. Everyone available was searching for Cerys, but I worried it would be too late when we found her. If Artur had harmed her in any way, he'd pay the ultimate price. Nothing would stop me from exacting vengeance, and I knew that Vadim would let me have it. Artur needed to be stopped. I'd known he was power hungry. It was the only reason he'd want his daughter matched with me. I'd been less than friendly with him over the years, and couldn't remember a time I'd said more than two words to his daughter.

A clean-up crew had been brought in to handle the dead bodies, and Ilya had been taken away for medical attention. I was thankful someone else had handled because all I could think about was Cerys.

My phone buzzed in my pocket. I pulled it out and frowned at the number on the display. It was local but not one I recognized.

I answered the call and put the phone on speaker, in case it was Artur. If the man was going to confess to his crime, then I wanted Vadim to hear it firsthand.

"Who is this?" I asked.

"Ian MacKenzie from the Southside Clinic."

My gaze locked with Vadim's. I couldn't think of a reason for the man to be calling unless he knew something about Cerys. Our connection was too new for anyone to know she was my wife, unless she'd told them. Did the doctor have my wife at his clinic? And if so, how bad off was she?

"What do you want?" I asked.

"Your wife needs you. Get here. Fast."

The call ended and I stared at Vadim. He gave a slight nod of his head and I was moving, through the door, bypassing the slow-as-fuck elevator, and practically running down the stairs. I rushed to my car and barely paused long enough for Vadim to slide into the seat next to me.

"I'm getting older, but I'm not dead," Vadim said. "But next time, take the elevator."

I snorted and put the car in gear, taking off so fast my tires squealed on the pavement and I left smoke in my wake. I took the corners too fast, nearly losing control, but I didn't let up. Pushing the pedal harder, the car shot forward again. Blowing through stop signs, lights, and nearly taking out a few pedestrians, I reached the Southside Clinic in fifteen minutes. I slammed on the brakes outside the front of the building, threw the car into park, and ran inside, not even stopping to shut off the car. No one in this area was dumb enough to steal my ride.

The sound of gunshots made my body go cold. I pulled my gun and noticed that Vadim was again beside me, his gun already at the ready. We moved farther into the clinic, peering around an open doorway. I didn't see Cerys, but the doctor lay on the floor with a spreading pool of blood under him. His back rose and fell, even though it was slight. He was alive for the moment.

Artur hadn't noticed my presence and stalked around the table in the center of the room. As he pointed his gun at the floor, I knew in that moment my wife was there, and this fucker was about to kill her.

"Artur!" I yelled out.

He swung his gun my way and I shot him through the shoulder. It was enough to make him drop the weapon. I advanced on him, not daring to look at where I suspected Cerys lay. If I saw her, saw what he'd done to her, I'd stop focusing on Artur and we could all die. It would only take a moment of distraction for him to get the upper hand. I slammed my fist into his temple, pulled back and hit him again across the jaw. I didn't stop, landing blow after blow. I made him bleed, made him beg, and still I went after him. His face was an unrecognizable mess, his bones broken, skin swollen and covered in blood. But it wasn't enough. He'd touched what was mine! Taken my wife!

"Viktor." Vadim's voice, firm and commanding, made me glance his way. "Your wife needs a hospital. And I believe the doc does as well."

I snarled at Artur and hit him again.

"Viktor!" Vadim said in a more biting tone. "I'll handle Artur."

I grabbed a white towel off a stack on a nearby table and wiped off my hands, then knelt beside Cerys. Her face was battered and bruised. I didn't take the time to check her over, just lifted her into my arms and carried her from the room. I didn't want her anywhere near Artur for a second more.

"Viktor," she said softly. "You came for me."

"Of course, *myshka*. I will always come for you."

She smiled a little, then winced. Her lip was bleeding freely, as were a few other places that I could see. I put her in my car and on the drive to the hospital I called for an ambulance to assist the doctor. My priority was my wife. I owed the doc for telling me where to find her, and for obviously trying to help her, but Cerys came first. She would always come first. The moment I'd discovered she was missing, had seen the blood in my penthouse, I'd known that she meant more to me than I'd admitted even to myself.

She moaned as I came to a stop in front of the Emergency Room.

"Easy, *myshka*. You'll be feeling better soon."

I got out and lifted my wife into my arms again, this time not putting her down until a nurse was ready to take her back. I refused to leave her side. The last time I'd walked out on her, she'd nearly died. This time, I wouldn't leave unless she was leaving with me.

"Mr. Petrov, we need to remove her clothes," the nurse said, fear flashing in her eyes as she looked at me. I knew my reputation preceded me, but I'd do whatever it took for my Cerys to be well again.

"Do it. Whatever she needs, see that she gets it, but I'm not leaving."

The nurse cast a glance behind me and I turned to see a doctor. His gaze locked with mine before turning to my wife. The way his features tightened, I knew he thought I was responsible for her wounds. I didn't care what they thought of me, but I wouldn't have them thinking Cerys was the type to stay in an abusive situation. She'd endured it with her father because she'd had no other options. He'd made sure of that.

"My wife was kidnapped," I said. "She hasn't spoken much since I found her. I don't know what…"

My throat grew tight. When I'd found her, her clothes had been torn, but were mostly in place. I didn't think she'd been violated, but I couldn't be certain. The thought of Artur doing that to her tore me up inside. My Cerys was sweet, and despite everything, had an innocence about her that I hoped she never lost.

I fastened my gaze on hers, even though she didn't know I was looking at her, and she lifted her hand, reaching for me. I went to her side and took her smaller hand in mine, giving it a gentle squeeze.

"He didn't hurt me that way, Viktor. He and his daughter hit me and kicked me."

There was a flicker in her eyes and I knew she was holding something back. He hadn't violated her, but something had happened, more than just hitting and kicking. I'd find out what, if not from her, then from Artur himself. I'd do whatever it took to make an example of him, ensure that no one came for my wife ever again, not if they wanted to live.

"Before we get started, is there any chance you're pregnant, Mrs. Petrov?" the doctor asked.

Cerys brow furrowed.

"We've only been married two days, but yes, it's possible she could be pregnant. We didn't use protection," I said.

The doctor hummed and made a note on the tablet in his hands. "Too early to tell then, but we'll take the proper precautions. Mrs. Petrov, we need to get you into a hospital gown. The police will also want documentation of your wounds."

"Documentation?" she asked.

"Photos," said the nurse, "but I'll take them."

Cerys paled and I could tell she didn't like the thought of someone taking pictures of her. She wouldn't be able to see what they were doing, and while she wouldn't admit it, I knew it made her feel vulnerable. These were medical professionals and were here to help her, but she couldn't see the kindness and worry in the nurse's eyes, or the glares the doctor had cast my way when he'd thought I was responsible for her current state.

"My wife is blind," I said. "You'll have to give her verbal instructions for anything you need. She won't see your gestures."

Sympathy crossed the nurse's face, as well as the doctor's, but I knew Cerys would hate that. If I'd learned anything about my wife, it was that she hated feeling like a burden. She didn't want pity. She just wanted to be considered normal.

"I'm not leaving her side," I said. "I left her earlier and she was taken from our home. A place she should have been safe. I'm not taking that chance again."

"The police will want to speak with you both," the doctor said.

I snorted. Not likely. Once the police knew who the victim was, they'd back off and let me handle this my way. Artur was already safely tucked away, waiting for his punishment. The police would never find him, not that they ever looked very hard at that part of town. They knew that side of town belonged to the Bratva. Nothing happened there without our permission, and if someone did cross that line, they were dealt with.

It bothered me that I hadn't even known about Cerys before entering her father's home that day. It hadn't been my first trip to her street. While I didn't go there for social visits, I did pick up chatter here and there, usually when people didn't realize I was lurking in the shadows. With the way her clothes had left little to the imagination, I would have thought at least the men would have let a comment or two slip. Not one soul had ever mentioned the blind woman, and her father had never said he had a daughter. Not until he was staring death in the face. Even then, I wondered how long it would have taken him to tell us about Cerys if she hadn't come tumbling into the room.

The doctor stepped out of the room and I helped

the nurse remove Cerys' clothing. Although, after the first cry of pain as she shifted, I decided to spare her the agony of taking anything off. Pulling a knife from my pants pocket, I sliced her clothes from her body.

"Easy, *myshka*. Don't move unless you have to. I'm sure you'll get something for the pain soon."

The nurse made a noise and I glanced over. Her pained gaze held mine.

"I need pictures."

I looked down at my naked wife, noting the dark bruising along her ribs, abdomen, hips, and legs. Although, the ones on her hips could very well be from me, or at least some of them. The ones from her father had started to yellow and were easily distinguished from the new ones. I wondered if there were more on her back, but I wouldn't ask her to turn over and show me until it was necessary. It made my gut clench when I saw the finger marks on her breast. I might have been a little rough before, but I knew those weren't from me. There would be a picture of that as well, something that other men would see. Even if they wouldn't look at her sexually, I couldn't contain my snarl of fury at the thought of other men seeing what was mine, and knowing she would feel humiliated over anyone seeing her like this. Hadn't she been through enough already?

The nurse lifted the camera to take a picture of the bruised breast, but I shoved the camera away.

"No. You've taken enough."

"Mr. Petrov, I have to take a picture of everything."

I growled and let her see the real Viktor Petrov, the one everyone feared. "No. You. Don't."

She gave a jerky nod and I gently eased Cerys onto her side, holding her as she cried. There was more bruising all down her back, but I limited the area the nurse could see, drawing the gown over Cerys' hips and covering her from her waist to her upper thighs. The nurse wasn't pleased judging by her pinched lips, but I didn't give a shit. When the nurse walked out, I helped Cerys into the hospital gown and tried to make her comfortable. It pissed me off that she hadn't been given anything for pain, but I understood they needed to run tests first.

"Viktor," she called softly.

I took Cerys' hand and lifted it to my lips, kissing it. "Yes, *myshka*."

"I'm sorry."

"For what? You did nothing wrong. None of this is your fault."

Her eyes turned glassy and a tear slipped down her cheek. "I tried to get away. If I could have seen him, maybe it would have been easier. I didn't know where to hit or kick, but I tried to fight back."

I brushed my lips against her forehead. "You did well. I'm proud of you, Cerys. You didn't let him break you, and when help arrived, you made sure they called me. You did the right thing, *myshka*. I should have protected you better."

"I want to go home, Viktor."

"Soon."

She took a shuddering breath as the doctor came in. He looked down at our joined hands, then focused on Cerys a moment. I could feel her trembling and wished there was a way I could soothe her. I didn't know what she needed from me. Until her, I'd never given women much thought. I'd bend them over, fuck them, then shove them out the door.

"We need to do a blood test to ensure they didn't give her any drugs at any point, then we'll need a CT scan. If your wife is pregnant, there's a slight risk to the baby during that procedure, but we need to rule out any internal damage from the beating she received. I'd also like an MRI since she mentioned them hitting and kicking her face and head. She's responsive, but I don't want to take any chances of a brain bleed or swelling." The doctor tapped on his tablet. "Once we get those results, we'll be able to decide where to go from there. I don't want to give her medication until I know what's going on internally."

Cerys squeezed my hand.

"Mr. Petrov, there are some people in the waiting area who asked to speak with you. If you would prefer to remain with your wife, I can tell them they need to wait." The doctor held his gaze. "One of them is Maksim Koslov."

I ran a hand through my hair and looked down at Cerys. I didn't want to leave her, but I needed to know if Maksim had news of Artur or his daughter. I hoped that Vadim had given him an update, if he wasn't still occupied with making a bloody mess of Artur. Cerys had said the bitch had joined in on the beating, and I would ensure that she paid the price for harming my wife.

"Go, Viktor. I'll be okay," Cerys said. The slight tremor in her voice belied her nerves over being left alone.

I focused on the doctor. "Anything happens to her, I will hold you personally responsible. Understood?"

He nodded.

Leaning down, I kissed Cerys gently on the lips. "I'll return soon, my *myshka*. I'm not leaving the hospital, only stepping outside to have a chat with Maksim."

She released my hand and I walked away before I changed my mind. I didn't turn to look at her. If she'd look scared or lost, I wouldn't have been able to keep going. I'd have turned around and stayed with her. Maksim wouldn't ask to speak to me unless it was important, and in the event my wife was still in danger, I needed to hear him out.

He was easy to find in the waiting room, along with Nikolai and Aleksi. The tension in their bodies alerted me to the fact something was wrong, other than my wife being in the hospital. I gave a nod toward the outer doors and Maksim followed. I waved a hand at Nikolai and Aleksi, wanting them to remain in the hospital in case Cerys needed anything.

"What couldn't wait until I knew if my wife would be all right?" I asked as we cleared the building and moved off to the side.

"Artur's daughter is missing. I sent men to pick her up and not only was she gone, but all her things were as well. Checked the airports, train stations, and even the bus stations. She's not a passenger for any mode of transportation leaving town."

"Did you see if Artur's car was missing?"

"We'll find her, Viktor." Maksim raked a hand through his hair. "There's something else. Vadim said that he's lifting your probation. You're in charge again, so we need orders, Viktor."

I sighed and looked up at the sky, trying to figure out where Tania Orlov would go if she were on the run. Once I put the word out, no one in the organization would aid her. My sweet *myshka* may believe that Tania had been shaped into a monster from what her father had done, that she had a reason for harming my wife, but I knew different. That spoiled, entitled woman was used to getting what she wanted. If she saw me as hers, then she'd do anything to keep me. Didn't matter that I'd never had an interest in her. Tania wouldn't care.

"Reach out to everyone, here in the US and home in Russia. Anyone who gives her sanctuary will be punished accordingly. She's to be brought to me, and I don't care what condition she's in as long as she's breathing."

Maksim nodded. "Very well. I'll see that it's done. And Nikolai? Aleksi?"

"I want Aleksi to remain here as extra security for Cerys. I need Nikolai to go to my penthouse and see that it's cleaned. Or send Feliks. I don't care who handles it, but I don't want any reminders of what Cerys suffered when I take her home. Fuck. Just… get rid of everything. Bring in new furniture, repaint the fucking walls. I don't care. Do whatever it takes to make the place look completely different."

"Do you think she'll be here long enough for all that?" Maksim asked.

"We'll go to a hotel for a few nights. I want twenty-four-hour security for her. Even when we return home, I'll need to increase security. Artur should have never been able to take her from my home."

Maksim tipped his head to the side. "This is more than you protecting an asset, isn't it? You're starting to actually care for her."

I waved a hand. I didn't matter why I was doing all this. It needed to be done, and that was that. I wouldn't discuss my feelings for Cerys with anyone other than her. It shouldn't make a difference if I cared for her or not. She was my wife and would need protection.

Maksim started to walk off but paused, not even

turning to face me. "You know, loving someone doesn't make you weak, Viktor. From what you've said, your Cerys is different from the other wives in the Bratva. She isn't after power or money. All she seems to want or need is you, Viktor. Don't be afraid to let her in."

Without another word, he left. I remained outside a moment, gathering my thoughts, then called Vadim. I needed to know that Artur was secured, and tell him that Tania was missing. I doubted she'd try to free her father, but anything was possible. The Vor needed to be prepared just in case.

"I'm busy, Viktor," Vadim said when he answered.

"Tania has disappeared."

He cursed and I could hear him pacing. "I'll send men after her. How's your wife?"

"They need to run tests. I don't know anything yet, but she's awake and talking to me. That has to be a good sign, right?"

Vadim was quiet a moment. "I know you want to handle Artur, set an example for anyone who comes for your family, but, Viktor, you need to focus on your wife and let me handle this. I promise that he'll suffer greatly, and I will make it known that any who harm your wife will suffer the same fate."

He was asking a lot. It was my right to exact justice for what Artur had done to Cerys. I could have lost her! A throat cleared behind me and I turned to see Nikolai waiting. The tension bracketing his mouth said that whatever news he had, it wasn't good. Vadim was right. Cerys needed to be my priority. If that meant remaining with her and letting someone else punish Artur, then so be it.

"Do it," I said. "But I want proof."

"Done. Go, Viktor. Once all this is over and your wife is on the mend, I'd very much like to meet her."

I ended the call and waited for Nikolai to gather his words. He seldom said anything he hadn't rehearsed in his head in various different ways, analyzing the outcome of each. It could be maddening.

"Tell me, Nikolai."

"They already took her for testing. The doctor refused to let either of us go with her."

Which meant she was alone, and Tania was on the loose. I went back into the hospital, not even stopping at the desk. I went up to the first doctor I saw and demanded to be taken to my wife.

"Mr. Petrov," a voice called across the waiting room.

I snarled as I faced the nurse hurrying toward me. I didn't have time for this shit! I needed to see my wife, to be there for her. She was alone, and I didn't like it. What if Tania came here? What if she made it past security and tried to hurt Cerys again?

"Sir, it's your wife." The nurse was wringing her hands as she stopped in front of me. "I'm sorry, but we think she's having a miscarriage. It's too soon to know for sure. This early it can resemble a regular menstrual cycle. She also has a concussion, but we haven't been able to run further tests."

It felt like someone had punched me in the gut. Cerys was losing our baby? She'd been pregnant when Artur took her?

"Take me to her," I said softly. "I need to see my wife."

As I followed the nurse, I tried to prepare myself. I didn't know how Cerys would feel about this, or what she'd been told. Whatever my *myshka* needed, I'd see that she got it. And as soon as we were alone, I'd tell her exactly how I felt. Maksim was right. If I waited, pretended that she was like every other Bratva wife, then I could lose out on something special.

I'd just promised to let Vadim handle Artur, but now I was second-guessing that decision. He'd cost me more than I'd realized. Not only had he kidnapped and beat my woman, but he'd quite possibly killed our child. What I'd done to Humes would pale in comparison to the hell I wanted to rain down on Artur Orlov. I quickly shot off a text to Vadim. *Leave some for me.*

* * *

I'd waited until Cerys was asleep; the nurse had given her something that would keep her calm for a few hours. After pressing a kiss to her cheek, I'd slipped on my jacket and left the hospital, leaving Nikolai and Aleksi standing guard outside her room. If she woke, if anything changed, I was to be called immediately. Otherwise, I had a problem that I needed to handle.

Vadim had taken Artur to a special warehouse we kept in the seedier part of town. I sped through the streets of town, blowing through a few stop signs and red lights. My car skidded to a stop in front of the rusty metal building, and I headed inside.

My steps echoed in the mostly empty building. There was a drain in the center of the floor for easy clean-up, and all our toys were kept in that vicinity. Artur was hanging in the center from a hook that descended from the ceiling. His bound wrists were looped over it, and blood flowed freely down his body. Vadim had stripped him and seemed to have had quite the party without me.

"When I asked you to leave me something, I'd hoped for more than this. He's mostly dead."

Vadim shrugged.

I glanced at the table of instruments, my eyebrows lifting when I noticed which ones were covered in Artur's blood. I circled my prey, taking in all the burns, cuts, bruises. The blood coating the backs of his thighs made me pause and my gaze caught Vadim's and held. That was savage even for him.

"I learned a few things I didn't like," the Vor said. "It seems Artur not only likes young girls and boys, but he made sure his daughter was well-groomed since the age of seven."

A red haze settled over my vision. That was a line I would never cross. To hurt a child was unforgivable, but especially to abuse them that way. I removed my coat, shirt, and even stripped off my shoes, socks, and pants. Left only in my underwear, I picked up the smallest of the knives. Artur hadn't even lifted his head to look at me. I wasn't certain he was even capable of such a thing. Vadim had, indeed, nearly killed him.

I dug the blade into his gut, carving out a piece of flesh. Artur didn't even make a sound. Frowning, I reached up and gripped his hair, lifting his head. Fucking hell. Vadim had taken his eyes and tongue. There was nothing left for me to do. Killing him now would be a mercy, and I didn't want that. I needed him to suffer as long as possible.

My gaze scanned him, stopping just below his waist. It seemed Vadim had left one part of him untouched. I picked up another tool and soon the scent of burning flesh and hair filled the air. It left me feeling unsatisfied. Even though I knew, could damn well see, that Artur had paid the price for his crimes, it didn't feel like enough.

"What am I supposed to do, Vadim?" I asked.

"Let go of the anger. Be with your wife. Help her heal." He shrugged. "If you can, love her."

Love her? I barely knew her. Perhaps while she healed, I'd use the time to learn more about my wife. I knew the sound of her cries when I was balls-deep inside her. I knew that she was sweet and innocent. But other than that, there was very little I'd learned about my wife in the two days we'd been together. And yet, I felt like I knew her better than any other women I'd ever met.

"I need you, Viktor. This organization needs you. For the longest time you've been a cold killer, unfeeling and remote. It's worked well for our needs. However, I think your wife may show you a way through the darkness, help you find another part of yourself. One you may not even know exists. Find that, and you'll be truly whole, and *then* you'll be unstoppable."

I gave Vadim a nod, used the hose in the corner to make sure I was free of Artur's blood, then stripped off my underwear and tossed them into the fire barrel before pulling my clothes and shoes back on. He was right. I needed to be with Cerys, and I needed to let go of the anger. Artur was punished. And Tania... I hoped she got the help she needed, but if the bitch came after my wife again, I'd end her. My sympathy only went so far.

Chapter Eight

Cerys

I hated hospitals. I'd never been to one before, but after my eight-day stay, I could honestly say I never wanted to go back. They'd kept me for observation and to help manage my pain. Although, I wondered if that had more to do with Viktor. I couldn't imagine other people staying so long for the same symptoms. Some had a tension in their voices when he was in the room. Even though he'd said he hadn't been the one to hurt me, and I'd told them the same, I'd wondered if they thought we were lying.

I'd often found myself pressing a hand to my belly. The doctors hadn't been positive I was having a miscarriage, but I'd told them repeatedly it wasn't time for my period yet. And if that's what the bleeding had been from, it had lasted much longer than usual. Even if they wouldn't say with any certainty that I'd lost my baby, I knew deep inside that's what had happened.

Viktor had been attentive, remaining by my side and handling business during the times I slept. He'd assured me that Artur wasn't a problem anymore. I wasn't naïve enough to think that meant he was still breathing. No, he was dead. Not by Viktor's hand, since he'd stayed with me, but I didn't doubt my husband had given the order. At least, I'd assumed he'd never left. He was always there when I woke.

Once I'd been released, he'd taken me on a trip to the ocean. He'd rented a home for us and I'd spent another ten days just enjoying the fresh air and the sound of the waves crashing on the sand. We'd grown closer, sharing more of our lives, learning what we liked and disliked. During that week, we'd become something more than lovers. More than husband and wife. We'd become friends. But our time had come to an end, and we'd flown back home.

When we pulled to a stop and the car hadn't started moving again, I'd known what it meant. We were outside the building where we lived. Viktor reached over to take my hand.

"We're home, *myshka*."

My body locked up tight. My heart started racing and there was a buzzing in my ears. I knew that Artur was gone, but it didn't stop the panic from rising over the thought of going up to the penthouse. I'd learned that Ilya would recover, but the security officers for the building had died from their wounds. If Viktor hadn't come for me when he did, Ilya would have likely been dead too. They'd feared he was already gone when they'd seen the blood, or so Viktor said. Thankfully, he'd only been unconscious and would heal from his wounds.

"I know you can't see the penthouse, but I had some changes made. New furniture, new paint. The place has been thoroughly cleaned. It will be like going into a new home, *myshka*."

I nodded, trying to let his words comfort me, but I was scared that I'd react badly once we were upstairs. Viktor left the car running and I knew someone would park it for him. He helped me from the car and led me inside. The elevator ride made my stomach flip. When the doors slid open and I stepped out into the hall in front of the penthouse, my hands started to shake and I seriously worried I might throw up.

Viktor opened the door and led me into our home. The smell of paint still hung in the air. Even though the memories of what happened here were still strong, it didn't feel as ominous or oppressive as I'd feared. It was just... our home. Viktor placed something in my hand and I felt along it, realizing he'd given me a cane.

"I had it delivered on our way back from Las Vegas. Maybe if I'd given it to you before I left that day…"

I pressed my hand to his chest. "No, Viktor. I've told you it wasn't your fault."

The gesture was sweet, and one I appreciated. The cane might have been handy at the beach, except he hadn't permitted me to walk very much. Viktor had watched over me carefully, and done his best to help me rest and heal.

"Come, *myshka*. There's something I need to discuss with you."

I used my cane to navigate the new layout and followed Viktor into the bedroom, his steps loud on the wood floors. A man in his position had to be able to move quietly and swiftly. I'd learned that he was noisier for my benefit, and it touched me, deeply. He drew me down onto the bed. The bedding even felt different. Softer. I ran my hand over the bedspread, trying to distract myself.

"Cerys, you're safe. I've made sure no one will ever get to you again."

I nodded. He'd told me as much several times while I was in the hospital. He'd hired extra security for our floor, as well as the building, and installed an alarm on the elevator to alert us to anyone even getting off on this floor, as well as inside the penthouse.

"I'm not a good man. Never will be. I've killed people, and I'll do it again. But meeting you, having you in my life, has changed me. I always used women and tossed them away, never caring about more than getting off."

I tried to look away, but he gripped my chin.

Even though I couldn't see him, he wanted me to look at him for whatever he had to say. The last thing I wanted to hear about were the women who had come before me. I'd known he wasn't a virgin, but it didn't mean I wanted it thrown in my face. It was silly to be jealous of them, but I was. Viktor was mine, at least in my heart and mind.

"*Myshka*, I've never met anyone like you before. You're sweet, innocent. My angel. You're the light to my darkness."

My chest ached and I found myself leaning toward him. He'd called himself dark before, but I didn't see him that way. To me, he was the man who had pulled me away from an abusive father. There were times he was cold and a little distant, but others... The other times, he made me feel warm and cherished.

"Cerys, I don't know what love feels like, so I can't say that I love you. I won't say those words without knowing that's what I feel. But I can tell you that no one has ever meant as much to me as you do. Without you, the darkness will swallow me whole and never let go. You give me a reason to keep going, a reason to come home." He ran his fingers through my hair. "You mean everything to me, *myshka*. Bringing you home with me that day was the best decision I ever made."

"I love you, Viktor. I don't expect you to say it back. It's crazy that I fell for you so fast and hard. We barely know one another! When Artur took me, it made me realize what you meant to me. Then all those days in the hospital, and our trip afterward. I loved hearing about your life in Russia, enjoyed finding out about your favorite books, that you dislike TV shows, and have never had a pet. I feel like we grew closer."

He took my hand and lifted it, kissing the back.

"Are you still hurting?"

My heart rate sped up. Was he asking because he wanted me? It felt like forever since he'd last made me cry out in pleasure. I couldn't call it making love, but it wasn't just fucking either. It was special, unique, like our relationship. Something that was just us.

"No. The bleeding stopped five days ago and all the tenderness is gone."

I'd been lucky and hadn't suffered any broken bones. The doctor had called it a miracle. I had to agree considering the beating I'd received. After the tests had concluded and I'd rested a little, I'd remembered the gunshots and asked about Mac. Viktor had assured me the doctor was recovering and would be fine. He was also being compensated for having helped me.

Viktor ran his fingers along my jaw, his touch light. "I want you, *myshka*, but not if it will hurt you."

"Just go slow?" I asked. I wanted him too, but I was a little nervous. The doctor had said it wasn't a good idea to try to have a baby again, not so soon. I wasn't sure how to bring it up to Viktor. He'd been in the room at the time, but did he remember?

"Want a shower? Or maybe a bath?"

I hesitated a moment. Did he intend to join me? Shower sex was nice, but it wasn't what I'd had in mind. Not after not being that close to him for so long.

His lips softly brushed mine. "I'm not stripping you naked and bending you over, *myshka*. We have all night. For that matter, we have the rest of our lives. You're more to me than sex, Cerys."

I reached up and fingered my hair. It was a little oily and needed a good scrubbing. At the beach, I hadn't washed it every day. There'd been little point when the salty air would just make it feel icky again.

"A shower would be nice."

"Wait here and I'll get the water warmed."

I felt the bed shift as he stood and heard his steps as he entered the bathroom. The shower turned on and after a few minutes, he returned for me, helping me stand. Viktor undressed me, taking his time. When I was completely bare, he led me into the bathroom and helped me into the shower stall. I didn't hear the door shut and a moment later I knew why. His hands slid around my waist as he pulled me back against his chest. His hard cock nestled along the crack of my ass, but he didn't make a move to do anything other than hold me.

"It felt like my heart was ripped from my chest when I saw the blood on our bed and on the floor. Knowing he'd taken you, hurt you, tore me up. I can't live through that again, *myshka*."

I reached up and curled my hand around the back of his neck, just letting him hold me. It felt nice to be in his arms. Viktor was my safe place. Maybe that was crazy. He was Bratva, a killer, but for me he was so much more. I'd been honest when I told him I loved him. He might never say the words back, and that was all right. The way he touched me, kissed me, worried over me told me enough. He might not know what love was, but I was almost certain that's what he felt.

"I'm right here, Viktor. I can't promise that nothing bad will ever happen to me, but I know you've taken every precaution, and I know you'll always find me."

He turned me to face him and kissed me, his lips teasing, coaxing. His fingers bit into my hips, as if he was afraid to let go, or perhaps worried I'd disappear again. I tangled my fingers in the hair at his nape and pressed closer to him. I'd missed this. Missed him. He hadn't left my side while I recovered, but it wasn't the same. I missed the intimacy, even though I'd only shared it with him so very briefly. The first time I'd been terrified. It had been different after our wedding in Vegas. That was the closest I'd ever felt with someone, and I wanted to feel that way again.

Viktor pulled away, breathing heavily. "I'm going to wash you, *myshka*. Only that and nothing more. Not right now. Going to take it slow, just like you asked."

I bit my lip and he tugged it free with his thumb.

"The doctor said..." I didn't know how to finish the sentence.

"I know. No babies for a little while. I'll protect you, my angel." He ran his hand through my hair. "While I prefer taking you bare, I won't do anything that could harm you. If we need to use condoms for a bit, then that's what we'll do. There's a box under the sink."

My body tensed at the reminder. He smoothed his hands up and down my arms, pressed a kiss to my brow, and pulled me close again.

"I'm sorry, *myshka*. My words were thoughtless. There's only you in my life now, in my bed. I don't want anyone else. I can't erase the past, Cerys, but I can promise you my present and future are yours and only yours."

"You don't need to apologize. It's silly of me to get upset over it. You didn't know me then, weren't married to me. And even now..." My heart ached at the mere thought, but he'd confessed while we were at the beach that it wasn't uncommon for the men to have someone on the side. It would kill me inside if Viktor ever did that.

"I'm not them," he said. "I should have never told you that, but you'll meet the other wives at some point and they may bring it up. I only meant to prepare you, *lyubimaya*."

"You've never called me that before."

He rubbed his beard against my shoulder before pressing a kiss there. The fact he didn't offer a translation worried me. As sweet as he was being, it couldn't be an awful word. Why wouldn't he tell me?

"Viktor? What's it mean?"

He was quiet and still. I didn't think he would answer.

"Beloved."

I couldn't stop the tears that gathered in my eyes. I rubbed my cheek against his chest and held on tight. Never in my life had anyone called me beloved. No one had wanted me once my mother died. Mrs. Popov had been nice to me, but she wasn't family. The day Viktor and his men had entered our home, I'd thought it was the beginning of the end. But meeting him, being part of his life, was the best thing to ever happen to me. Yes, it had put me in danger, but I'd finally experienced tenderness, found someone who cared, and loved me.

"Make love to me, Viktor," I said softly. "Please."

He kissed me again, then shut off the water and helped me dry. I heard him toweling off himself, then a cabinet opened and shut. I heard a *thunk* and assumed it was the box of condoms. Although, I honestly no idea what condoms would sound like hitting a counter. I'd never been around any before. The sound seemed to be a cardboard box, but I supposed it could have been something else. His hand grasped mine and he led me back into the bedroom and eased me down onto the bed.

I lay back against the pillows and Viktor stretched out beside me. I wished I could see him! I'd give anything to see the look in his eyes right now. Even if I only had my sight for mere seconds, it would be enough to last me a lifetime. I reached up, feeling the slope of his nose, the softness of his beard, brushed my fingers across his full lips.

He took my hand in his, then pressed it to his chest before sliding it down his abdomen. When he released me, I was frozen, unsure what to do.

"You can touch me, Cerys. Anywhere you want."

I felt my cheeks warm as I let my hand slide lower. I brushed over hair that was springy, then slid my fingers along the smooth skin of his cock. I wrapped my hand around him, stroking a few times. He groaned and I felt his body tighten. He'd always been in control, but this time he was giving the power over to me, even if just for a little while. I got up on my knees and ran my other hand up and down his thigh. Viktor rolled to his back and I settled between his legs.

"*Myshka*, there's only so much I can take."

I licked my lips and lowered my head. I felt his body tense and the vibration of his groan as I slid my lips down his cock. The musky scent of him filled my nose. I flicked at the underside of his shaft with my tongue before pulling back, only to suck him back in. Viktor trembled as I worked his cock, the taste of his pre-cum coating my tongue. It only made me want more, to make him come.

"*Myshka. Lyubimaya.* Stop. Please. I want to be inside your tight pussy when I come."

I pulled away and wiped the drool from my mouth.

Viktor grasped my waist and flipped me onto my back. I gasped, then giggled as he rubbed his beard along my ribs and hipbone. He placed tender kisses along my skin, traveling up until his lips closed over my nipple. The way he sucked and nipped at it had me moaning and arching my back, needing more. My clit pulsed and I was already slick with need.

"My beautiful wife," he murmured before teasing the other side. "So soft. Delicious. Sexy."

He licked between my breasts as he slipped his hand between my legs. The brush of his fingers against my pussy had me spreading my thighs more.

"Heels on the bed. Open all the way for me."

I swallowed hard and did as he commanded. His thumb stroked my clit as he thrust a finger in and out of me. It felt good, so good, but it wasn't anywhere near enough. I wanted his cock to stretch me, fill me. I whimpered and squirmed under him. Viktor gently bit my nipple as he added a second finger, curling them just enough to hit a spot inside me that had me panting and wanting to beg for more.

"That's it. Come for me."

I was close. So close.

"Now, *myshka*. Come for me now."

My body obeyed, pleasure ripping through me and leaving me breathless. He kept working my pussy and sucking on my nipples. It felt like my orgasm went on and on, little aftershocks starting to build to something bigger. When he slipped a third finger inside me and pressed a little tighter on my clit, I screamed out his name, my release soaking the bed beneath me.

He chuckled and kissed the side of my neck, then my lips.

"I want you on your knees."

I licked my lips. "Could we... Like at the hotel in Vegas?"

He went still, only his hand moving as he still worked his fingers inside me.

"Are you sure, *myshka*?"

"Yes, Viktor. Please. I… I liked it."

He released me, moving away. I felt the bed shift as he got up and heard him walk away. When he came back, I heard the clink of metal as he set the items on the bed. Part of me wanted to ask if it was wrong that I'd enjoyed it so much, but I didn't think it mattered. Viktor had been nearly feral that night, and I shivered at the memory. I wanted that again, wanted that wildness.

"I told you hands and knees."

I scurried to do as he said, sticking my ass up in the air.

"Grip the headboard, Cerys. Don't let go no matter what."

"Yes, Viktor." My fingers closed around the wooden slats. The first slap against my pussy had me yelping in surprise.

"Should have obeyed faster, *lyubimaya*. Now I need to punish you."

I could feel the warmth in my cheeks travel all the way to my toes. I couldn't see what he was using on me, but it felt like a paddle of some sort. He swatted my pussy again and I spread my legs farther. My clit pulsed and I had to bite my lip so I couldn't beg him to do more.

The bed shifted, then I felt cool metal that clinked as he snapped it around my wrists. Handcuffs. I tugged and couldn't break free. He'd fastened me to the bed with handcuffs. It turned me on even more.

Viktor moved behind me, his hands spreading me wider. The wet heat of his tongue as he lapped at my pussy was almost enough to make me come. He thrust it into me before flicking my clit. When he pulled away, I wanted to cry and beg him to stay. I heard a noise I didn't recognize, then felt his cock press against me, but it wasn't the same as before. The condom. He must have put one on. I didn't like the feel of it as he pressed inside me, but I knew it was necessary.

"Hold on, *myshka*. Gonna be hard and rough."

"Please, Viktor."

He growled and started driving into me, each thrust deeper than the last. The headboard banged into the wall as he possessed me, claimed me, took what he wanted. He snaked a hand under my body and pinched my nipple, twisting it. The spike of pain sent a warmth through my breast.

"Does my *myshka* need me to talk dirty to her?"

I nodded eagerly.

"My dirty girl? You're mine, *myshka*. You like getting fucked, taking my cock?"

"Yes! Yes, Viktor!"

"My wife enjoyed her spanking, didn't she? Likes getting that pussy smacked."

I moaned as he hammered into me, I couldn't hold out another moment. I came, a loud keening sound escaping me as I nearly blacked out from the pleasure. Viktor seemed to lose complete control, his hips snapping against me, his grip on my hip almost punishing. He gave a guttural cry as he came, pounding into me until he had nothing left to give.

Viktor slipped free of my body and I heard the pop of something. He gripped my hair and pulled my head back and to the side, then the wet head of his cock brushed against my lips.

"Open."

My lips parted and he thrust inside.

"Suck me clean."

I sucked and licked until every drop of his

release was gone. I could hear his ragged breathing and when he freed me, he collapsed on the bed.

"*Lyubimaya*, as much as I enjoyed that, I think I prefer being more gentle with you. You're not a whore, you're my wife. You're precious to me. Treating you like the others… it feels wrong."

I tugged on the cuffs and he released me. Curling against his side, I laid my head on his chest.

"I like the way you lose control when you have me tied down. I like that you don't treat me as if I'll break. When you're like that, it makes me feel like a normal woman. Not some blind girl who has to be coddled."

"Then I'll give you what you want, what you need." He pressed a kiss to the top of my head. "You're everything to me, *lyubimaya*."

"I love you, Viktor."

He tightened his hold on me, and my eyes slid shut. It wasn't long before sleep pulled me under. But as I drifted off, I thought I heard him utter something in Russian.

"*Ya ne mogu zhit' bez tebya.*"

I didn't know what it meant, but I hoped I remembered to ask. It sounded beautiful.

Epilogue

Viktor
Two Months Later

Cerys hid next to a potted plant, and I couldn't blame her. The other wives had been vicious when they thought I wasn't listening. But I'd heard every cruel word, and they would all pay. I'd already spoken to their husbands and ensured they would be kept on tighter leashes and given fewer freedoms for a while.

I crept up behind my wife, and slid my palm against her belly, drawing her back against me.

"Ya ne mogu zhit' bez tebya."

"Are you ever going to tell me what that means?" she asked.

I smiled and kissed the top of her head. I'd said those words to her countless times since the first time I'd uttered them, and she always asked what it meant. It was past time for me to tell her, but I had to admit it was a little fun watching the frustration enter her eyes, then kissing it away. We'd ended up in bed nearly each and every time she asked me the meaning.

Unless I wanted to take her in the bathroom, now wasn't the time or place, which meant that I needed to confess what it meant. I knew she needed those words, but I'd not been ready to utter them in English just yet.

"It means I can't live without you." I nuzzled her neck. "I love you, Cerys. In Russia, we don't say that often. What I told you that night, and have said many times since, is so much more than a simple I love you."

She melted against me. "I can't live without you either."

I rubbed her belly, wishing it was filled with our child, but the doctor had suggested we wait a little longer. Between the miscarriage and the trauma Cerys had suffered at the hands of Artur, I was more than willing to wait. I didn't want to do anything that would harm her.

"They don't like me," she said. I knew who she meant. The women hadn't been subtle.

"Their husbands will be handling the situation. None of them will be cruel to you ever again. If they are, then *I* will deal with them, and I can promise none of them want that."

She reached up and brushed her fingers over my beard. "My fierce protector."

"Always, *myshka*."

"I feel like I should thank my father."

I went tight at the mention of that man, fury filling me. "Why?"

My tone was harsher than I'd intended and I felt her retreat a little. I soothed her with my hands and a few kisses along her shoulder, and she began to relax against me again.

"If he hadn't gotten into trouble with your people, then you never would have come to my house that day. We might have never met, and you're the best thing that ever happened to me, Viktor. I would gladly endure all my father did to me all over again, as long as it meant we would be together in the end."

I turned her to face me, tipped her chin up, then kiss her soft and slow.

"We were destined to be together," I said.

"I was just collateral damage."

"No, you were the prize I'd been waiting for all my life. You own me heart and soul, Cerys. My light. My angel."

She pressed her lips to mine, and I pulled us farther into the shadows. Maybe finding an empty bathroom wasn't such a bad idea after all. I didn't think I'd last much longer without being inside my woman. I needed her like I needed to breathe.

I hadn't saved her that day. She'd saved me. And one day we'd have the family we both craved.

Unwanted Complication (Owned by the Mob 2)
Harley Wylde & Paige Warren

Raina -- A man took me from my home in Tahiti when I was five. They called it an adoption, but I know the truth. My parents sold me, pure and simple. My life has been one nightmare after another, a living hell I can't escape. When my owner gives me as payment to Feliks Sobol, I think it's just like any other time. But it's not. He's different. Under the darkness and danger, there's a tenderness I've never experienced. I want him. I shouldn't, but I do. He might be the one who ends up breaking me.

Feliks -- I'm the monster in the shadows, the man everyone fears. I've done unspeakable things, and I will do them again without a hint of remorse. I'm Bratva, born and bred. Hard. Unyielding. Yet when I'm around Raina, there's another side of me that emerges. One that's weaker. Wanting her could get me killed. Yet I can't let her go. Until my brigadier demands I choose. Raina, or the woman I wish to marry.

I decide to hold on to the power I'll gain by marrying Natalia Gorev. I didn't realize it was too late. Raina is already under my skin, and when she's taken, I know I've made the wrong choice. I'll bathe the city in blood if that's what it takes to get her back. I only hope she can forgive me.

Chapter One

Raina

Someone once told me, "As long as you're hurting, you know you're alive." If so, I was definitely alive. My wrists and ankles ached from the constant presence of the shackles that bound me. I preferred that pain over the other, though. I just didn't understand why anyone would want to live like this. I'd prefer to die than continue in this hell.

"There's my little slut."

I cringed as I turned to face the man who had *adopted* me. I liked to think my family wouldn't have given me away if they'd known why he'd paid so much. Maybe it was a fantasy. My parents could have been just as awful as the man who'd bought me.

"Come here. Now."

I walked over, knowing my chains would reach as far as the doorway. He grabbed my chin as I stopped in front of him. I knew better than to look him in the eye. Nothing good ever came of it. He'd punish me for such insolence.

"It's time to get you clean and prepped. I have a special guest coming."

Which translated into he owed someone money or a favor, and the best way to pay them back was to let them use me how they saw fit. He'd turned me into his personal whore, and if I dared to disobey or fight back, then it got much worse. In the twisted mind of Gary Leeds, I owed him for the food he gave me and the roof over my head. And he took payment however he wanted, whenever he wanted.

He pulled the keys from his pocket and unfastened my cuffs. The first time they'd rusted, he'd cursed about me costing him additional money. Now he freed me when it was shower time, but I didn't dare try to run away. I rubbed at my wrists as he hauled me to my feet and began shoving me in the direction of the bathroom.

Gary twisted the shower knob, only the cold one. He got a perverse pleasure out of watching my nipples get hard under the icy spray. With a grin stretching his lips, he jabbed me until I stumbled under the water, then reached for the soap. Every time he washed me, I went somewhere else in my mind. His hands lingered in places I tried not to think about. When the water turned off, I quickly dried myself, braided my long hair, then went back into the bedroom. He'd said this was a special client, which meant he'd take me to the playroom.

Gary put another set of cuffs on me, prettier ones to showcase his merchandise, then led me downstairs. He unlocked the door to my worst nightmare, then pushed me inside. The lights came on, nearly blinding me, and I tried not to look at everything in the room. I already knew what was here. I'd experienced it all firsthand.

He led me over to the waist-high table, then forced me over it. Once he'd secured my hands at the middle of my back and anchored me to the table, he kicked my legs apart and fastened my ankles to two O-rings on the floor. Shackled and unable to move, I stood bent over the bench and spread wide for whatever his *guest* wanted to do. It also would give them access to my mouth. I hated Gary. Hated his friends. Hated my life.

Gary leaned over me, his breath against my ear, his cock pressing against me. "Let's get you ready, shall we?"

I stared blankly at the wall ahead of me. He took

great pleasure in lubing me, then inserting the largest anal plug he owned. It was silver, and the metal was cold as it entered me. I winced as it burned and stretched me but crying out only gave him a thrill. He loved to make me suffer.

A knock at the door drew Gary's attention. I heard a murmur of voices when he went to the hallway. He typically liked to leave me like this for a while before anyone arrived. He'd look at me, touch me, let his favorite guards do the same. After his guest finished with me, he'd allow any of his staff to fuck me.

The room was chilly, and my nipples were so hard they hurt. That was the main reason for the temperature of the room. Gary loved seeing the tips of my breasts harden into peaks. Even if it wasn't from desire, he got off on it. Enjoyed touching them.

I heard a loud voice drawing nearer and realized the man had a thick accent. *Russian*? Oh, hell. My nape prickled. If Gary had borrowed money from the Bratva, I didn't think the offer of my body would be enough. I'd heard stories of how ruthless they were. The man entered the room. I didn't dare look at him, but I was aware of his presence. It was a tangible thing, his voice like a caress against my skin.

"What is the meaning of this?" the man demanded. "I can have a whore without relieving your debts. Did you forget the Bratva-owned brothels are the best in this city?"

"Of course not, Mr. Sobol. I meant no disrespect. I've had many compliments over Raina and thought only to offer her to you as a down payment on the amount I owe. As a *kryshas* for Mr. Petrov, I thought perhaps we could come to an agreement. In exchange for an hour with her in the playroom, you lessen my debt by, say… one thousand?" Gary asked.

The Russian snorted. "*Nyet.*"

"Come, Mr. Sobol. At least look her over. She's still nice and tight, and she can take a hard ass-fucking. I've also been told she has the best cunt in the neighborhood."

The Russian grunted. I heard his footsteps draw closer, then the light touch of his fingers as he dragged them down my arm, across my hip, then settled his hand on my ass cheek. He flicked the anal plug with his finger, making me gasp at the twinge of pain.

"She's already prepped, as you can see." Gary moved closer. "If you don't wish to make use of her mouth, I have a ball gag. Unless you like it when they scream. She has a good set of lungs."

"Such beautiful golden skin," the Russian murmured.

"She's from the islands. Tahiti. Bought her when she was only five."

The Russian turned sharply. "You've been whoring her out since she was a child?"

Gary lifted a hand. "Of course not, Mr. Sobol. She didn't get broken in until she'd gotten her period and become a woman."

The Russian growled, and every hair on my body stood on end. "Leave us," he demanded.

I heard Gary hasten to comply, and the door click shut. The Russian turned toward me again, his touch light as he caressed my shoulder, my back, my hip. Then he spread my ass cheeks and removed the anal plug. I whimpered and tried not to show fear.

"Easy, *lastachka.* You ever feel pleasure when men take you?"

I hesitated, and it must have been the wrong thing to do. He spanked my ass hard enough to make me yelp, but it really only stung. He'd surprised me but hadn't seriously hurt me.

"Answer, *lastachka*."

"No. I never experienced pleasure when men fuck me. I'm only here to be used."

I heard the clink of his buckle unfastening, then the sound of a zipper lowering. I tried not to tense, knowing that would only make it worse. What I didn't expect was the feel of his naked cock in the crevice of my ass. But he didn't enter me. He leaned over my body, then slid his hands between my torso and the table. "Are you always chained?" he asked.

I nodded. I didn't know why he'd asked. Did it matter? I'd thought men liked it when a woman was helpless.

The Russian cupped my breasts and tugged at my nipples. My eyes went wide as a spark of pleasure hit me. He rolled the hard tips. I'd had men touch me there before, but it had never felt… good. The Russian mumbled soft words in his native tongue, things I didn't understand, but the tone was clear enough. He thrust against my ass, his cock feeling impossibly big and hard. I knew he'd split me in two when he entered me.

He rolled my nipples again before giving them another tug. With a shift of his hips, he worked his cock between the lips of my pussy. Every thrust made the head bump against my clit. Soon I was panting for breath, my body going tight, and I couldn't help but make a keening noise. It felt so good, yet not good enough.

"Beg me, *lastachka*."

"Please," I said. "I want… I want…"

"To come?" he asked.

"Yes! Please, I want to come."

He leaned down again, pressing his shirt covered chest to my back and bound hands. "Are you clean, *lastachka*? Do I need a condom to fuck you?"

"Gary makes everyone wear one. They're… They're in the cabinet near the door."

"Not what I asked." He pinched down hard on my nipples, and I cried out, coming for the first time in my life. Tears slipped down my cheeks from the intensity of the feelings.

"I'm clean. I get tested."

He grunted and the next thing I knew, I felt his cock pressing into my pussy. It burned as he stretched me, but I didn't experience the pain I typically felt. The slide of his cock as he stroked in and out of me had my nipples hardening more. I gasped when he hit a certain spot inside me, and nearly saw stars. He did it again and I whimpered. I bit my lip and moaned as my pussy clenched down on him.

He growled and thrust into me faster. I cried out as I felt the gush of my release, and my cheeks warmed. I'd never done such a thing before. Would he be angry?

The Russian leaned down and kissed my cheek, rubbing his chin along my shoulder. "Such a good girl." He pulled free, and I felt him spread my ass cheeks again. I tensed, worried he'd hurt me now, that it had all been a ruse. He rubbed the tight hole and crooned to me in Russian before I felt the head of his cock press there instead. Slowly, he worked his hard length into my ass. I whimpered at how large he was, but the Russian was oddly gentle as he used shallow thrusts until he filled me. He ground his hips against me, muttering words I didn't understand. Cupping my breasts in his hands, he began stroking in and out of me. At first, he was slow, almost gentle. Then he began playing with my nipples again, and I clenched down on him.

The Russian growled and started slamming into me, taking me hard and deep. "Going to ride this gorgeous ass, then fuck your wet cunt until I come again," he said. His voice was rougher than before.

His hips jerked, and I felt the hot spurts of his release. The big man growled again, not stopping as he roughly claimed me. When he pulled free, I heard him panting for breath. My pussy throbbed and ached in a way it never had before. I wished he'd come inside me there. He'd said he would, and I wondered if he'd meant it.

Although my ass hurt, he'd been more careful than anyone had before. He could have ripped me apart, but he hadn't. I pressed my lips together, trying not to feel anything. I couldn't let one encounter with this man undo all of my training. I knew what happened if I let my emotions get the better of me. I needed to be numb. It was the only way to survive.

I heard him pull some wipes from a nearby canister. Gary kept several around the room for the men to use. No one cared how messy I got. The Russian must have cleaned his cock, then I felt the heat of his body over mine.

"Keys, *lastachka*? Where are they?"

"Gary keeps them."

He reached down and turned my face toward him, and his beauty dazzled me. I'd never seen a man so handsome before. Even the scruff along his jaw was sexy.

"I wish to turn you over."

I shook my head. "You can't."

His gaze narrowed. "Why?"

I licked my lips, hating to confess just how dirty I

was. I might not have tested positive for any diseases, but I was still just a whore and nothing more. "When you're done, the men get to have me. I have to stay locked down."

Anger tightened his features. I felt him grip the shackles at my right ankle and with a *snap*, he broke it. My body went still. He'd just broken metal. With nothing but his hands!

He freed my other ankle and the chain binding me to the table, then helped me stand. His touch was gentle as he fingered the handcuffs on my wrists. With a hard yank, he broke the connector. While the cuffs were still on my wrists, my arms were no longer bound behind me.

Pain surged through my arms as the blood rushed through my veins. I wanted to shake them out, but I didn't dare. This man was an unknown to me. I didn't want to risk making any sudden moves. I knew his type. If he mistook something as a threat, it would be dealt with before I could make an explanation.

"He called you Raina."

I nodded. "And you're Mr. Sobol?"

"Call me Feliks." He eased me onto the edge of the table, then caged me between his arms. The heat of his body made me shiver. Feliks leaned in closer, his lips near my ear. "Do you want this, *lastachka*? Do you want my cock in your wet cunt?"

"You're asking?"

He nodded. "I can give you more pleasure. Give you a proper fucking. Every woman should experience pleasure at least once."

His coarse words should have turned me off, but they didn't. When he said them, it only left a lingering heat inside me. I didn't know if my reaction was because of his kindness or something else. He could have hurt me. Could have raped me without a care for whether I enjoyed what he did. But Feliks hadn't done that. He'd made me come -- for the first time in my life -- before taking his own pleasure. It didn't change what I was, or that I'd had no choice but to be taken. And yet, I knew it was doubtful I'd ever have another man ask me such a thing. I'd be a fool to decline his offer. "Yes, Feliks."

He lowered his lips to mine, his kiss harsh and demanding. I felt the slide of his cock along my folds, then he plunged inside. He didn't take me slow. Wasn't gentle. He was rough. Dominant. The way he gripped me, shoved his cock into me, should have scared me shitless. But his touch wasn't one of anger or power. Yes, he was powerful, but he was also... considerate.

He shifted his hips on the next thrust so that he rubbed against my clit with every stroke of his cock. He powered into me, his hand braced at my hip, the only thing keeping me in place. "Come for me, *lastachka*. Come now."

I obeyed his command, and I felt my release soak the table under me and slick my thighs. Feliks groaned and took me harder. Deeper. He made me come twice more, and still he didn't stop. I'd never been with anyone like him.

"*Lastachka*, look at me." I lifted my gaze to his and held it. He tweaked my nipple, then angled his thrusts so that he hit some special place inside that made me see stars. I tried to hold his gaze, but my eyes slid shut, the pleasure almost too much to bear. He tapped my cheek with his fingers. "*Nyet, Lastachka.* Eyes on me. Know who is making you come, who owns your body."

I tried to focus on him, but my mind was hazy. I

felt his release as he came inside me, and a chill raced down my spine. No one had ever taken me bare. I could feel his essence leaking out of my ass and pussy. His cock twitched inside me, and he lightly stroked my cheek.

He'd asked if I was clean, and I was, but I should have told him I wasn't on birth control. Would he be angry when he found out?

"Thank you, Feliks," I whispered. Maybe it made me crazy to thank him, but this was the first time I hadn't feared my captivity, hadn't been hurt by the man taking me. Any kindness was a welcome one.

"I'm not a nice man, *lastachka*. I've killed. Raped. Done what the Bratva demanded. I'm a man who takes what he wants when he wants it." I shuddered at his words. He'd shown me a kindness, but he'd hurt other women the way Gary's men hurt me. "But you… that's all you've known. The ugliness of the world. I'm going to take you again. And again. We're not done, *lastachka*."

"Gary will return. He said an hour."

Feliks gripped my braid, using it to tip my head back. "I take what I want. I will fuck you as many times as I wish, and you will like it, won't you?"

"Y-yes. I've never…" I bit my lip.

He kissed me again, his lips firm. He swept his tongue into my mouth, proving he owned my body, that I was his to command. I leaned into him, still aching and needing more. I wasn't this woman. Had never wanted a man's touch. What was wrong with me? Had someone drugged me? No. That had happened before. This was different.

"Mr. Sobol, I'm going to need the little slut back," Gary said from the doorway. "I'll get your payment to you shortly. She's good, isn't she? I bet she can earn the cash quick enough."

I tried not to let my fear and revulsion show. Feliks' cock twitched inside me again. He pulled free, then turned me over. Without a word, he thrust into my pussy. I didn't know how he was still hard. With Gary watching, he fucked me. From the mirror on the back wall, I could see Gary pulling out his cock and stroking himself, getting off on watching. Feliks came inside me, then pulled out and spread my ass cheeks wide. He wasn't gentle this time as he entered me, making me cry out.

Feliks gripped my hips as he slammed into me. He was rough as he fucked me, his hot cum filling me up within minutes. When he pulled out, he held me open and grunted.

"You're beautiful, with my cum smeared over your ass and cunt."

Gary gave a shout. "No! You can't take her bare!"

"Too late." Feliks snarled at him. "You offered a payment. I accepted. On my terms. Gave her a thorough fucking, and I don't like condoms."

My heart hammered in my chest. Jesus. If he didn't like condoms, had he just given me something? When he'd asked about *me* being clean, I hadn't considered he wouldn't be. Not that it mattered. My refusal wouldn't have ended well. I knew if I contracted a disease, Gary would sell me off to a brothel and wash his hands of me. And it wouldn't be an upscale place. No, he'd dump me in the worst whorehouse he could find.

"Mr. Sobol, I'll need to be compensated. She'll need the morning-after pill, and..." Feliks lunged at him, and I fell to the floor without the support of his body. I watched in horror as Feliks threw Gary into the wall, the plaster cracking. Seeing the violence, he was capable of reminded me he was no less a monster than the man who had bought me.

"Morning-after pill?" Feliks asked, his voice almost deadly. "She's not protected against pregnancy, but you whore her out?"

"I'll take care of it! I promise, Mr. Sobol. Please, don't kill me," Gary begged and blubbered.

Feliks stalked back over to me, wrapped his hand around my throat, and lifted me to my feet. My heart raced, and I wrapped a hand around his wrist, hoping he wasn't about to strangle me. He pressed his fingers to the pulse point in my throat, a smile ticking up the corner of his lips. "So frightened, *lastachka*. I could snap your neck. Or maybe I could just fuck you again. The damage is done already."

At that moment, I knew what choice I needed to make. It was the only one that would ever free me. I tried to swallow, but his grip tightened. "Do it," I said, my voice almost a whisper.

His brow furrowed, and he squeezed tighter.

"Kill me, Feliks. Make it end."

"You want to die, *lastachka*?"

"Yes." I felt a tear slip down my cheek. Then another. "Death would be kinder than living."

He growled, lifting his lip in a snarl. Leaning in closer, I felt the heat of his breath against my face. "You wish to die? What if instead I take you with me? Every time you utter such foolishness, I spank you, then fuck you."

"Not foolish." How could he understand? I doubted he'd ever been owned, humiliated, treated like trash. His grip was tight enough now that black dots swam across my vision.

"Sleep, *lastachka*." I felt my body grow heavy, and then everything went dark.

Chapter Two

Feliks

Raina wasn't a complication that I needed. It was possible she carried my child within her already. I'd come inside her multiple times and planned to do it again soon. But a pregnancy could pose a problem. A rather large one. I'd had my eye on a certain lady who would make an excellent wife, especially for someone wanting to climb the ranks of the Bratva. While she might turn a blind eye to me keeping a mistress, a child would be an issue if Raina became noticeably pregnant before I sealed the deal with Natalia Gorev. Her father, Fedor Gorev, had the ear of the Vor.

I didn't normally keep a mistress, but I had an apartment I kept for just such a purpose. Having nowhere else to take her, I'd brought Raina here and placed her on the bed. Pacing the room, I wasn't coming up with any ideas on how to handle the problem. As much as I didn't need a child with her, the morning-after pill wasn't a possibility. There were some lines even I wouldn't cross, that being one of them. I would never kill my child, especially before they had a chance to be born.

I could keep them both here, but if I didn't sign papers and have an official engagement with Natalia before Raina showed -- if she was even pregnant -- then the entire deal would unravel. Having been raised around the Bratva, Natalia knew what I expected of her. Her family had trained her to become the wife of someone like me. She'd turn a blind eye to any indiscretions and be on my arm for all events and parties. She'd run my home, do charity work, and whatever the hell else the other wives did in their spare time.

Folding my arms, I came to a stop next to the bed and stared down at Raina. Although she was a little too thin, her hips and overall bone structure told me she'd fill out nicely with some regular meals. I couldn't help but reach out and run my fingers over her silky skin. She was beautiful in her own way, and she captivated me. Which made her incredibly dangerous. If I were smart, I'd keep her here long enough to ensure there wasn't a child, then give her to someone else.

Apparently, I wasn't smart because I had no intention of giving her up. While I'd always worn condoms if I fucked any of the whores in the brothels, I detested them. I'd always been careful and ensured I protected my paramours against pregnancy, and I got tested frequently, and made sure they did the same. But Raina was different. For whatever reason, I'd listened to my baser instincts and taken her bare. It had been foolish. Even if she'd claimed to be clean, what if she wasn't?

The way her previous owner had reacted when he'd seen me fuck her without protection made me think she was safe. No, it was clear he always made men wear a condom when he'd let them fuck her. It didn't make it foolproof. Condoms broke and accidents happened. The fact he'd had her since she was so small had infuriated me. I knew that had to be part of why I'd lost all reason. Knowing he'd allowed men to have her, to treat her like a whore, when she'd likely still been a young teen, if even that, made me see red.

I was no angel. Never pretended to be. I'd done unspeakable things in my life. Usually at someone else's order, but it didn't change the fact I'd harmed women, killed men, and had done it all without a hint of remorse or guilt. The things the Bratva had ordered me to do were jobs and nothing more. A man doesn't pay his debts or try to cheat the Bratva? Fine. We take his wife as payment and use her in front of him to drive home the point -- *we* are in charge.

Leeds giving Raina to me, or anyone else he owed a debt, was no different. If I hadn't had easy access to pussy anytime I wanted, his offer might have tempted me. I hadn't accepted because of his debt. It had been her. Seeing her bound, on display, had made me hungry for her. Learning she'd been used since she'd been much younger had infuriated me. But after I started with her, and she said the others would use her when I was finished... it had twisted something inside me, made me want to be someone other than the monster she'd see when she closed her eyes. Not one woman had ever seen me as anything more than a creature of darkness. They feared me, even when they wanted me. Or rather, the power that would come with tying their names to mine. They wanted wealth and a certain level of protection. None of them had cared about me personally. Only what I could give them.

I loosened her braid and ran my fingers through her hair. It was long, thick, and beautiful. It wasn't silky and smooth like most of the women I dealt with, but in this case, different was good. The strands were still wet, and slightly coarse. I feathered my fingers over her cheek, wondering when she'd wake up. I'd been as gentle as I could, but I'd needed her unconscious for the journey here. That and she'd pissed me off by telling me to kill her.

I didn't know how old she was. My stomach twisted at the thought she might still be underage. I hadn't stopped to ask. Leeds had said she'd become a woman before they'd used her, which meant she'd had her period. Didn't mean she was eighteen or older now. Shit. I should have clarified. Even monsters had rules, and I'd never knowingly harmed a child.

My phone rang, and I answered, seeing Viktor's name on the screen.

"What do you need?" I asked, knowing he wouldn't call without a reason.

"Why am I hearing from Leeds about his debt being reduced?"

I pinched the bridge of my nose, wishing the asshole had waited. This wasn't a conversation I wished to have with Viktor just yet. I needed to figure things out. Mostly, I needed to know what I wanted to do with Raina.

"I'd planned to discuss it with you tomorrow. I lowered what he owes by one thousand dollars." I paused. Leeds hadn't demanded more when I'd left. I knew the man feared me. Now that I was gone, would he try to get Viktor to lower the debt more? If he did, I'd discuss it with Viktor. The asshole should be grateful I let him live.

Viktor growled, and I heard him slam his fist onto his desk. "And why would you do that?"

"He had a girl chained up. He'd stripped her, locked her to a table, and offered me the use of her to reduce what he owes." I ran a hand through my hair. "Viktor, he's had her since she was only a child. All she's known is pain."

"And where is she now?"

I glanced at the bed. "The apartment I keep for my mistresses. I didn't find out until after I'd accepted his offer she wasn't on birth control. It's possible she's pregnant."

Viktor started cursing, and I heard him pacing. "Are you telling me you fucked a child?"

"What?" I turned away from the sight of Raina in my bed. "Of course not! Although, I didn't ask how old she is now. As far as I know, she's at least eighteen. I need to keep her here until I know if she's carrying my child."

"And your engagement?" he asked.

"This complicates things. I need to lock down an agreement with Gorev before anyone finds out about Raina. His daughter knows to look the other way. However, I can't guarantee her father will give me her hand if they find out I may have gotten Raina pregnant. I need that marriage to go through, Viktor."

Viktor didn't say a word, which didn't bode well for me. When my brigadier went silent, bad things happened. Ever since he'd married, some of his hardness had smoothed out. He was no less capable of killing when the occasion called for it, but when it came to women and children, something had changed.

"I'm sending Aleksi to your apartment."

"Why?" I asked, my brow furrowing.

"As you said, this girl is a complication you don't need right now. If she's in fact carrying your child, we can deal with that later. For now, I think it's best if someone else handles her care."

"*Nyet*. Viktor, you can't just come in here and take my..." I didn't know how to finish the sentence. My what? She wasn't my mistress. Certainly not my wife. She was an inconvenience. I should be thankful he wanted to have someone take her off my hands. So why wasn't I jumping at the chance? "Give me some time. At least a few days. She's had a shock and we should ease her into this."

"Feliks, I've known you a long time. It wasn't very far in the past, you insinuated you'd fuck my wife when I tired of her. Why should I leave that poor girl in your care?" Viktor asked.

Even if they hadn't been married yet, I still remember my words to his wife. I'd like to say I'd changed since then, but I hadn't. I heard a gasp behind me and whirled to find Raina sitting up in the bed. Her eyes were wide, and her hand went to her throat as she looked around. Her gaze landed on me and she froze. A tear slipped down her cheek, then again. Fuck! I didn't know what to do with a crying woman.

"Viktor, I need to go. Raina is awake."

"Aleksi will be there within the next three days and not a moment later," Viktor said. "I'll give you that much, but nothing more. You're pushing it already, Feliks. You know the right thing is to give her up -- or forgo the marriage to Natalia. Don't ask for more. You won't get it."

The call disconnected before I could tell him the fucker wasn't needed.

"Where am I?" Raina asked.

"Somewhere safe." I scanned her body, enjoying the sight. It would be a pity to cover her, but I knew she needed clothing. Walking over to the dresser, I pulled out the drawers until I found what I wanted. A discarded nightgown from a previous lover. I'd shred it once I bought her new things, but with Aleksi arriving at any moment, I needed her to dress in something. "Put this on."

She took the garment from me and pulled it over her head, running her fingers over the silky material. "Is it mine? I mean, can I keep it?"

"*Nyet.* I will buy you something better." I sat on the edge of the bed and reached out, lightly touching her cheek. "You have nothing to fear, *kroshka*. You're safe here."

"Is this your home?" she asked.

I shook my head. I didn't know how to tell her I intended it for my mistress. After all she'd been through, I didn't want to hurt her more. And yet, I didn't want to lie to her either.

"What is this place?" she asked, wrapping her arms around her middle. "Is it where…"

"Where what?"

"Am I in one of the brothels you mentioned?" she asked softly.

The thought of her working on her back, letting other men touch her… anger surged inside me. It made little sense, but now that I'd tasted her, brought her pleasure, I felt a bond of sorts. Or perhaps it had to do with the potential child growing inside her. Whatever the case, I'd never allow her to work in one of those places. Not after all she'd suffered.

"*Nyet*. You are not a whore, Raina. You're… mine." My brow furrowed. I hadn't meant to say that, and yet it was true. I didn't want to let her go.

"Yours?"

I nodded. "Yes."

She looked around the room again. "This isn't your home, so it's… mine? If I'm not a whore, does that make me your… I don't know what to call it."

"Mistress," I said. "Would that bother you?"

She stared at me a moment. "Are you married?"

"Not yet, but soon. An engagement should be announced within the week. You will not be a prisoner here, Raina. You may leave and go shopping, go out to eat. Whatever your heart desires. I'll provide you with funds and a driver."

"Will your wife know about me?" she asked.

"Natalia's family has trained her to look the other way. She'll be a proper Russian wife and know what's expected. When I need to attend an event, she'll be on my arm. But when I need passion, I'll be here with you."

She looked around the room again, seeming to take it all in. I knew such an offer would offend some women. But those women hadn't been through the horrors Raina had. Leeds had treated her as a whore long before she should have ever known the touch of a man.

"Is that common? Keeping two women?" she asked.

"For men like me? Yes. Some keep more than one mistress. Will it bother you? Knowing I'm married to another?" Her answer wouldn't matter. If I wanted to keep her, I would. Besides, where else would she go?

She hesitated, but I could tell she thought over the question. At least she hadn't blurted an answer. When she finally spoke, I'd know it was a decision she hadn't come to lightly.

"You won't let others use me?" she asked. "I'll be with you and only you?"

"Of course, *lastachka*. Any man who touches you will answer to me."

Her shoulders sagged, and she blew out a breath. I still didn't feel certain about her answer. Was she pleased with this turn of events? Pissed? Had I hurt her feelings? I knew women to be emotional creatures, and yet Raina seemed more reserved than most.

"What happens when you don't want me anymore?" she asked.

I cupped her cheek. "*Kroshka*, I don't see me tiring of you soon. Possibly never. We'll worry about that when the time comes, but I won't throw you out onto the streets with no way to care for yourself. That much I can promise."

She placed her hand over mine and leaned into

my touch. "Thank you, Feliks."

"Would you like to shower? Are you hungry?" I tipped my head to the side and studied her. When had she last eaten? "I can order out and have something delivered. We'll stock the kitchen tomorrow."

"Anything would be good. All Gary let me have was plain oatmeal or buttered bread. He said anything else was a waste."

My poor Raina. So abused and mistreated. I'd treat her like a queen, for however long I had her. It might take me a while to convince Viktor to allow her to remain with me. I didn't want to relinquish her to Aleksi or anyone else. Raina was mine, and I'd see to it she had everything she needed. "I'll have a few dishes delivered. Go ahead and start the shower, Raina. Use as much hot water as you like." After my last mistress, I'd cleaned the place out. All new bedding, towels, and even the soap and hair products were new. I didn't know what scents Raina would like, but the ones available would suffice for now.

I helped her stand and pressed a kiss to her forehead. "I'll check on you in a moment."

She gave me a nod and slight smile before going into the bathroom. She left the door open, and I watched her as I ordered our food. Even now, my cock hardened, and I wanted her again. I couldn't remember the last time I'd been so attracted to a woman. Usually once would be enough to get them out of my system. Even my mistresses hadn't inspired me to take them more than once or twice, and I'd come inside Raina multiple times already.

The thought of risking a pregnancy should have been a deterrent. Now that I knew she wasn't on anything, I should be more careful. And yet... I enjoyed the feel of her without a barrier between us.

While I needed Natalia, the idea of Raina carrying my child made my cock hard. I wanted to fuck her again and again, until I knew my seed had taken. Until her, I'd have never done such a thing.

I didn't know why or how, but she was different from anyone I'd met before. I hoped I had enough time to figure out why I wanted her as much as I did. Viktor could be persistent. The few days I'd asked for may or may not be granted. But until someone showed up to take Raina away, I'd spend as much time with her as I could.

* * *

Raina

I'd never had a hot shower before. The water felt like heaven, and I wanted to cry at how something so simple could mean so much to me. I reached for the shampoo and lathered my hair, then used the scented soap to wash my body. I'd never had such luxuries before. Even though Feliks hadn't said I had to leave the door open, or the shower, I'd done both out of habit. At least with the sexy man in the other room, I didn't mind him watching me. In fact, his gaze made me feel warm all over.

When he entered the bathroom and began removing his clothes, my heart beat a little faster. Other men or chains had always held me down. Before Feliks, no one had freed me before fucking me. What would it be like to be intimate with him outside that environment? He'd been the only man ever to care if I enjoyed his touch. Whatever he wanted, I'd give it to him.

"Was the open door an invitation?" he asked, cupping my cheek as he stepped into the shower. It was the first time I'd seen him naked. At Gary's, he'd only unfastened his pants.

I ran my fingers over his chest and down his abs. They weren't as chiseled as some men I'd seen, but I liked that bit of softness. Then again, so far I liked everything about Feliks. He'd been honest with me about where I stood. And he'd promised I wouldn't be a whore again.

"You've given me more than anyone else ever has," I said. "I would give you anything you asked."

He lowered his head to mine and kissed me. His lips brushed mine softly at first, then more demanding. I melted against him, opening and letting him in. Clinging to his shoulders, I worried my knees would buckle. I'd never felt this way before. Of course, the only kisses I'd received had been painful. They hadn't been passionate or sweet.

"I only want you, *kroshka*." Feliks picked me up and urged my legs around his waist. He pinned me to the shower wall and reached between us, rubbing my clit. I whimpered as his mouth devoured mine and pleasure shot through me. Soon, I found myself moving my hips, wanting more. I needed him inside me. It was a foreign feeling, actually *wanting* a man.

"Please, Feliks. I need you."

"Soon." His lips brushed mine twice more. "Come for me, Raina."

He slipped a finger inside me, then another. I worked my hips as he teased me, and soon I was screaming out his name. My nipples tightened, and I panted for breath as aftershocks rocked me.

"Beautiful, *lastachka*. Now you may have what you want."

He eased his fingers from me and pressed the head of his cock into me. Using short thrusts, he went a little deeper each time, until I'd taken all of him. The gentle way he touched me, the way he seemed to care… It was almost too much. I felt tears prick my eyes, but I refused to cry. Not right now. I'd cherish this moment. Always.

Feliks gripped my hip and thrust into me. Every stroke put just the right amount of friction on my clit. I knew I wouldn't last long. His powerful body surrounded me as he took what he wanted. But he also gave me what I needed.

"Don't stop. Please don't stop," I begged.

"Never."

He kissed me once more as he fucked me against the shower wall. He took me harder. Deeper. And soon I was coming again. The moment my pussy squeezed his cock, he grunted, and I felt the heat of his release. It felt magical, sharing something like that with him.

"Are you sore?" he asked, pressing a kiss to my jaw, then my shoulder.

"No." I didn't want to tell him he'd been the gentlest of anyone. The other men had thrived on causing me pain. They liked it when I had to lie helplessly beneath them while they violated me. Not once had I ever wanted to give myself to someone until Feliks.

I wondered if he knew the power he had over me. I'd already said I'd give him anything. Not only had I meant it, but I wanted to give him *everything*. I'd have given him my soul if it were possible. This beautiful man had done the impossible. He'd freed me and given me a new life. I'd thought I would die in the hell I'd been living in since Gary bought me. Had prayed for death.

And now I had a reason to live.

"Let's clean you up again, then we'll eat. The food should be here by now."

"You said it was being delivered. Didn't you need to answer the door to get it?" I asked.

He smiled. "You didn't see the building since you were passed out."

Right. Because he'd choked me until I'd blacked out. I might have been angry over it, or at least scared, if it had been anyone other than Feliks. He spared my life when I begged him to kill me. I didn't understand why. I was nothing to him. He'd been so angry to learn I could be pregnant. Wouldn't letting me die have solved the problem? Even now, his touch was soft and his kiss tender. Everything I'd learned so far made me trust him. Stupid? Probably. But living life the way I had made me see the world differently, and the people in it.

"The elevator requires a code to enter this floor. Our food will be waiting outside the door," Feliks said. "I'll work on buying some clothing for you tomorrow. For now, you'll have to wear the nightgown."

I was more than all right with that. It might not seem like much to some. For me, it gave me a little of my dignity back. Something I hadn't experienced, even though I'd seen it in others.

"Thank you, Feliks. For saving me."

He kissed my forehead and ran his nose down mine. "I couldn't have left you there, Raina. I think I would have had a hard time walking away whether or not Leeds said you might be pregnant. Even if I'd left the room, I'd have returned for you."

"Why?"

"I don't know." He frowned, and I could tell he told the truth. He might have wanted to rescue me, but he didn't understand why any more than I did. It honestly didn't matter. I was safe. And for the first time in my life, I felt happy.

I reached for the soap and quickly washed, then helped Feliks clean up as well. My cheeks flamed as I cupped his cock. The heat flaring in his eyes told me he already wanted me again. My stomach growled, and he pulled back.

"Later, *lastachka*. Food first."

He shut off the water and helped me out. Picking up a fluffy towel, he dried me off and dropped the nightgown over my head, tugging the material down my body. It only fell to the tops of my thighs, but it was the best gift anyone had given me. Well, other than my freedom.

Feliks pulled on his boxers and his pants but left the rest of his clothes on the bathroom counter. I couldn't wait to see what he'd ordered. Anything was better than oatmeal and buttered bread.

The scent from the sacks he brought into the apartment made my mouth water. He unloaded everything onto the kitchen counter and motioned for me to sit at the small table nearby. I pulled out a chair and waited eagerly.

My lips parted, and my eyes widened at the large bowl of pasta. It looked like bits of shrimp and something else were in the creamy white sauce, and I couldn't wait to take a bite! He added a piece of garlic bread on the side and brought me a glass of ice water.

"I'm sorry, but water is all we have tonight."

"This is amazing, Feliks. It looks incredible." I took a small bite and gasped at the flavor. "Oh, my gosh! It's... indescribable. I love it!"

He smiled as I ate more, and I noticed he had something different to eat. He noticed my stare and lifted the fork to my lips. I accepted the bite and moaned at how wonderful it tasted. He offered me more and I shook my head. As little as I'd eaten over the years, I didn't think I'd be able to finish my meal, especially if he kept offering me his.

"Eat as much as you want, *lastachka*. I will have breakfast delivered in the morning. Whatever we don't finish can go in the fridge in case you want to snack on it later," Feliks said.

"I keep waiting for something bad to happen," I admitted. "All this seems too good to be true. A man like you wanting me? Being nice to me?"

He reached across the table and caressed my hand. "I only wish someone had saved you sooner. A child should never endure what you did. That's a line I won't cross. I'm not a good man, Raina. Not even a little. But I can promise I've never knowingly harmed a child."

He might consider himself evil, but to me, he was my knight in shining armor. He'd stormed the tower, fought the dragon, and carried me off to safety. I'd once dreamed of such a thing happening. Eventually, those dreams died as my reality weighed me down. I'd realized no one was coming, and I would likely die lying under some disgusting man who liked causing pain.

"I say knowingly, partly because of you. Raina, I don't know how old you are."

"I'm not entirely sure. Time passed differently while I was with Gary. There wasn't much point in counting the days, and I never celebrated my birthday. Not after my family had sold me to him. The last time I had a birthday cake was when I turned five."

"Do you think you're at least eighteen? That's the legal age for consent in most states. Some states are a little lower, but usually when the two people are close in age." He seemed worried about it.

"I think so. I know the men who preferred

younger girls stopped coming around about two years ago. Something about it not being fun anymore."

He growled softly and ate another bite of food, chewing so forcefully I worried he'd crack his teeth. We finished our food and Feliks cleared the table. I didn't know what to do with myself. I tried to help, but he shooed me away.

"When did you last watch TV?" he asked.

"Gary allowed me to watch something once a day, but I could pick either one movie or two episodes of a show. The rest of the time I either slept, or…" I pressed my lips together, not wanting to admit what I'd been doing. I knew Feliks was already aware, especially since Gary offered me as payment. It didn't mean I wanted to remind him about it.

"Pick anything you want, *lastachka*. We can watch in the living room, or there's another TV in the bedroom. As badly as I want you again, I think it's best you sleep tonight. It's been a long day."

If he kept being this sweet, I'd be in love with him in no time. I didn't know if he'd planned it that way, or if he was just being himself. For someone who seemed to think he was a monster, he'd treated me with kindness. Choking aside. And I blamed Gary for that one. He'd pushed Feliks. I hoped it wasn't something he would do again. I didn't plan to give him a reason to hurt me. He didn't seem to be like the others. I didn't think he'd cause me pain intentionally unless I angered him.

I went over to the living room and sank onto the soft couch. Curling my legs beneath me, I picked up the remote and found a movie I hadn't seen before. Feliks joined me, tugging me against his side. I rested my head on his shoulder and did my best to enjoy the moment. I didn't know how many of these I'd have, and I wanted to remember them forever. A day might come when he no longer wanted me. Something told me Feliks would end up breaking my heart.

Men like him didn't keep women like me -- not long term.

Chapter Three

Feliks

Three days with Raina and I knew I wanted to keep her. She'd gotten under my skin, and I'd discovered I loved seeing her face as she experienced new things. I hadn't gotten around to buying her clothing yet. She said she didn't care, and I often caught her running her hands over the nightgown I'd given her.

I'd held off Viktor as long as I could, but I knew time was running out. He'd called again this morning, saying Aleksi would come for Raina. I hadn't told her. How could I? She finally felt safe, and I could see her relaxing a little more each day. Now I had to tell her she couldn't stay? It seemed cruel.

A knock sounded at the door, and I knew Aleksi had arrived. I went to answer and yanked it open, glaring at him on the doorstep.

"Viktor sent me," he said. "Where's the girl?"

"Raina isn't going anywhere," I said. It would kill me to hand her over. Would she think I'd betrayed her? So many had hurt her before. I hadn't wanted to add my name to the list.

"Viktor claims otherwise. I'm not defying him, Feliks."

I felt a small hand on my back and turned my head to look down at Raina. She'd come up behind me and pressed herself close. I felt a slight tremor run through her and knew Aleksi's words had scared her. She didn't know who Viktor was, or why he'd sent Aleksi. She likely thought he wanted to haul her off to a brothel.

"Raina, the man I answer to has decided you can't remain with me. I want you to know I'm not like

Gary. I don't own you, and I haven't sold you. But I'm being ordered to let you go," I said.

Aleksi stiffened, and I heard him growl. "What the fuck do you mean someone owned her?"

I took a step back, pressing Raina farther into the apartment so Aleksi could enter. Once I'd closed the door, I took Raina's hand and laced our fingers together. I wanted her to feel safe. She needed to know I still wanted her, would protect her. Except, I couldn't. Viktor was making sure he separated us, and I doubted he'd change his mind.

"Gary Leeds purchased Raina when she was small. He's held her captive ever since. Three days ago, he offered the use of her body as a down payment on what he owes Viktor. I accepted, then brought her here."

I rubbed my thumb over her fingers and gently pulled her from behind me. The nightgown she wore covered everything important. She stood beside me, refusing to look at Aleksi. I wondered if they had trained her that way, or if she truly feared him.

The dark marks on her wrists were visible as I looked down at our joined hands. I'd thought they were from being chained to the table, but now I had my doubts. The bruising was deeper than I'd realized, and I noticed scars on her skin, as if they had chained her for years. She had spoken little about her time with Gary, unless I asked a question. She'd answer, and then we'd move on to something else. I hadn't wanted to push too hard.

"Raina, please tell Aleksi about what it was like living with Gary Leeds?"

She pressed closer to me. "He adopted me when I was young. Paid my family. I've been his whore for a long time. He uses me to pay his debts or buy extra time to get the money together."

"He said he'd have her earn the money for us," I told Aleksi.

"He kept me chained in a bedroom. Never let me have clothes. When he wanted me to shower, he'd make the water ice cold, and he washed me himself. He got off on causing me pain or watching others do it. He was going to let his men have me once Feliks was finished."

"So you rescued her?" Aleksi asked, his eyes full of disbelief and a hint of concern. "Feliks, this doesn't sound like you at all, especially with the engagement not yet solidified. Does she know you're planning to marry Natalia Gorev?"

"He told me," Raina said. "I'd rather be his mistress than be forced to be a whore again. Feliks has been kind to me, and I enjoy being with him."

Aleksi took a step back, shaking his head. "You know I need to call Viktor. He's not going to let you have a mistress. Not if you plan to remain in this area. As your brigadier, he's going to insist you remain faithful to your wife. Now that he has Cerys, things have changed."

"What will you do with her, Aleksi? Take her to your home?" I held her hand a little tighter. "How long before she's in your bed?"

"Feliks, be reasonable. I'm not trying to marry into an influential family. In fact, I have no intention of marrying at all. Let me take Raina with me. I'll watch over her, see that she has everything she needs. Once we know if she's carrying your child, we can discuss her options." Aleksi pulled the phone from his pocket. "Or I can tell Viktor you're refusing to cooperate."

Motherfucker! If he told Viktor I was being difficult, it would jeopardize everything. I'd worked too hard to wreck things now. As badly as I wanted to keep Raina, I knew I needed to let her go. At least, for now. Once I spoke with Viktor, I could smooth things over and make him see reason. Raina would be better off with me.

"Fine!" I released her hand and stepped away. "Take her if you must. But if she's carrying my child, she'll be returned to me. Understood?"

Aleksi stared me down. "Not my call, or yours. You know Viktor would make sure you had access to your son or daughter, Feliks, but he will not let you keep Raina and Natalia. You're going to have to choose. The mother of your child, or an icy bitch whose family can advance your career."

I wanted to curse him, but I needed to play this right. I couldn't bear to look at Raina. Did she feel as if I'd betrayed her? I'd have talked to her more about the situation if I'd thought Aleksi would be leaving with her. I'd hoped I could convince him to leave Raina with me. It seemed my plans were unraveling.

Aleksi held out his hand. "Come along, Raina. I promise no harm will come to you."

Raina backed up and refused to go to him. Aleksi sighed and surged forward, gripping her wrist and tugging her into the hall. Raina cried out, eyes wide with fright, as she reached for me. I fisted my hands at my side, forcing myself to remain still. As much as I wanted to bring her back into the apartment, Aleksi was right. I couldn't afford to anger Viktor right now, and he'd never let me have them both.

Natalia was my future. This wouldn't be the first, nor the last time I'd have to make a sacrifice to earn a higher place in the Bratva. So why did watching Raina leave feel as if a part of me had been ripped out?

Her eyes would haunt me for a while. I could see

the fear and helplessness, and I fucking hated it. There was no harm in her remaining here. Especially right now. I hadn't been officially engaged to Natalia yet. Why couldn't they have left Raina a while longer? After I finalized things with Natalia's father, then perhaps I could have let Viktor move her elsewhere until after the wedding.

I went to the kitchen and started emptying the fridge. I wouldn't be back here soon. Not unless Viktor returned Raina to me. There would be no point in leaving the fridge stocked with items that might spoil. After I tied off the trash, I set it in the hall for someone to pick up later.

I wished I'd taken the time to purchase some things for Raina. Now she was gone and didn't have a reminder of our time together, except the nightgown she wore… a garment which had belonged to another woman. I hated myself even more for that slight. She deserved so much, and I'd given her nothing.

Yes, I'd brought her here and removed her from Gary Leeds' home, but it wasn't enough. I should have showered her with gifts, bought her expensive clothes, and given her jewelry, so she'd known what she meant to me.

My phone rang, and I answered after seeing Viktor's name.

"Why?" I asked.

"You know the answer already, Feliks. We'll discuss this more in person, but I'm not changing my mind. You can't have them both, so you need to think long and hard about which woman you wish to keep. The whore you freed, or the woman you wanted to marry."

I hated him at that moment. I'd known the choice he'd give me. But was it really a choice? If I kept Raina,

I'd never advance in the Bratva. No one would take me seriously when my wife had been a whore. More than half the unsavory men in this town had likely touched her at one point or another. I couldn't walk into a room with Raina on my arm. Not and hold my head high. They would whisper about her and me.

"I'll see you soon, Viktor. I'll think about what you said and let you know my decision."

Or rather, I'd do my best to come up with a way to keep both of them. Natalia was a means to an end. But Raina… she had a spark, an inner fire I wanted to see more of, to taste. After only a handful of days, I already knew I wanted to keep her.

I could only hope when I saw her next, she'd be happy to see me, and not think I'd given her up to Aleksi. I'd sooner cut off my hand than let another man touch her.

For the moment, there was nothing I could do. Nothing except wait and hope for the best.

* * *

Raina

I didn't know the man who'd taken me from Feliks. Fear filled me as he dragged me onto an elevator and out to his car. He put me in the passenger seat, buckled me in, then shut the door. My heart raced and I couldn't help but stare at the building we'd just left. Feliks hadn't stopped him. He'd said I would be his mistress. I'd be safe! And now he'd let a stranger take me.

For the first time since Gary had purchased me, I'd had hope that things might be different. Now I felt like I was spiraling again. What would happen when we reached our destination? I didn't know where he was taking me. Feliks had asked if the man was taking me to his home, and he hadn't answered. What if he took me to the man they'd called Viktor?

Feliks had admitted the Bratva owned brothels. I didn't know where they found the women they put in those places. If Viktor, or the man currently driving me away from Feliks, decided I was a liability, would they put me in one of their brothels? I'd sooner die than live that way any longer.

I rubbed at my wrists. The chains may have been removed, but it felt like they were still there. I was no more free than I'd been at Gary's house. Feliks had said as his mistress I'd be able to go where I wanted, and he would give me money for the things I needed. It had sounded like heaven. And now that shot at freedom had been yanked away from me by the orders of a man I'd never met.

"Stop fidgeting, *rypka*. No harm will come to you." He glanced my way. "I'm Aleksi. The man who sent me to collect you is Viktor. Neither of us will hurt you."

"Where are we going?" I asked.

"For now, my home. Viktor didn't tell me anything other than to get you from Feliks. What I told him was true. Viktor will never allow him to keep you on the side. Since getting married, he's learned to appreciate women a little more. He wouldn't risk Feliks' fiancée being hurt by your presence in his life."

I swallowed hard. I hadn't thought of it that way. I'd only been worried about myself. And yet, Feliks had said the woman he was to marry wouldn't care if he kept a mistress. Had he been lying? Or did he not realize the woman would be brokenhearted over another woman in his life?

"Can you tell me about her?" I asked. "The woman he's going to marry?"

Aleksi shrugged. "I don't know her well. Her name is Natalia Gorev, and her father is a high-ranking member of the Bratva. He has the ear of the Vor, which is what attracts Feliks the most. If you're asking if he loves her, then *nyet*."

He delivered the words so matter-of-factly, I wondered if he was even human. Did any of these men feel emotion? Aside from anger... I'd thought Feliks was different, but now I realized I'd been wrong. "So it's a marriage of convenience?"

Aleksi nodded. "As far as I know. At least, as far as Feliks is concerned. If Natalia has feelings for him, I'm unaware of it. The few daughters I've met at the various functions seemed more like little dolls. All dressed up and emotionless."

I somehow doubted they were unfeeling. If what Feliks said was true, about Natalia having been groomed to be the perfect wife for someone like him, then maybe she was just as caged as I'd been most of my life. Perhaps Viktor was right to be worried about her feelings. I would hate to be the reason she had an unhappy marriage.

I wished there was a way to meet her, to see if she liked Feliks. I knew it would never happen. I wasn't the sort of woman allowed to attend the functions Aleksi had mentioned. If I ever lived a life outside of prostitution, it would still mean I remained in the shadows. I'd always be someone's dirty little secret.

Remaining silent for the rest of the trip, I tried to watch my surroundings. I hadn't been outside of Gary's house since he'd first brought me home. Well, he'd permitted me in the backyard when I'd been younger. But I'd never explored the city. I did not know where we were. Seeing the street names meant nothing to me. When I'd been much younger, Gary had often let other people help care for me. If you could call it caring. One of them had taught me to read. I'd only had enough lessons to manage the basics, but I could sound things out if I didn't know the word.

Aleksi pulled up in front of a wrought-iron gate and rolled down his window. I didn't see the code he punched in to make the gate open. As the car pulled through and the gate closed, it felt like I'd just been locked in another prison. He stopped in front of a large home and turned off the engine.

"We're here, *rypka*. Ready to see where you'll be staying?"

I nodded. Might as well get it over with. I opened the door and got out, then waited for Aleksi. He came around and led the way up the steps to the front of the house and unlocked the double doors. He pushed one side open and motioned for me to enter.

An older woman came bustling into the entryway, her lips turned down and her eyes narrowed. "Mr. Voronin, what's the meaning of this?"

He arched an eyebrow and stared the woman down. "Mrs. Sims, last I checked, I was your employer and not the other way around. Who I bring into my home is none of your business."

The woman grumbled something under her breath and turned to leave.

"Wait, Mrs. Sims. Raina will stay here for an indefinite amount of time. I want you to treat her kindly. If I hear you've said or done something you shouldn't have, the consequences will be dire."

"Very well, Mr. Voronin." She left as quickly as she'd arrived, her displeasure still thick in the air.

I glanced at Aleksi, wondering if he regretted bringing me here. "You didn't have a place like the one

Feliks had? I could have stayed there. You didn't need to bring me to your house," I said.

He rubbed the back of his neck. "I do, but it's occupied."

I blinked at him. "Won't she be upset if she hears I'm staying in your house?"

"Most likely." He sighed. "I was about to release her, anyway. Come, *rypka*. I'll show you to your room."

I followed him up the stairs and down a long hall. He stopped near the end of the hall and pushed open a door. I padded inside and looked around. The neutral colors made me wonder if it was a guest bedroom. Did he live in this vast house all by himself? Or did Mrs. Sims live here too? Did he have other staff who remained at the house?

"Do you know what size you wear? I can order clothes for you," Aleksi said.

I turned to face him. "I've never had clothes until Feliks gave me this," I said, running my hand over the soft material covering my body.

"Never?"

"Not since…" I pressed my lips together. I couldn't bring myself to say the words, *not since Gary made me a whore*. Even when I got my period, he didn't permit me to wear anything. He'd given me a box of tampons and told me to figure it out. In fact, I'd need some soon. It had been about two weeks since I'd last had one.

"I'll need your measurements in order to purchase some clothing for you. Can't have you running around in a nightgown all the time." He stepped back into the hall. "I'll return in a moment."

He left me alone, and I went to the window. It felt strange to look out at the world and not have a view of bars. Gary had made sure I couldn't escape through any windows after my first attempt to get away. The second dash for freedom had resulted in me wearing chains. I'd learned my lesson.

Aleksi returned with a measuring tape in his hand. He motioned for me to come closer. I stood in front of him, arms out, and stared at the ceiling while he measured me. His fingers brushed my breasts as he measured me for a bra, then he lightly touched my waist as he tried to determine my pants size. He never once seemed to notice me as a woman, despite where he'd had his hands. When he'd finished, he typed everything into his phone.

"We'll order some things online, but I'll have a few items brought to the house tonight. You'll need something in the morning." He glanced at my feet. "Hold your foot up. I'll need an idea what size shoe for now."

He lifted my leg and placed his measuring tape along the sole of my foot. After he released me, I went to sit on the edge of the bed. My thighs had dried cum on them. I hadn't bathed since Feliks had fucked me earlier.

"There's a bathroom through there," Aleksi said, pointing to a door on the opposite wall. "You're welcome to shower or soak in the tub. I'll bring you some clothes within the hour. Are you hungry?"

I nodded. "I haven't eaten today."

He frowned and folded his arms. "Feliks didn't feed you?"

"We hadn't had a chance to eat yet before you arrived. If you're asking if he's been starving me, the answer is no. He's taken good care of me." I placed my fingers against my throat. "Except for when he forced me to pass out, and I woke in the apartment."

He eyed my throat. "When you say he made you

pass out… are you telling me Feliks choked you until you blacked out?"

"Well, yes, but…" I bit my lip. I didn't know how he would react if I told him what had happened. "He didn't take it well when he found out I wasn't on birth control. He never asked, or I'd have said something. I told him Gary wanted everyone to use condoms and where to find them. He refused after he found out I was clean."

"And he choked you?" Aleksi asked, reaching into his pocket and pulling out his phone. "He said nothing to Viktor about that."

Aleksi began dialing a number, and I had a feeling he was calling Viktor. I didn't want Feliks to get into trouble and reached out to place my hand over the phone. "Stop. Please."

Aleksi shook his head. "*Nyet, rypka.* He needs to know Feliks is still out of control. He should have never accepted the use of your body to lessen a debt, and he damn sure shouldn't have choked you until you passed out."

"I asked him to kill me," I said. "He refused. Instead, he took me from Gary."

"That's only because of the child you might be carrying." Aleksi held my gaze. "Do not think for a moment he wouldn't have left you there if he didn't worry you might carry his child. That's the only reason he freed you from Gary Leeds. He has little honor when it comes to women, *rypka.*"

I digested his words and removed my hand from over his phone. If what he said was true, then Feliks wasn't the man I thought he was. I didn't know why he'd offered to make me his mistress. Was it only because of the possible pregnancy? He'd have truly left me in that hell, even after I told him what would happen to me? My stomach twisted, and I thought I might be sick.

I rushed into the bathroom as Aleksi made his call and emptied the contents of my stomach into the toilet. After several dry heaves, I could finally stand again. I rinsed my mouth and stared at myself in the mirror.

"Just a dirty whore," I mumbled. "That's all you'll ever be, Raina. Stop hoping for something better."

Feliks hadn't seen me as something special. I'd just been another hole for him to fuck. Nothing more. I reached out and touched my reflection. I had no idea how old I was. My face remained unlined and youthful, but my eyes... I looked to be fifty or older. Instead of innocence, all I saw was darkness and pain. Was that what others saw when they looked at me?

I removed the nightgown and started the shower. When steam rolled out, I stepped under the spray. No matter how hard I scrubbed, I knew I'd never wash away the filth. It clung to me, had sunk all the way into my soul, and it wasn't something I'd ever escape. Feliks' soft touch had made me feel different for the past few days. Now I knew he truly was a monster, and he'd lied to me. What reason would Aleksi have to make me hate Feliks? No, what he'd told me must be true. Even Feliks had admitted to being an evil man. I'd just chosen not to believe him.

Aleksi stepped inside the doorway and froze, averting his gaze when he realized I was showering. The glass cubical left nothing to the imagination. "I'm going out to purchase a few things for you, Raina. Please make yourself comfortable. Mrs. Sims is going to leave a tray on the bed for you. Eat as much as you want."

"Thank you, Aleksi."

He nodded and left, closing the door behind him. I stayed in the shower until the water ran cold, then I got out and dried off. I stared at the nightgown. When Feliks gave it to me, I loved it. Now I couldn't stand the sight of it. I'd thought it was a gift. Instead, it was just another reminder of who and what I was. *Never enough. You'll never be enough for anyone, Raina.*

I shook the thought from my mind and wrapped the towel around my body. I tucked it so it wouldn't fall off and went into the bedroom. Just as Aleksi had said, a tray had been left on the bed. Mrs. Sims had made a sandwich and included a cup of soup, as well as a glass of water.

I carefully sat and started with the soup before devouring the sandwich. I drained the glass of water, then set the tray out in the hall. From my first encounter with Mrs. Sims, I knew she didn't want anything to do with me. She'd been here first, so I'd do my best to stay out of her way.

By the time Aleksi came back home, I'd fallen asleep. I felt a gentle touch stroke down my arm, and it jolted me awake. I sat up, rubbing at my eyes as panic set in. For a moment, I'd forgotten where I was.

"You need to get dressed, Raina. I bought two things for you to sleep in, and two outfits as well as undergarments and a pair of shoes. Tomorrow, we'll go shopping."

"This is plenty," I said, standing and reaching for the cotton nightgown. The blue material felt soft and stretchy, and I knew it would be comfortable. I let the towel drop and pulled the nightgown over my head before reaching for the package of panties. I ripped it open and took out a pair, slipping them on.

Aleksi had averted his gaze once more, refusing

to look at my naked body. I'd never had a man not ogle me, and I wasn't sure what to make of him. He'd said he had a mistress but would release her soon. For someone who would be without companionship, I'd expected him to lure me into warming his bed next. Not that I really would have a choice. I had nowhere else to go.

"If you need anything, I'm right next door," he said. "Goodnight, Raina. I hope you sleep well."

"Goodnight, Aleksi."

He left, shutting the door behind him, and I pulled back the covers on the bed. I'd thought I'd fall back to sleep easily, but I didn't. Instead, worry ate at me. I had no idea what would become of me. If I carried Feliks' child, did that mean they would return me to him? Or would they take my baby from me and give it to Feliks to raise? I knew nothing about these men, only that they were powerful. And expected to be obeyed. Then again, all men I'd known wanted obedience.

Eventually, my eyes closed, and I fell into a fitful sleep. Nightmares of being tossed into a brothel plagued me. By the time the sunlight woke me, I'd decided I'd rather die than be a whore any longer. Once I knew I wasn't pregnant, I'd make sure no man would ever hurt me again. Until then, all I could do was wait.

Chapter Four

Feliks

My hands fisted at my sides as I faced Viktor. He'd called me to his home before the sun had risen, and I'd known it wouldn't be a happy meeting. No, he'd read me the riot act over my treatment of Raina, and other women. I found it hypocritical the man helped run the brothels in town, and yet he didn't like the fact I visited them. Or that I'd removed Gary's whore from his house.

More accurately, he didn't like the way I'd gone about it, or my reasoning.

"You'd have left her there, wouldn't you?" Viktor asked, his hands steepled in front of him. "If Leeds hadn't said something about the morning-after pill, you'd have walked away, knowing what they'd do to her once you were gone."

"I'd given her pleasure, Viktor. Made her come multiple times. It was a kindness none had given her before. I didn't fall in love with her." I knew what he hoped for. It wouldn't happen. "She's not Cerys. You took your wife in exchange for her father's debt. A pure girl. This is different."

"You're right. It is. For one, I'd have never treated Cerys the way you're treating Raina. What did you plan to do with her, Feliks?"

I didn't like this line of questioning. Viktor saw too much, and yet not enough. Did he expect me to declare my undying love for the woman? We were strangers. I'd enjoyed the use of her body and hadn't wanted those men to hurt her. The thought of them using her since she'd been a child had been abhorrent to me.

"She seemed eager to be my mistress," I said,

folding my arms over my chest. No sense in hiding the truth. Or at least, most of it. "She'd have been given freedom to do as she pleased, as long as she didn't sleep with other men. And I'd give her an allowance. It's more than she's ever had before, Viktor. Don't make me out to be a monster."

"Leeds is the monster, Feliks, but I'm not sure you have an ounce of compassion in you. Or any decency. Yes, I kill, and I help the Bratva earn money from women lying on their backs. It doesn't mean I agree with the practice, but I do as I'm told." He leaned back in his chair. "I think you get off on taking women by force. Do you enjoy causing them pain?"

Inwardly, I seethed. I'd done the things they had commanded me to do. It didn't mean I enjoyed hurting women. Did I bend a few to my will? Yes. But they spread their legs willingly. Just as Raina had come apart for me so sweetly. And yet, I couldn't put her in the same category as the others.

"We're not so different, Viktor. Do you remember what you were like before your precious Cerys tamed you?" I asked.

He nodded. "I do. It doesn't make the things I did right. At least I never raped a woman. Can you say the same, Feliks?"

I hated him at that moment. He'd bring up my worst sin, one they had forced me into. I'd been nothing more than a tool the Bratva had used. And he damn well knew it! He was only rubbing salt into an open wound. I'd hardened myself, or tried to. I couldn't let those women's screams affect me. The Bratva would sniff out my weakness and use it against me.

"You know I can't. Did I do it because I wanted to? *Nyet*. I followed orders, same as you, Viktor. The

Vor made the demands. If you have an issue with how the women are treated, take it up with him."

"Watch your tone," Viktor warned.

I knew I needed to tread carefully. Viktor could easily marry Raina off to someone, or send her to another city. She'd be far out of my reach, and I'd never see her again. My jaw tightened at the thought of that happening.

Viktor pointed at me. "There. That expression. What thought just crossed your mind?"

"Never seeing Raina again," I admitted. "You've made it clear you won't let me keep her. Not if I marry Natalia. I'm not like you, Viktor. I don't already hold power in this organization. Keeping Raina as anything other than my mistress is out of the question. I need the alliance with Gorev, and you damn well know it."

"I do," he said. "But I have to think of the woman as well. Both women. How do you think Natalia will feel when you're staying with Raina? Or how will Raina feel if you only spend an hour or two in her bed, then run home to your wife and legitimate children? What happens when you tire of Raina?"

I didn't think it would be possible to *not* want Raina. But I understood where he was going with this. "You think I'm going to toss her out like unwanted trash?"

Viktor leaned back in his chair. "Will you? I can't remember you hanging onto a woman for longer than a year. Most don't make it past a few months. What makes you think Raina will be any different?"

"I don't know, Viktor. I can't promise I won't tire of her, but if she's carrying my child, I'll see to it they both have a home. I won't turn my back on either of them."

"I'm glad to hear it. Still doesn't solve the issue of

Natalia Gorev. You realize as your brigadier, Gorev will come to me before signing any documents with you. He won't offer you his daughter without first making sure I'm all right with it."

It hadn't occurred to me. I'd thought I only needed to win over Gorev. Knowing I needed Viktor's approval made things more difficult. He'd never let me have both women. Choosing Raina wasn't an option.

"What do you want from me, Viktor?"

"Agree to let Raina go, and I'll make sure the engagement with Natalia goes through without issue. Decide to keep Raina, and no one will offer you their daughters, sisters, or any of their female family members. You'll remain unwed, and in the same position you're in now." He stared me down again. "Is being my *kryshas* really so terrible?"

"Of course not, Viktor. I only wish to climb higher in the Bratva. One day, I'd like to be a brigadier and have my own *kryshas*. Not in this town, obviously. Is it wrong to want more?"

"Not wrong at all, Feliks. It seems you've made your decision. You'd rather have power and an alliance with Gorev than keep Raina. I'll start making arrangements for her."

I had to bite my tongue so I wouldn't say something I shouldn't. I didn't know how soon he'd called Aleksi and tell him the news. What would Riana think? I needed to see her, even if this was the last time. Once Viktor excused me, I left his home and went straight to Aleksi's house. I didn't care if he was home. I'd push past him if need be, just to speak with Raina.

Mrs. Sim, his housekeeper, answered the door, offering me a smile. "Welcome, Mr. Sobol. I'm afraid Mr. Voronin isn't home."

"That's all right, Mrs. Sims. I'm here to see the

young lady he brought home last night."

Her lips thinned, and she nodded. Interesting. It seemed she didn't like Raina. I wondered what had transpired between the two.

"She's upstairs. Room next to Mr. Voronin's," she said.

I took the steps two at a time and hurried to find Raina. Opening her door, I saw her lying on the bed, staring at the ceiling. The nightgown she wore was different from the one I'd given her. I didn't know if Aleksi had taken it from her, or if she'd opted not to wear it. I didn't like the thought of her wearing clothes another man had given her, but I didn't have the right to say anything.

"Raina," I called softly. She jolted and stared at me. For a moment, she seemed happy to see me. Then her expression blanked. "*Lastachka*, are you all right?"

"I'm fine," she said.

"Aleksi is treating you well?"

She nodded, fingering the nightgown she wore. Had he bought it for her? Rage filled me at the thought of him assisting her into the garment. Had he seen her naked? Touched her?

"Why are you here?" she asked. "I thought Viktor said you couldn't keep me."

"He did, and we've come to an agreement."

Her eyes lit up. "I get to go back to the apartment with you?"

I curled my fingers into my palms so I wouldn't reach for her. "*Nyet*. You will remain here until Viktor makes other arrangements. I only wished to see you one last time, Raina. To make sure you were all right."

"I see." She looked away. "You chose her, then. The woman you want to marry."

"Yes."

She sighed and refused to look at me.

"Raina, are you angry?"

"No," she said. "I knew this would happen. When Aleksi told me Viktor would make you choose, I already knew it wouldn't be me. Why would you want the filthy whore when you could have a well-bred wife?"

I didn't like her speaking about herself that way, but it was no longer my place to correct her. Even now, I wanted to taste her. Touch her. Slide my cock inside her and make her scream in pleasure. I took a step closer. Then another. Reaching out, I ran my fingers through her hair and over her bare arm. "Is there a chance you're pregnant?"

"I won't know for a few weeks," she said. "Why? Are you going to steal my child from me? Will they force me to give up my baby so you can have them? How will your wife react? Will she want to raise the bastard you had with a whore?"

I growled but didn't respond. Every point she made was valid. Natalia would never raise a child I had with Raina. I could force the issue, but I knew the child would be the one to suffer. "*Nyet.* Natalia would never raise a child you and I had together. I wouldn't ask it of her."

She nodded. "Right. So what happens now? Are you going to ship me off to a brothel? Make sure I earn back the money Gary owes?"

"What the fuck is going on?" Aleksi demanded from behind me. I turned and noticed the bags in his hands. He'd been shopping. Most likely for Raina.

"I came to see Raina one last time," I said.

"So you chose Natalia," he said. "I thought you might. You need to leave, Feliks. All you're doing is making things worse for Raina. How do you think she feels, hearing you say you chose someone else? You've let her know she means nothing to you. Is that what you wanted?"

I paused. No, I hadn't wanted that. I honestly hadn't considered how she'd react. Not to that extent. It didn't occur to me it might be painful for her to hear what I had to say, or know I was abandoning her. Perhaps Viktor was right.

I was a monster.

Her monster.

And if there was one thing I never wanted, it was to see fear in Raina's eyes when she looked at me.

"Leave, Feliks. Leave now and I won't tell Viktor," Aleksi said.

"Fine. But so we're clear, you're not keeping Raina. Even if she doesn't carry my child, I had her first. Do you really want my leftovers, Aleksi? Do you want Gary's whore in your bed?" I snarled at him. "I know you. You'd never be able to touch her, knowing how many had fucked her. So stop pretending to care about her. She's a job to you and nothing more."

"You've gone too far," Aleksi said, his voice soft. "You need to leave, Feliks."

I spun to look at Raina one last time, and the stricken look on her face, the tears rolling down her cheeks, nearly took me to my knees. I'd done that. My careless words had caused her pain. I didn't like it.

Even worse, I hated the fact I cared whether I'd hurt her.

I turned and walked away, refusing to look back. I'd made my choice, and now I needed to live with it. I'd meet with Gorev tomorrow and hope I could sway him. Within a few months, Natalia would be in my home, with my ring on her finger. And soon, I'd have everything I wanted.

"Feliks," Aleksi called out. "Don't come to my house uninvited again."

I kept walking until I'd exited his home and gotten into my car. I forced myself not to look at the house as I drove away. This was for the best. Raina would understand that one day. Perhaps Viktor would find her a husband in another city. Another state. I wanted her to find happiness. To be safe.

If I couldn't have her, then I at least owed her that much.

I pressed the button on my steering wheel and told the car to call Viktor. He answered almost immediately, and I heard his daughter crying in the background.

"What?" he asked instead of saying a normal hello.

"If you're going to send Raina away, I want you to make sure she's cared for. She's had a hard life, Viktor. She deserves some peace, and to feel secure."

"I'm not an idiot, Feliks, and unlike you, I have a heart. She's not in danger of being whored out, if that's your worry."

It was, but I wouldn't admit it. "Thank you."

Some of the tension eased from me, knowing Raina wouldn't face that fate. I'd still prefer to keep her with me, but it didn't seem to be an option. Viktor was adamant, and I knew I couldn't convince him otherwise.

"If that's all, I need to go. Cerys has taken to bed with a migraine, and Alina won't stop crying. I'm afraid she wants her mother and no one else will do," Viktor said.

"Take care of your daughter. Just remember your promise."

I ended the call and went home.

To my empty house.

Even though I'd never intended to bring Raina here, I still wondered what it would be like to come home and have her greet me at the door. Would she welcome me with a kiss? Not now. I'd shattered whatever trust she had in me. I was no longer her savior -- just another man who'd used her.

I closed my eyes and attempted to see Natalia. I'd thought her beautiful, and she was, classically. Long blonde hair. Slender curves. Long legs. And empty. I'd never seen genuine emotion in her. I wondered if she ever felt anything. If there was passion inside her, I hadn't seen it yet. She didn't seem to be the type to greet me with any sort of enthusiasm when I came home. She'd probably be polite and reserved.

I'd known marrying her wouldn't be about physical satisfaction. I'd bed her, and hopefully put a kid or two in her belly, but I didn't think I'd enjoy it. Hell, even now, I couldn't get hard seeing her in my mind. It would be wrong to close my eyes when I fucked her and picture Raina lying under me instead. But just the thought of the golden-skinned beauty had my cock stiffening.

Stay the course. I needed this. Natalia was a means to an end and nothing more. Perhaps one day, I could reason with Viktor. Once he saw how unhappy my marriage was, I hoped I could convince him I needed Raina or another woman on the side. Someone to give me the things Natalia could not. Although, with him sending Raina away, it was doubtful I'd ever see her again. The thought displeased me.

I went into the house and straight up to my suite. I didn't bother shutting the bedroom door. There was no point. No one was here except me. Stripping off my clothes, I let them fall in a trail behind me as I entered the bathroom and started the shower. I sneered at my reflection, remembering the words my father said each time he shoved me into a shower so hot I thought my skin would melt. *Time to wash away your sins, Feliks.* Even as a boy, I'd had certain needs. It had taken little to convince those girls to give me what I wanted. Then one had gone crying to her father, and my life had gone to hell.

"Soon you'll have everything you want," I told my reflection. Except, I didn't believe a word of it. I'd never have *everything*. Power? Yes. A respectable wife? Certainly. But I'd never have Raina. I'd seen to that. Not only by my agreement with Viktor, but by hurting her. I could never unsay the words she heard today. I had a feeling she'd never forgive me.

I won't forgive myself either.

Chapter Five

Raina
Two Weeks Later

I stared at the stick on the bathroom counter, my stomach churning. No matter how long I looked, it didn't change. Two pink lines filled the window. Pregnant. I didn't know what it would mean for me. Feliks had walked away, chosen someone else. I'd remained with Aleksi for five days before Viktor had found another place for me. He'd sent his *byki*, Ilya, to remove me from Aleksi's home, and I'd been staying with the bodyguard ever since.

Viktor had demanded I call when I knew if there was a baby. I couldn't bring myself to do it. What if he tried to take the child from me? I'd never thought I'd be a mother. I didn't really remember much about my parents. As the years passed, it became harder and harder to recall what they even looked like. With no role model, what if I made a terrible mother?

I placed my hand over my belly and tried to breathe in through my nose and out through my mouth. My hands shook and my knees felt like they'd give out at any moment. I left the bathroom, not bothering to throw the test away. Not yet. I might need to see it again, to prove there was really a baby inside me.

I had mixed feelings about it. At first, I'd wanted to remain with Feliks. Thought he'd cared about me. It had all been a lie. He was no different from any other man I'd ever known.

Ilya lounged on my bed, and I froze. When had he gotten here? Yanking my hand from my belly, I hoped he didn't know what I'd been doing in the bathroom. He'd tell Viktor, and I wasn't ready for that yet. Maybe never.

"I take it congratulations are in order," he said. "So what happens now, Raina?"

"Don't tell anyone. Please. I need more time," I said. I didn't know if pleading would do me any good, but I had to try. My life had been one nightmare after another. I couldn't handle much more.

"Time is not something you have." He stood and reached inside his suit jacket, pulling out some papers. "We could locate your birth record. However, to make you a citizen is another matter entirely."

I stared at the documents he held. Watching him, I couldn't see so much as a crack in his armor. It was like staring at someone wearing a mask. No emotion showed. No hint of what he was thinking. I should have become used to this by now. All the Russians I'd dealt with were the same. Emotionless. Soulless.

"I don't understand. Gary said he adopted me. Wouldn't that make me a legal resident of this country? He's American."

Ilya nodded. "Yes, if that's what happened. Except Gary Leeds lied to you. He purchased you in Tahiti from a couple claiming to be your parents. Whether they were, I cannot say. What I know is he never officially adopted you. There's no paperwork saying you belong to him as a daughter. Only a bill of sale. Which means the US government doesn't consider you his child."

The room spun a little, and I swayed. Ilya jumped up and grabbed my arm, leading me to the bed. I sank onto the side and tried to make sense of it all. He'd lied to me. It shouldn't surprise me. Had he only done it to make me more compliant? He'd been right. I'd listened and obeyed, thinking he was my adopted parent and that I had no choice.

I'd thought Feliks was different. He'd been the only man to show me kindness, but he'd ended up being like all the others. Cold. Heartless. Without a conscience.

"Why do any of you care what happens to me?" I asked.

Ilya placed his hand on my belly. "You carry Feliks' child. The baby is part of our family."

Right. Of course. They weren't doing any of this for my well-being, only for the baby inside me. A child they hadn't known existed until just now. What if I hadn't been pregnant? If the test had been negative, how would they have reacted? As badly as I wanted to know, I was too scared to ask.

"Why did you bring up my citizenship?" I asked.

"Because you need to marry in order to remain in this country," he said. "If your child is born here, he or she will be a US citizen. But the moment they realize you're undocumented, they'll deport you. Without your child.

"You sound American. If we forge some records, enough to get you a marriage license, and you marry, then we may be able to avoid all the unpleasantness. Think of your child, Raina."

My stomach churned, and I pressed the back of my hand to my mouth. Oh, God. They'd force me out and make me leave my baby behind? I couldn't even imagine such a thing. I did not know if he spoke the truth. The question was whether I was willing to risk it all being a lie. And I wasn't. Not even a little.

"What do I do? What about Feliks?" I looked up at Ilya. "Is he engaged to that woman?"

He hesitated, which told me enough. I wrapped my arms around my stomach. I'd told myself it didn't matter. Convinced myself it wouldn't hurt when I found out. I'd been wrong. My eyes burned with unshed tears. I shouldn't want anything to do with him. He'd been an asshole. The things he'd said had broken me. And yet, if I had to marry someone, I'd have preferred it to be him. I knew it was screwed up.

"Right. So who am I supposed to marry? You? Aleksi? Some other cold-hearted Russian who has the emotional capacity of a thimble?" I pressed my hand to my mouth and shook my head. "I'm sorry. I just..."

For a moment, I saw a flash of something in his eyes. He seemed human until the mask slipped back into place. I didn't like all the unknowns. At least with Gary, I knew what to expect every day. More pain and suffering. I still hurt, but these men liked causing a different sort of pain. Perhaps *liked* wasn't the correct word. I wasn't certain they even realized their words could rip someone apart.

Had Feliks known when he'd said all those things?

"When is he getting married?" I asked.

"Three months. Natalia wants a quick wedding. She's... eager."

I nodded. Of course, she was. Feliks was attractive, and I'd imagine he'd been charming to her. He wanted her as his wife, and I knew he'd put in every bit of effort to make it happen. Had she fallen in love with him already?

It felt like a dagger had pierced my heart and I took a breath. Then another.

Ilya came to me, reaching out. His fingers feathered through my hair a moment before he pulled me against him. As his arms came around me, the dam inside me broke, and I couldn't hold back my tears any longer. I sobbed against him, holding on, and wishing the pain would end.

"He should have left me there," I said. "No one wants me. Why would they? Gary made me a whore. I'm dirty. So very dirty. No matter how hard I scrub, I never feel clean."

"Hush. None of that. The one thing Feliks did right was take you from Leeds. I doubt he regrets it, Raina. The man is stupid." I tensed, but he smoothed his hand down my back. "Hear me out. He wants Natalia Gorev for her family connections. I've seen the two of them together. She may enjoy his company, but he's putting on an act. He doesn't care for her. One day, he'll realize life without passion isn't worth living, and that's what he's signed himself up for."

"What are you saying, Ilya?"

He cupped my cheek and forced me to look him in the eye. "Feliks can never care for her. You've already gotten under his skin. The bastard looks miserable. He's asked for pictures of you. Why? Because he needs a glimpse, even if it's not in person. He needs you, Raina. Every bit as much as you need him. I only hope he comes to his senses in time."

"He said awful things. Told Aleksi I was so used and dirty he'd never sleep with me." I tightened my hold on him. "What if he meant those things? Is that how he sees me?"

"Would you like to find out?" Ilya asked. "Feliks will be at an event this evening. A charity dinner. I can ask Viktor's permission to take you. We can buy you appropriate clothes, take you for a spa day so they can style your hair and whatever else women do before these events."

"Really?" I asked. "I could see him?"

Ilya nodded. "I'll call Viktor now. Stop crying, Raina. Until Feliks says his vows, not all is lost."

I nodded and backed away. "Even if this is the

last time, I'd like to see him in person. He should know about the baby."

"Get ready to leave. I'll check with Viktor, but I think he'll permit you to go. We'll leave in the next fifteen minutes."

I hurried to do as he said. By the time I'd combed my hair, braided it, and changed my clothes, he stood by the door waiting for me. He led me out to his shiny car, and we pulled away from my temporary home. Since we had little time, I let Ilya pick my clothes, and he informed the ladies at the salon where we were going. They fussed over me, and I felt like a different woman when they'd finished.

They'd painted my nails, deep conditioned my hair, and styled it with pretty clips. I almost didn't recognize myself as I stared at my reflection. The dress Ilya picked hugged my body. I'd filled out some since Feliks had taken me from Gary. My breasts were larger, my hips fuller, and my skin seemed to glow. The necklace around my throat felt heavy as I lightly touched the cool stones. Diamonds! I'd never thought to see such a sight, much less have something so fancy around my neck. I touched my wrists, wondering if I needed bracelets, but the bruises had faded. Perhaps no one would question any of my scars.

"You look beautiful, Raina. Are you ready?" he asked, holding out his hand.

I nodded and slid my fingers against his, letting him lead me to the car. During my transformation, he'd changed into formalwear. I had to admit he looked nice, even if he didn't make my pulse race the way Feliks did.

"What should I expect?" I asked.

"With Feliks, I have no idea. If you mean the event itself, it's a charity dinner. There will be a silent auction, perhaps a bit of dancing, and an overpriced meal with wine." He reached over and patted my knee. "Don't worry, Raina. I won't feed you to the wolves. You'll be safe tonight."

I hoped so. It wasn't just myself I had to consider now. While the dark thoughts and doubts still crept in, I tried pushing them away. I didn't like the idea of marrying a stranger, but I owed it to my child to make sure he or she had a good life. I couldn't give it to them on my own.

"Feliks commented on needing a wife for these events. Aren't people going to look at me funny? Or say something about my presence?" I asked.

"*Nyet*. As a spouse? Perhaps. Tonight, you're merely my guest. They may believe you're my mistress, or that I'm seeking a buyer for you. I'll handle anyone who approaches."

Ilya pulled up to the curb outside a hotel and got out. I waited, letting him open the door for me, then he escorted me inside. Everything looked like it cost a small fortune and I felt like a fraud even walking through the doors. He seemed to know exactly where he was going and led me to a banquet hall on the first floor.

"Be prepared for anything, Raina. I'm not sure what Feliks will say or do. But once we walk through these doors, we're here for the duration. Do you still wish do to this?" Ilya asked.

"Yes. I need to see him, even if it's the last time."

He nodded and opened the doors, ushering me inside. He placed my hand in the crook of his arm and strode across the room, approaching a small group of men. Feliks stood with them, and my heart beat faster. I curled my fingers into Ilya's arm. Seeing Feliks was harder than I'd expected. Especially with the beautiful woman on his arm.

"Is that her?" I whispered.

"Yes. Natalia Gorev. His fiancée."

I nodded and pressed a hand to my stomach, willing the butterflies to stop swooping around. I'd come this far. Now I needed to see it through.

"Viktor," Ilya called out as we drew nearer. All the men turned to face us, and I recognized Aleksi right away. I couldn't bring myself to look at Feliks' face. "I don't believe you've met my date for this evening. Viktor, this is Raina. Raina, Viktor is my brigadier. He's the one who issues my orders, and the man I protect at all costs."

I held my hand out and Viktor lifted it to his lips, kissing the backs of my fingers. "A pleasure, Raina. You already know Aleksi and Feliks, correct?"

I nodded, my gaze skirting over to Feliks. The heat staring back at me nearly made my knees buckle. A woman came up to Viktor, looping her arm through his. I noticed she had a cane and seemed to stare at nothing in particular.

"Raina, this is my wife, Cerys. She's blind, so please don't feel slighted that she didn't greet you immediately," Viktor said.

"It's a pleasure to meet you," I murmured.

Cerys smiled at me warmly, and I knew I'd like her. At least, until she found out who I was. I had a feeling everything would spiral out of control once that information made the rounds. I'd already noticed more than one man who'd used me at Gary's. How long before they came over and said something?

The woman next to Feliks pressed herself closer to him. "Aren't you going to introduce me? Viktor said you'd met her before."

"Raina, this is my fiancée, Natalia."

"I can't wait to marry this man," Natalia said, smiling widely. Her words hit me like darts, and I knew I'd made a mistake in coming. It was too late to back out, but I felt incredibly foolish.

"Perhaps you should get Raina some wine, Ilya," Feliks said.

Ilya placed his hand over my mine, giving it a slight squeeze. It was enough of a warning not to run, and I looked up at him before turning to Feliks once more.

"She can't have wine tonight," Ilya said. "I'll have to make sure the servers have other options."

"Can't hold her liquor?" Natalia asked, smirking at me.

"*Nyet.*" Ilya gave Feliks a chilling smile. "It's not good for the baby."

Feliks stiffened, and his gaze locked onto me. And now he knew. As the seconds ticked by without a word being said, my nerves unraveled. Cerys, bless her, seemed to realize it, even though she couldn't see me.

"Raina, I can show you to the ladies' room, if you'd like? When I was pregnant with my daughter, it seemed I always needed the bathroom." The blind woman held out her hand, and I took it, thankful for the lifeline.

"That would be great, thank you."

I felt Feliks' gaze boring into me as we walked away. It wasn't until we'd left the room the tension finally drained from me.

"Want to tell me what's going on?" Cerys whispered as we stepped into the hall.

"The baby isn't Ilya's. It's Feliks'."

"Ah. I can see what the drama is about now. Did he know there was a chance you could be carrying his baby before he proposed to Natalia?" she asked.

"Yes." I swallowed hard. "He made his choice. Feliks wanted power more than he wanted me."

"And tonight?" she asked, leading me farther into the hotel.

"I needed to see him one last time. I didn't realize she'd be with him. I'm not sure I can go back in there."

Cerys led me into the bathroom and leaned against the row of sinks. "If you need to leave, I can arrange it. But I need to know what happened. How did you get mixed up with Feliks, of all people? The man is, forgive me, an asshole."

"He took me in trade," I whispered. "The man who owed a debt offered the use of me in exchange for a lesser amount. Feliks accepted. Then he discovered I wasn't on birth control. I blacked out and woke up in an apartment meant for his mistress."

Cerys mumbled something under her breath. "I swear the men working with Viktor are idiots."

"I have nowhere to go," I admitted.

"We'll figure this out, Raina. I'm so angry with Feliks, but it shouldn't surprise me. I've never liked him. When we first met, he grabbed at me and told me he'd get to have me when Viktor grew bored. I'd never been so scared in my life."

The more I heard about Feliks, the more I questioned my sanity. Why did I want the man to like me? He seemed abhorrent, and he'd clearly made his choice. He didn't want me. I shouldn't have come tonight.

"Do you need another minute?" Cerys asked. "I can try to help you, but not right now. All of Viktor's men are in that room. There's no one to take you home. Unless you want me to tell Ilya you don't feel well?

Perhaps he could leave and take you with him."

"Please. Can we try?"

Cerys nodded. I took her hand, and we left the bathroom. As we neared the doors to the banquet hall, a sense of unease filled me. My nape prickled, and I tensed, feeling like prey.

"Cerys…"

"I feel it too," she mumbled. "Stay close."

She reached for the doors, and as she pulled them open, someone grabbed me from behind. I screamed and lashed out, but the man only laughed.

"We meet again, little whore." I froze. I'd know that voice anywhere. My heart slammed against my ribs. If the Italian enforcer had me, then all was lost. No one would find me in time, and I knew he'd kill me. I tried to scream again, but he cuffed me upside the head and the world went dark.

Chapter Six

Feliks

I watched the doors, waiting for Cerys and Raina to return. I wanted to curse Ilya for letting them leave without an escort. Viktor didn't seem concerned. Perhaps he thought the hotel was secure enough. Whatever the case, I didn't feel quite so at ease when it came to Raina's safety.

Yes, I knew it made me a hypocrite. I'd pushed her away. Made her hate me.

I could feel the tension building in Natalia and knew I needed to pay her more attention. She sensed something about Raina, or perhaps it was the fact I couldn't take my eyes off her. I'd known she would clean up nicely. The battered girl I'd brought home was a far cry from the stunning creature who'd entered the room on Ilya's arm. It made me want her even more.

Not that the fancy dress and makeup mattered. Even bruised and resigned to life as a sex slave, she'd been beautiful to me. I'd found it hard to look away once Leeds had shown her to me. Then he'd made me an offer I couldn't refuse, not after knowing the pain she'd suffered for so long. It was the only time I'd thought of someone other myself. At least, that I remembered. At heart, I was a selfish creature, and cared for no one else.

Until Raina.

I couldn't get her off my mind. Even when Natalia tried to sink her claws deeper into me, it was Raina who held me spellbound. She'd been in my thoughts from the moment I'd carried her out of Leeds' home, and I wondered if it would always be that way.

I swallowed the knot in my throat. Did I make

the right choice? With Natalia came many benefits. I knew she'd bend to my will, give me anything I wanted. But therein lay the problem. I didn't *want* anything from her, except her father's connections. Raina was different. I enjoyed touching her. Wanted to hold her. Natalia felt more like a job.

"Feliks, you aren't listening," she whined, tugging on my arm.

I held back a growl. Barely. The woman was in her mid-twenties, and yet she acted like a spoiled child. Once we were wed, I'd set some rules. She'd fall in line or pay the consequences. The thought of spending the next few decades with the simpering idiot made me grind my teeth. I couldn't stand being in her presence. How I'd father a child with her was a mystery, unless I closed my eyes and pretended she was Raina.

When Cerys re-entered the room, alone, I knew something had gone horribly wrong. I shook off Natalia and went to Viktor's wife.

"Cerys, where's Raina?" I asked.

She appeared pale and shaken. "I don't know who took her. A man called her a little whore, and I heard her cry out. There was a bit of shuffling, like maybe he picked her up? Then nothing. I think they must have hurt her. Feliks, she sounded so scared."

Her hands trembled, and her lip quivered. I saw tears gathering in her eyes and knew Raina's abduction hit her hard. They may have just met, but Cerys had always had a soft heart, and it seemed she liked my Raina.

Shit. *My Raina.*

I'd known it all along, and yet I'd tried to lie to myself. I'd pushed at her, called her names, made her feel like nothing. Less than nothing. I'd been such a fool. And now, my Raina would be the one to pay the price. Bile rose in my throat, and I pushed it down. I couldn't falter now. She needed me.

Viktor came from behind me and took his wife into his arms. He began crooning to her softly, trying to ease her fears. My pulse pounded loud enough I worried people could hear it across the room. Someone had taken Raina. A man from her past. It couldn't have been Leeds. He wouldn't have been able to get into an event like this one. The hotel wouldn't have permitted him to even cross their threshold. So who?

"What's happened?" Aleksi asked as he joined us, with Ilya on his heels.

"Raina's gone. Kidnapped," I said, my words clipped. I was barely holding on. I wanted to beat the hell out of someone. Make them bleed. If they hurt Raina, I'd make them suffer a hundred times more.

The fact I knew I'd feel nothing if Natalia were the one taken said plenty. I'd fucked up. No matter how much I wanted the connection to Fedor Gorev, I couldn't marry his daughter. Not when I wanted Raina with every breath I took.

"I'll check with hotel security," Aleksi said. "Ilya, stay with Cerys and Viktor. They were likely just after Raina, but until we know for certain…"

Ilya nodded.

"I'm going with you. I need to see who took her," I said.

Aleksi held up a hand. "Feliks, you left your fiancée standing across the room. You need to remain with her. Remember, you wanted power instead of Raina. She's no longer your concern."

His words, though coldly delivered, got their point across. If he'd thought it would dissuade me, he was wrong.

I roared and punched him in the stomach, then

took another swing. He blocked me and slammed the heel of his palm into my nose, making my eyes tear up. Thankfully, he hadn't hit it right, or he'd have broken it. He shook me loose and straightened his clothes. Inwardly, I seethed. The asshole knew I wanted Raina. I'd made it clear I'd planned to keep her until Viktor had demanded I choose between the women.

"I believe Natalia is in good hands," Viktor said. "Maksim is consoling her. But Aleksi is correct, Feliks. You wanted to marry Natalia Gorev. Threw Raina away so you could advance in the Bratva. You need to stand down and let others handle this."

"You heard what Ilya said. Raina is pregnant. With *my* child."

What was wrong with these men? Didn't they understand? Whoever took Raina hadn't only taken my woman, they'd taken my unborn child. I wanted to bathe the city in blood, tear the world apart, and I'd do exactly that until she was back by my side. I should have never walked away. I'd do anything to have her safe again.

Viktor nodded. "Yes, and you knew there was a chance she was pregnant when you threw her away like garbage. It's time you stopped trying to be a stingy kid holding onto all the toys. You can pick *one* woman, Feliks. I made that clear in my office, and you said to make arrangements with Natalia's father."

"You don't understand," I said. My throat felt like it was closing, and the room spun a little. The longer we stood here, the farther they could take Raina. I needed to know who had her so I could get her back. The horrors she'd faced before… Were they doing that to her now?

"I think I do." Cerys pulled away from her husband. "You finally found a woman you want to protect. Is that it, Feliks? You want to keep her safe?"

"Yes." I smoothed out my lapels. At least someone saw reason. It wasn't lost on me. The one person who could see the situation clearly was completely blind.

"And you think about her when you're apart?" she pressed.

My brow furrowed, and I sensed a trap, and yet I knew I needed to answer. If I refused, Viktor would take issue with it. "Yes, I think of her often."

More like every second of the day.

"How would you feel if Raina were with another man? If she let him touch her. Kiss her. Raise your child?"

I growled and fisted my hands at my sides. Cerys smirked at me, and I took a step back. I didn't like that look. Not even a little.

"You're scaring him, *myshka*," Viktor said.

"He should be terrified. He's already falling for her, and he's made a mess of everything. For whatever reason, she wanted to see him one last time. In the bathroom, she confided in me. I know how they met, and how he's treated her. I don't understand why she likes him. Feliks is easily my least favorite of your men."

I folded my arms and tried not to take offense. "The longer we stand here, the more distance between us and Raina."

"He's right," Aleksi said. "We can hash this out later. If he wants to come with me, let him."

Aleksi charged out of the room and headed for the security office. I followed in his wake and hoped we'd be able to get to Raina in time. I could only imagine how scared she must be. When we reached Security, it only took Aleksi a few minutes to figure out who had Raina.

The look he gave me didn't bode well. "What? Who has her?"

"Paulo Bini. The Italian mob enforcer for this region."

"He's used her before," I said. "Why else would he have called her little whore? He had to have been offered her as payment by Leeds. It's the only explanation. I don't understand why he took her now. Did Leeds put out a bounty on her? I don't see how he could afford it."

"You said the men who'd accepted her in trade previously had all hurt her. I don't think we have a lot of time, Feliks. We need to find her. Now!"

I followed Aleksi from the room and only paid half attention as he shouted orders to more of our men. We stepped out of the hotel, and he called for his car. I didn't bother asking for mine. It was only the two of us. Two Bratva soldiers rushed down the sidewalk in opposite directions. I knew they'd take their own vehicles and do their best to locate Raina. But would four people be enough?

"We need more men, Aleksi."

"What we need is a fucking miracle. I can't believe you, Feliks. If you hadn't hurt her the way you had, then none of this would have happened. You could have kept her from the beginning. You know Viktor wouldn't have stood in the way. But not you. No, the mighty Feliks needs to marry above his reach, *and* try to keep the woman he actually wants to be with."

I fisted my hands, knowing he was right. It didn't mean I had liked hearing it. The fact was Raina had been placed in danger, and the blame lay solely at my feet. If I'd married her, protected her, then no one would have dared harm her.

"You're right," I said.

The car swerved as Aleksi glanced my way. "I'm sorry. Did you just agree with me?"

I nodded. "It's my fault someone has kidnapped her, and I *will* get her back. I'll break the engagement with Natalia."

"Fedor Gorev won't handle that well. He'll claim you've made a fool of him and his daughter," Aleksi warned.

"I'm aware." I looked out the window. "Do you have any idea where you're going?"

"The docks. The Italians have a big shipment heading out today. There's a chance Raina is on that boat. If she's not, then one of the others will find her. But I'd rather hit the biggest threat first. If they get her on that ship and leave, you may never get her back." His hands tightened on the steering wheel. "If you did, you may not want her anymore. Their cargo is of the human sort. Once Paulo is finished with her, he'll sell her."

"She'd rather die than live like that again," I said. "The day I brought her to the apartment, she'd asked me to kill her. I'd been so furious, I'd wrapped my hand around her throat. She'd looked me in the eye and begged me to end it all."

"I think if she hadn't discovered she carried your child, she may have tried to kill herself when she heard about your engagement. I wasn't there, but I could tell how much she cared about you. I'd imagine it destroyed her to see you with Natalia tonight. That's probably why she escaped with Cerys to the bathroom."

Yet another sin I needed to atone for. I seemed to hurt Raina at every turn. I'd taken her bare when she'd said I needed a condom and had gotten her pregnant. For that matter, I'd never used protection with her. I'd only thought of how incredible she felt with nothing between us. Then I'd let her be taken from the apartment. I'd chosen another woman over her and said cruel things when I next saw her.

If she never wanted to see me again, I'd understand. It didn't mean I'd allow her to leave. She'd forgive me, eventually. I'd shower her with gifts. Move her into my home. Help her set up a nursery. She'd see I planned to keep her, to cherish her. Wouldn't she?

"What are you thinking?" Aleksi asked as we drew closer to the docks.

"Of ways to keep Raina by my side," I said.

He snorted. "You might start by telling her you're an asshole, an idiot, and that you're sorry you ran off the only woman you've ever loved. Anything short of that…"

"I know." I'd never been good at expressing my feelings, unless it was anger. How would I tell her all that? I wasn't sure I was capable of such a thing. The Bratva had made me cold. Hard. If I still had a heart, it had blackened with each sin I'd committed.

Aleksi skidded to a stop, and I scanned the area. With so many ships docked, how would we know which one to approach? We hadn't had time to plan. I hated going in blind, but in this case, it couldn't be helped.

"Let me do the talking," Aleksi said. "I'm more rational right now."

I cast him a glare as we exited the car. I kept pace with him, since Aleksi seemed to know which ship we needed.

"*Scusami.* We're looking for Paulo," Aleksi said.

One of them stepped forward, scanning Aleksi

from head to toe and back again. "What for?"

"Business." Aleksi shoved his hands into his pockets, looking completely relaxed.

"Paulo's busy." The man smirked. "Won't be available for a while."

So, he'd brought her here. I advanced on the man, shoving Aleksi aside. Rage filled me as I thought of all the vile things he could do to my Raina right now. And this fucker was keeping me from saving her. Wrapping my fingers around the asshole's throat, I lifted him off the ground. "Paulo has something of mine, and I'll be taking it back. You can either tell me where to find him, or I can make you."

The others moved closer, but I saw Aleksi pull his weapon. He forced them back, leaving me to deal with the arrogant fuck who thought to keep me from Raina. The man spit at me and sneered. "I'll tell you nothing."

"Very well." I grabbed him and tossed him farther into the shadows. Aleksi moved the other two as well. The fewer witnesses, the better. I shoved him to the ground and kneeled on his chest. He thrashed but couldn't dislodge me. The stench of liquor told me plenty. He'd probably had enough alcohol he'd not only dulled his wits, but he'd be slower too. Perfect.

I slammed the man's hand against the concrete and he cursed at me. I did it again. Then a third time. I felt the bones give as they cracked, and he screamed like the little bitch he was. "Last chance. Tell me where Paulo took Raina."

"Fuck. You."

I sighed. I didn't have time to play with this fucker. Any other time, I'd draw things out. Torture him for a while. But I needed to step things up. "Remember, you did this to yourself."

I pulled a knife from my pocket and flicked it open. I kept it extra sharp just for this very reason. As he squirmed, I noticed Aleksi pulled a second gun and pointed it at the man lying under me. He stilled, staring down the barrel. Fool! It wasn't Aleksi he needed to fear, but he hadn't figured that out yet.

He would.

Pressing the blade against his index finger, I shoved down hard and severed it from his hand. The man screamed and bucked. Blood spurted and pooled on the ground. The spray missed me. If this asshole got blood on me, and I scared Raina when she saw me looking like I'd stepped out of a horror movie, I'd bring him back to kill him again. And yes, he would die. I just needed information first.

"Ready to talk?" I asked. He shook his head, but I saw the fear in his eyes. I cut off another finger, then a third. The man still wouldn't speak. He'd gone pale, as his blood flowed freely. The pussy would likely pass out from the pain soon enough.

The other two men began speaking rapidly in Italian. Their eyes were wide as they watched what I did to their friend. I ripped open his shirt and slid the blade down his chest, splitting his skin open. He still refused to utter a word.

Aleksi knew their language well and peppered the other two with questions. The man beneath me sagged, clearly thinking he'd be safe now. Was he so new to this way of life he didn't understand he'd be sent to hell tonight? The other two seemed to realize it. Resignation filled their eyes as they stared at Aleksi.

"Your friends are quite helpful," I said. "Pity you weren't."

Before he understood what I meant, I sliced the blade through his throat, letting him choke on his own blood. I wiped the knife clean on his clothes before standing and brushing myself off. Someone would find the body later, but no cops would be called. Things didn't work that way in this part of town. If the Italians even thought to retaliate, I'd be happy to show them the error of their ways.

"If you're finished playing, I know where Paulo is," Aleksi said.

"And those two?" I asked.

Aleksi shot them both in the head, the bodies dropping to the ground. "They've outlived their usefulness."

"Where's Raina?" I asked.

"She's on board. Lower level. You understand this won't be easy. There's only two of us, and many of them. We can't just walk past them and go searching for her," Aleksi said.

"Then call in backup, but I'm not waiting. Every second she's with him is too long."

Aleksi nodded. "Very well, Feliks. Do what you must."

With my knife in one hand and my gun in the other, I approached the ship. I walked up the ramp, being careful not to make unnecessary noise. The sound of voices overhead gave me an idea of how many men I'd have to slip past. If I stayed in the shadows, it would help. Thankfully, I'd worn solid black to the charity event.

Keeping my back to the ship, I eased up the ramp. When I reached the top, I froze and waited. Peering around the corner, I saw four men, smoking and laughing, as they stacked boxes on one of the decks. I waited until their backs were turned and snuck onto the boat. Moving quickly, I found the hatch that led below into the bowels of the ship, and knew I needed to act fast.

I knew little about ships, but I hoped I could cause enough damage to stall them. We couldn't leave the docks. Not until I had Raina safely tucked in the car and far from here. I studied the various mechanics. Smashing the butt of my gun into some dials and a few buttons, I hoped it would be enough. Sparks shot out, and I hid my face with my arm. Creeping farther into the depths of the ship, I looked for a set of stairs.

Making my way to the cabins on board, I searched each, hoping to find Raina. At the end of the hall, I heard muffled curses and slowly turned the knob. The door opened a sliver, enough for me to look inside. I recognized Raina's shoes on the floor, and her dress pooled closer to the bed.

My stomach knotted, and I ground my teeth together. If he'd already raped her, I'd make him die slow. I opened the door farther, but the big bastard had his back to me. He had no idea anyone had snuck up on him. I silently crept nearer to the bed and saw Raina. Her head had fallen over the side of the bed, and her chest rose and fell steadily. Inching closer, my hand tightened on my knife when I saw what he'd done. I knew when she woke, she'd be in immense pain.

"You shouldn't have touched her," I said, my voice little more than a growl.

Before he could turn, I buried my knife in his back, then yanked it free. Paulo whirled to face me, his soulless eyes taking me in. Fucker didn't even seem to notice he'd been stabbed. This man needed to suffer. As badly as I wanted to put a bullet in him, I wanted him to hurt for far longer.

Shouts elsewhere on the ship told me Aleksi had arrived with backup. I hoped they'd keep the others busy. Backing to the door, I shut it and twisted the lock. Paulo grinned when he saw the move, and I knew he thought he had the upper hand.

"Raina is mine," I said. "Perhaps Leeds forgot to mention it?"

"The whore carries your brat. Everyone knows," Paulo said. "Her cunt can still take a cock. Until she's showing, she can earn some extra cash. Once the kid is born, I'll sell them to the highest bidder, and make sure they send you a video of your child being taken again and again. I have a buyer picked out who will be perfect. He likes boys *and* girls."

I gripped my gun so tight I worried I'd crack it or break my fingers. He wanted me to react out of rage. I was close. So very close to giving in to that urge. But if I did, not only would Raina and our baby pay the price, but I'd most likely be tortured to death. I couldn't let that happen.

"Fuck you, Paulo! You'll never sell my child because Raina will leave with me."

He stepped to the side, waving a hand at her, like a game show host displaying a prize. "Don't you like what I've done?"

I refused to look. I'd already seen her. My beautiful Raina. She'd be devastated, assuming the pain didn't drive her mad.

"You'll pay for hurting her, both now and before. She told me of the men who harmed her. I know you were one of them."

He smiled, flashing his teeth like a shark. "Of course, I was. And I will be again. In fact, I'll let you watch. As you lie dying in a pool of your own blood, your last vision will be of me fucking your whore. I don't care if she's awake or not."

My hands shook as I fought to control myself. I

wouldn't make the first move. I couldn't. I needed to keep a level head, even if I wanted to slit him open and pull out his guts while he still breathed. I wanted him to feel every second of pain, and know it was payback for what he'd done to Raina.

"Did you know I was one of her first?" Paulo asked, licking his lips. "Her young, tight cunt felt so good. Her ass felt even better, and the way she choked on a cock? Mmm."

He closed his eyes, an expression of bliss crossing his features, and I knew... I couldn't wait. As much as I wanted to gut him alive, he needed to be put down. I aimed my gun and fired, hitting him in the stomach. He dropped to his knees, his eyes flying open. His mouth opened, but no sound came out. The knife may not have bothered him, but a bullet certainly got his attention.

As he toppled to his back, I decided I had just enough time for a little revenge. I ripped open his shirt and used my blade to slice him from clavicle to groin. He gurgled and I saw the light fading in his eyes as I reached in started pulling out any organs I could tear from his body. I left a pile beside him as he exhaled his last breath. Only then did I allow myself to focus on Raina.

I didn't dare touch her, covered in his blood. I stripped out of my clothes, and as loathe as I was to use anything of the Italian's, I found a pair of pants and quickly pulled them on. I washed off in the bathroom sink before carefully lifting Raina into my arms.

"I've got you, *liubimaja*. Please don't wake until I can get you medical attention." I pressed a kiss to her forehead and carried her from the room, leaving the carnage behind me.

Chapter Seven

Raina

Everything hurt. All I felt was immense pain when I struggled to open my eyes. Panic filled me when I couldn't see anything. I reached up to touch my face, and a powerful hand gripped mine.

"Easy, *lastachka*. The doctor has taped your eyes shut to help them heal faster."

I recognized the voice. *Feliks*! Had he come for me? I opened my mouth and felt his finger press against my lips. When he released them, I felt something cold. Opening, I realized he'd given me some ice chips. I savored them for a moment, my throat aching as if I hadn't had a drink in days.

"What happened?" I asked, my voice croaking. The pain in my throat made me wince.

"Do you remember the charity event?" he asked.

I nodded slowly. I did. Cerys seemed so sweet when I met her. Then on our way back to the men... I gasped, bolting upright.

"*Lastachka,* you're safe now. I have you and no one will harm you again." He brushed his lips against my fingers. "Not even me."

"The Italians," I whispered.

"Yes. Paulo had you. When I found you..." I heard him audibly swallow. "I'm sorry I didn't find you sooner, *lastachka*. The fact he didn't have time to rape you gives me a small amount of comfort, but he did so much damage before I reached you."

I reached toward my face and stopped. "My eyes?"

"Yes. They had to operate. Even so, there's a chance you'll lose your sight. There's fresh scarring on your body. He'd stitched your lips shut and used a knife to carve the skin of your breasts, belly, and inner thighs."

I swayed. It was too much! I'd known Paulo's cruelty before, but Gary had always stopped him from damaging me too much.

"He hit you in your temple and you had bruising elsewhere." I felt his lips on my hand again, then my shoulder. "I'm so sorry, *lastachka*. Please forgive me. I've been a fool."

"I don't understand, Feliks. Shouldn't you be with your fiancée?" My breath caught, and I placed a hand against my belly. "The baby…"

"Is fine. The doctor said to watch for bleeding and to be cautious the next week. As for Natalia, I told Viktor to cancel my engagement. I've pissed off Fedor, and I'm sure I'll have to meet with him soon. I'm hopeful an explanation will smooth things over."

"What could you possibly tell him?" I asked.

"That I discovered I had a child on the way, and it didn't seem fair to ask his daughter to a raise a child who wasn't her own. I promised I wouldn't take our child from you, *lastachka*, and I meant it. But Fedor doesn't know that. The thought of his precious daughter raising the child of my mistress might be enough to sway him that this was the right decision."

"Mistress?" I asked. "I thought… You said…"

"I know." I kissed my cheek softly. "I'm sorry for so much, *lastachka*. The words I said were cruel and thoughtless. I hurt you. Even knowing I wanted to keep you, I still made the deal with Fedor to marry his daughter. It was wrong, and I didn't realize it until I'd lost you."

My mind was spinning, and I felt like Feliks had thrown too much at me all at once. I couldn't process everything he'd said, nor what had happened to me. It explained why I hurt everywhere. How did I not remember any of it? When he'd hit me, had it knocked me out that much? Surely the pain would have woken me when he'd started cutting into me?

"I can't handle all this right now. I'm tired, Feliks."

Feliks helped me lie back again. He smoothed my hair from my face and gently kissed my brow. "You will hear things in the coming days. It will make you think of me as a monster. Just know everything I did was for you."

I wanted to ask what he meant, but I was too scared. Instead, I pretended to sleep. I heard his footsteps echo on the floors, then the door opened and shut. I didn't know if he'd left for certain, so I continued to feign sleep. It felt like hours passed before I heard whispered voices.

"Can you believe he did that?" a woman asked.

"They say he's one of the most brutal men in the Bratva. For this area, anyway. He tortured those men!"

I didn't recognize either voice. They bustled around my room, and I wondered if they were nurses. The scent and beeping told me I was most likely in a hospital. Considering Feliks said I'd had surgery, it made sense. Although, I could just as easily have been in a Bratva-owned makeshift hospital facility. I knew those men were injured regularly. Well, I didn't know about the Bratva specifically, but the mafia in general.

Once they'd left again, I breathed a little easier.

"They weren't wrong," said a voice. I squeaked and tried to sit up, holding my hands out. Who the hell had slipped into my room now?

"I apologize for startling you. I slipped in as they were leaving. We met so briefly, I'm not surprised you don't recognize my voice. I'm Viktor. My wife, Cerys, was with you when you were kidnapped."

"H-hello, Viktor."

"Would you like to know what happened when you were taken?" he asked.

Did I? The way those women were talking, I wasn't certain. My hesitation was enough to keep him from speaking for a moment. I heard the creak of a chair as he settled himself nearby.

"I demanded Feliks return to his fiancée when he found out you were missing. The second he saw my wife return without you, he nearly ran across the banquet hall to reach her, needing to know where you were."

I digested his words. Feliks had been worried about me? I hadn't been sure he'd even notice if I'd decided not to return to the room at the charity. It seemed I'd been wrong. He'd been the first to react to my disappearance, other than Cerys since she'd been with me.

"When he learned someone had kidnapped you, he wanted to charge after you. I told him more than once to go back to Natalia, and he refused. My wife helped him see the light. I don't think Feliks realized until then exactly how he felt about you."

"I thought he hated me," I whispered.

"*Nyet*. Far from it. He and Aleksi went to find out more about your abduction, and they left once they knew who had you. Do you want to know what he did to the Italians?"

"I-I don't know."

Did I? Was that what the women had spoken of? Had Feliks hurt people? I knew he hadn't kept his hands clean, not working for the Bratva, and he'd admitted as much to me. I had a hard time picturing him hurting someone because of *me*.

"It's bloody and violent. He tortured one for information. Once he knew your location, he killed the man, and Aleksi shot the other two men with him. And Feliks went onto the ship, without backup, because he refused to leave you there another minute. Instead of waiting for help to arrive, he snuck onto the ship, disabled it, and went in search of you."

My throat hurt from the emotions welling inside me. "He did all that?"

"More," Viktor said. "Paulo is dead. I'll spare you the details, but Feliks sent the man to hell in a vicious way. I think seeing what the monster had done to you unhinged him a bit more than usual. If he hadn't been worried for you, he would have taken more time and made Paulo suffer longer. I can guarantee it."

He'd done all that for me? Between Viktor's words, the mumblings of those women, and the way Feliks acted while he was here… Was it possible he truly regretted what happened between us? Did he want me to stay with him now?

A sick feeling filled me. No. It wasn't me. He hadn't been the least bit ready to leave Natalia until he learned about the baby.

"It's not me he wants," I said. "It's because I'm pregnant."

"I mentioned that to him," Viktor said. "I guess the only way we'd have known for certain would have been for you to *not* be pregnant when all of this happened. But we can't turn back the clock. I guess you'll have to have faith in Feliks. Can you do that?"

Could I? I felt conflicted. I'd have been content as his mistress. It would have been a step up from my life before. An enormous step. And I had to admit, being without him had been miserable. The thought of marrying someone else had sent me running straight to Feliks. I'd said I needed to see him one last time, but hadn't he done exactly as I'd hoped? He'd left Natalia to be with me.

So why didn't it feel like I'd won?

"What is it, Raina?" Viktor asked.

"I wanted him to leave her, to choose me." I licked my lips and winced when it hurt. "Now that he has, it feels... wrong. Did I break up their engagement?"

"Yes and no," Viktor said. "Truthfully, I don't believe Feliks would have lasted long with Natalia. He didn't like her. I could tell she grated on his nerves. In time, he'd have regretted his decision even if he hadn't seen you at the charity dinner. You only sped up the timetable."

"Does she know?" I asked.

The door to the room slammed against the wall, and I startled, nearly falling from the bed. I felt Viktor's hand on my arm, steadying me.

"I'd say she does," Viktor murmured. "Natalia, why are you here?"

"To see the whore who stole Feliks from me. Father said she's carrying his brat. Is it true?" I could feel her glaring at me. "Why is she so ugly right now?"

Her harsh words might have made me cry before. Now, I only curled my fingers into the blankets and tried to remain calm. I didn't know why she'd come here. Oh, I'd heard her words, but I thought she might have a bigger reason than what she'd admitted. If she'd hoped to harm me, I had a feeling Viktor's presence would stop her plans.

"Raina got kidnapped from the charity dinner. It's why Feliks rushed off," Viktor said. "You need to leave, Natalia. I doubt your father would want you here, and I know Feliks will be angry."

I heard her labored breathing, then a sob. I tensed. Was she crying?

"Don't I deserve to be happy?" Natalia asked, sniffling. "I've adored Feliks for years. When he asked to marry me, I knew all my dreams were coming true. But *she* had to wreck it all."

"I didn't ask him to leave you," I said. "In fact, I'd just told Cerys it had been a mistake to attend the event with Ilya when the Italians took me."

"But you're p-pregnant. With Feliks' baby." More sniffling. "I can't compete with that. I heard what he told Father tonight and had to come straight here. He said he didn't want to force your child on me, that he'd expect me to raise it, to treat it like my own if we were to marry. Can you believe it?"

I could because he'd already told me his plan. I wasn't going to tell her it had all been a lie. Feliks would have broken the engagement even if she'd agreed to raise my baby. He'd have found another reason they shouldn't be together. I might not have known him for long, but I could tell he was stubborn and used to getting his way.

"Natalia, go home," Viktor said, his voice brooking no argument.

I heard her whirl and flee the room. If anyone expected me to rest, they'd need to lock the door. At this rate, I worried the rest of Viktor's men would show up, and possibly Cerys and anyone else I'd met in the past two weeks.

"You're tired," Viktor said. "Rest, Raina. I'll remain until Feliks returns. He doesn't want you to be left alone right now. The Italians could retaliate. It would be foolish, but since he took out their enforcer, the odds aren't in our favor. I'll keep you safe."

"Thank you, Viktor. And thank your wife too? She was nice to me," I mumbled.

I felt his fingers lightly touch my cheek. "You're easy to like, Raina. Sleep."

I sighed and did as he commanded.

Chapter Eight

Feliks
Three Weeks Later

I lay in bed watching Raina sleep. She'd curled on her side, her hand protectively resting over her still-flat belly. Her vision hadn't returned fully. The doctor said it was possible she could gain more back in the upcoming weeks or months, but I could tell it distressed her. Faint scars marred her lips where Paulo had stitched them shut. The marks on her body were pink and raised. In time, the doctor said they would fade with the thinner ones becoming fine white lines. I'd offered to pay for plastic surgery, but she'd refused.

Running my fingers over her cheek, I smiled. I'd have never guessed I'd feel happy having a woman sleep in my bed. Then again, until Raina, I'd seldom stayed the night with a woman. I used them, got what I wanted, and left. Even my mistresses hadn't kept my attention all night and into the next day. Since her abduction, I hadn't touched Raina intimately. I wanted to. Burned for it.

But she wasn't ready.

While she hadn't shied away from sharing a bed with me, and I doubted she'd turn me away if I tried anything, I could tell she still hurt. My brave Raina tried to hide her pain, but I saw the winces here and there. If I could bring Paulo back from the dead and kill him again, I would.

"I didn't think I had a heart, Raina, but I was wrong. Because you have it," I murmured. Loving her didn't make me weaker. If anything, I felt whole for once in my life. Although I knew my enemies could use her against me. It only meant I had to keep her safe.

I'd hired protection for her. Two men I trusted a great deal would shadow her at all times. Even now, one remained in the house, ready and waiting for any trouble that might come knocking. If only I'd done things differently. Turning back the clock wasn't possible, but if it were, I never would have given her up. How could I have thought spending the rest of my life with Natalia had even been an option? Sending Raina away had been like cutting off my hand.

My phone rang, and I reached for it, hoping to answer before the sound woke Raina. I spoke softly. "Hello."

"I need you to come to my home. We need to discuss your broken engagement," Viktor said. "Fedor isn't pleased by the turn of events. I have a feeling his spoiled daughter is pitching a fit."

"I need to shower and dress. I'll be there shortly." I reached to touch Raina's cheek. My beautiful, Raina. Every time I had to leave the house without her, I worried I'd come home and find her gone. After the cruel way I'd treated her, it wouldn't surprise me if she left.

I disconnected the call and went to get ready. By the time I'd showered and put on a suit, I walked into the bedroom to find Raina awake and sitting up in bed. She looked adorably disheveled, and I smiled, just admiring the view.

"I need to meet with Viktor. You'll be all right on your own for a while?" I asked.

She nodded. "Other than getting something to eat, I'll probably spend the day in bed. I'm feeling more tired than usual."

I pressed a kiss to her forehead. "Rest, *liubimaja.* I'll return as soon as I can. There's one stop I need to make after I leave Viktor's, but I'll try to be quick."

"Stay safe," she said.

"Always."

Before I got the urge to blow off Viktor, I left the room and didn't look back. If I had, I may have never left. On my way out the door, I stopped to get coffee from the kitchen and spoke briefly with Ivan, the current guard on duty.

"Raina said she's going to rest," I said. "Please check on her in an hour. If anything goes wrong, or she needs me, call immediately. I may not be able to get out of this meeting with Viktor, but it doesn't mean I won't leave if Raina needs me."

"I'll take care of her," Ivan said.

I took my coffee and went out to my car. The drive to Viktor's gave me time to think. I didn't know how to handle the situation with Fedor. I'd thought he understood, and agreed, breaking the engagement with his daughter was for the best. Not only for me, but for Natalia as well. Now it seemed he'd changed his mind. So what did he want?

He had far more money than I did. It couldn't be something that simple. So what?

I pulled up to the gate at Viktor's home and waited to be let in. The cars in the drive told me more than Fedor had arrived at the house. For the same meeting? Or were the others here for something else? I recognized one of the vehicles. Vadim Ivanov. Why had the Vor come to Viktor's house? A chill skated down my spine, I hoped I hadn't lied to Raina when I said I'd return. If Fedor petitioned the Vor, I could easily be locked up, beaten, or even killed for breaking a contract.

I entered the house, coffee in hand, and went straight to Viktor's office. I saw the Vor's personal *byki* standing outside the door and my feeling of unease grew.

"Viktor asked to see me," I said, and the man knocked on the office door.

"Enter," Viktor called out.

I stepped inside and scanned the room quickly. Viktor, Fedor, Maksim, and Vadim. I felt like asking if I needed to make arrangements for my family but didn't dare. It would be seen as a sign of weakness.

"I apologize I couldn't get here sooner," I said.

"Have a seat, Feliks," Vadim said. "We have a few things to discuss."

I sat and wished I could turn the chair to put my back to the wall and my eyes on all the men in the room. For the first time since working for Viktor, I didn't feel safe in this room. What would happen to Raina if I didn't return? Even worse… if they wanted to truly punish me, they'd use Raina to do it. I hoped they didn't realize exactly what she meant to me.

"You agreed to marry Natalia Gorev, correct?" Vadim asked.

"Yes. I did."

"And you signed a contract?" Vadim asked, pulling a set of papers off Viktor's desk. A quick glance told me it was the marriage contract.

"Yes, I signed those papers. I did so before finding out my mistress became pregnant."

Vadim held up his hand. "I didn't ask for an explanation. Not yet. You admit that you broke your contract with Fedor Gorev?"

"I admit it," I said.

"Did you read the fine print?" Viktor asked.

I opened my mouth then shut it. Had I? I tried to recall, but I'd been in a hurry at the time. "*Nyet.*"

"In the event you broke the contract to marry Natalia, you agreed to give the Gorevs anything they asked. An open-ended favor so to speak," Vadim said.

I felt sweat start to gather under my suit and hoped no one could see how nervous those words made me. What the hell did the man want?

"I see. And the price he's asking?" I kept my gaze on Vadim and refused to look at Fedor. If the bastard looked smug, I might very well hit him.

"Natalia has made a request, and I've decided to honor her wishes," Fedor said. "She wants to carry your child."

My mind blanked for a moment. My child? But Raina already carried my baby. What the hell did he…" Are you asking me to impregnate your daughter?"

"It's what she wants." Fedor shifted in his seat. "To ensure it happens, she's asked to spend thirty days in your bed. I hear you've moved your whore into your home. You'll have to make her leave during that time."

I was shaking my head before he'd even finished his statement. "*Nyet*. I will not remove Raina. She carries my child, and I have every intention of marrying her. It's not *my* house any longer, but *ours*."

"If you refuse, Fedor has agreed to an alternate solution." Vadim stared at me. "But you'll like it even less."

"What does he want?" I asked.

"To fuck your whore while you watch." Fedor gave me a chilling smile. "I'm hoping she's a fighter. I like it when they struggle."

I fisted my hands, my rage rising by the minute. I no longer saw the men in the room. A red haze settled over my vision. He planned to hurt my Raina. To brutalize her the way others had before. It was no longer Leeds' blood I wanted. I'd kill everyone in this room if it was the only way to keep my Raina safe. I'd make Cerys a widow without a moment's hesitation.

The door opened, and I heard soft footsteps. The moment Natalia spoke, something inside me snapped.

"Did he agree?" she asked, sounding too cheerful considering what she'd asked of me.

Shaking, I rose to my feet. Before anyone could stop me, I yanked the knife from under my jacket and threw it at Natalia, watching as the blade sank into her chest. Her eyes went wide, and she staggered back, blood trickling from the corner of her mouth. My gun was in my hand almost instantly, and I shot Fedor between the eyes. It was a better death than either had deserved.

Pointing my weapon at Vadim, I kept my finger on the trigger and stared him down. "Will you be next?"

He only smiled and remained seated. It was almost as if he hadn't noticed I'd killed Fedor and Natalia in front of him. Neither Viktor nor Maksim had made a move either. I scanned the three of them, waiting for them to move. One inch, and I'd put a bullet in them.

"I'm not permitted to marry Natalia and keep Raina as my mistress, but you'd allow them to ask such a thing of me?" I demanded. "And Fedor… He got off far too easy."

"I told you," Viktor said, turning to Vadim. "Satisfied?"

"Yes." Vadim stood slowly, buttoning his suit jacket. "Feliks, you may ask one favor of me. Only one. Today, you did me a great service."

"I don't understand," I said, lowering my weapon. "You're not going to kill me for what I've done? Punish Raina?"

Vadim shook his head. "*Nyet.* Fedor crossed a line and never even realized it. Your Raina isn't the only woman he's done that to. The last one happened to be related to me. I'll let her parents know she's been avenged."

"Is that why you called me here? You knew what he'd ask of me?"

Vadim nodded. "I did. He made his wishes known before we came here. I asked Viktor to arrange this meeting and bring in Maksim. We needed as many witnesses as possible to tell the story. Natalia made a scene. Her father killed her in a fit of rage, and we were given no choice but to put him down when he lost all reason."

"You used me," I muttered. "I sat here, fearing for Raina's life, and it was all for nothing? So you could be the puppet master and yank my strings?"

Vadim shrugged. "It all worked out."

Viktor stood and pulled a briefcase from under his desk. He handed it to me. The weight told me it contained more than a few papers. Opening it, my brows lifted at the amount of money inside.

"Consider it a bonus, in addition to the favor," Vadim said. "I hope you'll invite me to the wedding, Feliks. I look forward to meeting your bride."

The Vor left and I stared at Viktor. "It's over? No one will be coming for us?"

"Not within the Bratva," Viktor said.

"I'm about to tie up a loose end." I shifted the case to my other hand and put my gun away. "Gary Leeds has lived far too long, don't you think?"

"Let me handle him," Maksim said. "I would consider it an honor. Go home to Raina. You've done enough for today, Feliks."

I thanked him and took my leave. He was right.

Being with Raina was more important. And the money in the case would be put to good use. I'd put some aside for our child, and the rest would help pay for the wedding. I hadn't asked her to marry me yet, and knew I needed to make one last stop before I went home. I needed to retrieve something from the safe at my bank.

* * *

Raina

I didn't know why I felt so tired. I'd spent most of the day in bed, and still couldn't seem to find the energy to do much of anything. It felt like Feliks had been gone forever. According to Ivan, it had only been a few hours. My bodyguard had brought me a bowl of soup with some crackers. I'd eaten them, then slept for an hour. When I'd woken, I'd stayed in bed, staring at the ceiling.

My vision wasn't one hundred percent yet, but it returned a little more each day, or so it seemed. The doctors wanted to give it more time before deciding if I should check into getting glasses or contacts, or possibly have corrective surgery. I'd spent enough time at the hospital, I wasn't sure I would want to have another procedure done anytime soon. I'd be glad when the need for doctors would be over.

Something felt off, and I couldn't figure out what it was. Feliks had assured me no one would take me from him again. He'd been sweet and doted on me. And yet, I wasn't certain I felt as if I belonged here. He'd moved me into his home. Bought a massive wardrobe for me and had already started setting up a nursery. So why did I feel as if I were a visitor?

Because he walked away once before. What if he does it again?

I knew Viktor had given him an ultimatum before. Me or Natalia. He'd chosen to marry for power. What if the same thing happened again? How long could he possibly be happy with someone like me? I was nothing. Less than. Just some unwanted child who'd been sold and turned into a whore. I knew Feliks could do so much better. I'd seen Natalia. She'd been stunning and had clearly wanted him.

What if she didn't give up? What if she demanded he keep their engagement?

My heart would break. In fact, it already felt battered and bruised. It wouldn't take much to crumble it entirely. Only Feliks had that sort of power over me. I didn't care what anyone else said or did. They meant nothing to me, but Feliks... I loved him.

The side of the bed dipped, and I looked over. Feliks had removed his jacket and rolled up his sleeves. He leaned onto the bed, bracing his weight on his elbow. "Did you sleep well?"

I shrugged a shoulder. What could I say? No matter how much I napped, it was never enough. I'd thought it was the pregnancy. Now I wondered if it was something else. Could I be depressed? Or was I merely resigned to my lot in life?

"I have a gift for you." He reached out to run his finger down the bridge of my nose. "Gary Leeds will no longer be breathing by the end of the day. Maksim is going to take him out, and he'll likely suffer before he dies. You'll never have to worry about seeing him again."

He'd done that for me? Arranged for my biggest abuser to die? It had to mean something, didn't it? He wouldn't have done such a thing if he didn't care. It gave me hope my fears had been for nothing.

I reached and laced our fingers together. "Thank

you, Feliks."

He pulled something out of his pocket, holding it in his closed hand. "Raina, I screwed up when we first met. I let you go when I should have held on tight. Made you feel as if you weren't important. *Lastachka*, you're the other half of my soul. Without you, I'm incomplete."

Tears burned my eyes at his words. It was everything I'd wanted to hear from him, but was it true? Did he really mean it? I'd give anything to be someone important to him, to possibly have his love. He'd said the words before, but I hadn't believed him. I'd been mostly asleep and convinced myself I'd dreamed it all. What if I hadn't?

He opened his hand and I gasped at the beautiful ring he held in his palm. I reached out and lightly touched it, wondering about the significance. I didn't need jewelry. If he thought I needed him to buy me expensive things, he was wrong. I only needed to know he wanted me. Needed me. Nothing else mattered.

"It belonged to my grandmother," he said. "I'd be honored if you'd wear it and promise to marry me as soon as it can be arranged."

"Wh-what?" I lifted my gaze to his. He couldn't be serious. Could he? "Feliks, are you… you're asking me to marry you?"

He nodded. "Not the most romantic proposal, and for that I'm sorry, but it's heartfelt. I don't want to spend another day apart from you. Please, Raina. Marry me. Be my wife. The mother of my children."

"Feliks, I…"

He pressed his lips to mine in a gentle kiss. "I love you, Raina. You're my heart. My very reason for living. Please."

"Yes, Feliks. I'll marry you."

He slipped the ring onto my finger, and it suddenly felt like everything was right in my world. Had this been what was missing? Had I felt off-kilter because I'd worried he'd never marry me?

"There are things you need to know, *lastachka*. But not right now. You have shadows under your eyes and are still healing. I'll run a bath. Maybe after soaking, you'll feel better."

I bit my lip. "Feliks, would you get in with me? The tub is big enough."

He cupped my cheek and pressed his forehead to mine. "I'd be honored, Raina. Wait here."

He stood and went into the bathroom. I heard the water running a minute later and lounged on the bed while he filled the tub. I knew it would take a while. The first time I'd seen the bathtub, I'd joked he had a mini pool in his home. Not only could Feliks and I fit in there, but there was enough space for far more people in the tub.

I admired the ring on my finger, feeling warm inside. He'd actually asked me to marry him! I smiled and snuggled into the bed a little deeper. Until I'd met Feliks, I'd thought I'd die in pain. Unwanted. Unloved. And now I'd met the most incredible man. He had his faults, and he'd broke my heart. But he'd also saved me more than once. How could I not love him?

"Come, Raina. It's ready," he called out.

I stood and went into the bathroom. Quickly stripping off my clothes, I climbed into the tub in front of him. He'd already sunk into the water and leaned back against the side of the round tub. As I stepped in, he reached for me, tugging me down and pulling me back against him. He trailed his fingers along my thigh, up my arm, and over my shoulders before repeating the pattern. Slowly, I began to relax. My eyes shut, and I drifted on a haze of bliss.

"That feels good," I murmured.

"I want to spoil you, Raina. You and our child. I will do everything in my power to keep you safe and make you happy. Just please don't ever leave me. I'm not sure I'd survive it."

I tipped my head up and kissed his jaw. "Promise."

I wanted to demand the same of him, to ask he be faithful to me. If he'd been willing to marry Natalia and keep me as his mistress... My stomach knotted. Could I share him now that I'd fallen in love with him? Before, he'd been my savior, and had promised a better life. This was different. Being his wife meant something to me.

"Feliks..." I nibbled my lower lip. Did I dare make such a demand? Or perhaps I could just ask his intentions.

"What it is, *lastachka*?"

"Before, when you were going to keep me as your mistress, you still intended to marry Natalia."

His hand stilled where he'd been lightly stroking my skin. "And you wonder if I'll keep a mistress now that you're to be my wife?"

I nodded. "I know I don't have a say in the matter. You made that clear before. I just... I'd rather be prepared than surprised later."

He kissed the side of my neck and rubbed his whiskered jaw along my shoulder. "The only woman I want is you, Raina. You're my sun, my moon... you're more beautiful than all the stars in the sky, and every bit as captivating."

I reached up and wrapped my fingers around the back of his neck. "I love you, Feliks. You have no idea how easy it would be for you to hurt me. I've tried to be tough, to be strong… but you're my weakness."

"*Nyet*. Not a weakness. Together, we're stronger than we are apart. There's something I should tell you."

"What?" I turned slightly to see him. "Did something happen while you were gone?"

He nodded. "Viktor called a meeting. Fedor, Natalia's father, wished to make some demands. In response, I killed both him and his daughter. Not only in front of Viktor, but also Maksim and the Vor. I'd thought they would kill me, or worse, hurt you in retaliation. Instead, the Vor thanked me for solving a problem for him and offered me a large amount of cash. We'll put half into a trust for our child. Something they can have when they turn eighteen."

"Killed them?" I asked, not certain I'd heard him correctly. "You murdered a woman?"

He stared at me, his gaze chilling more by the minute. "Do you want to know why? Ask me, *lastachka*. Ask why I didn't hesitate to end both their lives. What could they have possibly wanted that would pull such a response from me?"

"I…" I didn't know. Did I want to find out? I stared at him and realized I needed to hear his reasoning. "Yes. Tell me."

"Natalia demanded I toss you from our home and take her to my bed for thirty days, to ensure I impregnated her." He cupped my cheek. "I could never do that to you, nor did I want anything to do with her."

"So you killed her?"

"Only after I heard her father's demands when I refused to touch her. He planned to violate you, in front of me. I had to choose. Fuck his daughter or watch him rape you. I decided they both needed to die and handled the matter."

I pressed my finger to my mouth, holding back my cry. The world he lived in was brutal, and savage when it came to women. We were merely possessions. Toys for big powerful men to use as they saw fit.

"And now you know," he said. "I will never let another man touch you, Raina. And I don't want anyone but you. Touching her would have been abhorrent, and I'm not sure I could have gotten hard. But the thought of him hurting you that way? *Nyet*. I couldn't stand for it."

I turned and straddled him, cupping his cheeks in my hands. "Thank you, Feliks. For protecting me. As horrible as it was to hear what they intended, I'd rather know than live in the dark. Don't hide enemies from me. Isn't it better for me to be prepared?"

He nodded. "You're right. Beautiful *and* smart. I'm the luckiest of men."

"Make love to me? Please?"

"Right here? Or do you prefer the bed?" he asked.

"Here. Now."

He ran his hands up my sides to cup my breasts, his thumbs stroking over my nipples. He released me, placing his hands on the sides of the tub. "Would you like to be in charge this time, Raina? You've always had men take from you. Ride me. Take your pleasure."

My body heated at his words and my cheeks flushed. I reached between us, wrapping my fingers around his cock. The man seemed always to be hard. Even now, after speaking of murdering two people, he felt like steel in my grasp.

I sank onto him, moaning as he filled me. Placing my hands on his shoulders, I used him as leverage to lift and lower myself. My breasts bounced with each stroke, and I liked the way he stared at them. The hunger in his gaze made me burn hotter, ache for him even more.

"Feliks… touch me."

"Here?" he asked, leaning forward and capturing my nipple in his mouth. He lightly scraped his teeth across it before sucking hard. He released it with a *pop.* "Or here."

He rubbed his fingers over my clit. I cried out, my hips jerking. "Both! Please. I need you. Make me come."

He toyed with my body, lavishing attention on my breasts while his fingers strummed my clit. My orgasm was so strong I saw stars, the water around us sloshing as I rode him hard. My pussy clenched down on him, and he groaned. I knew he was close too. I shuddered and sucked in a breath.

Feliks lifted me off him, spun me to face the side of the tub, then thrust into me from behind. I clung to the porcelain as he pounded my pussy, taking what he wanted. What we both needed…

"Yes! Don't stop. Feliks, I… I'm going to…" A long keening sound escaped me as I came again. This time, I felt the heat of his release as he pumped his cum into me.

He panted for breath and pressed his forehead to my shoulder. "You'll be the death of me, Raina. I can see my headstone now. *Here lies Feliks. His wife fucked him so well, she drew his soul from his body.*"

I couldn't stop the snort that escaped me, or the giggle that followed. "Did you just infer I'm a succubus? I didn't suck out your soul!"

"You're right." He sighed. "Besides, I'm not entirely certain I have one anymore. But if I did, you'd be welcome to it. Everything I have is yours."

"All I want is you," I whispered.

He kissed my shoulder, then my neck and my cheek. "And you have me."

He helped me clean up before we got out of the tub. As we lounged in bed, both sated and content, he started talking about wedding arrangements. The thought of testing wedding cakes, picking out flowers, and going dress shopping might have excited some women. For me, I felt panic welling inside me. I didn't know how to do any of that!

"Feliks, could we hire someone to do those things?" I asked, giving him a tentative look. "I wouldn't know where to start, and it sounds overwhelming. I'd be happy with a quiet ceremony."

He shook his head. "The Vor asked to receive an invitation. We must have a proper wedding, *lastachka*. But if you don't want to handle the details, I'll ask a wedding planner to come to the house. You can discuss some options and I'll give them a budget. Will that work?"

"Yes. Thank you, Feliks."

"Anything for you." He kissed me softly. "My beautiful soon-to-be wife."

"Don't forget the appointment with the doctor tomorrow. I've never been to one before and you promised you'd go with me."

He nodded. "And I will. I'll make sure Viktor knows I won't be available during your visit. I'm just as eager to find out more about the baby as you are."

I wasn't certain eager was the right word. More like terrified. But now that I knew Feliks loved me, that he wanted a future with me and our child, my anxiety had lessened a great deal. As long as he stood beside me, I knew I could face anything. Even motherhood.

Chapter Nine

Feliks

As I looked around the waiting room, I realized there were few husbands or boyfriends attending these appointments. One man had clearly come with his mistress. Another seemed to be the girl's parent. If I had a daughter, she wouldn't be pregnant until after she'd wed. I'd forbid any man from looking at her and shoot anyone who dared. He clearly didn't know how to protect his family. Imbecile.

"Raina Sobol," a nurse called out from an open doorway.

"That's us, *lastachka*."

She whispered in my ear as she stood, "That's not my name yet."

"I wasn't going to permit you to put Leeds down, now was I? Besides, we'll be married in a few weeks."

I held her hand as we followed the nurse. She had Raina stand on a scale, noted her weight, then led us to a room. As they checked Raina's vitals, I glanced at the posters on the walls. After the nurse left, I went to Raina and took her hands in mine. Lifting them, I kissed her fingers before pressing my lips to hers.

"Excited?" I asked.

"Nervous," she admitted.

"There's nothing to be scared of. You'll see."

"The doctor is a woman, right? You made sure?" she asked.

And then I understood her stress. My sweet Raina worried a man would be checking her or delivering her baby. I'd never permit such a thing. No one would dare see her body again, except me. As it was, anyone we ran into who had hurt her in the past wouldn't remain living for long. I'd take them out, one at a time, until I'd rid the world of their filth.

"Mr. and Mrs. Sobol?" a man asked as he entered the room. "I'm Dr. Gray. I'm afraid Dr. Pierce has been called out for an emergency C-section, so I'll be handling the exam today."

I felt Raina tense and knew she was about to panic. The doctor seemed kind enough, his gaze merely clinical as he studied Raina. But I knew we'd have to return when the female doctor was available.

"My apologies, Dr. Gray, but my wife will be uncomfortable if you perform her exam. We'll reschedule for a time when she can meet with Dr. Pierce."

"I can assure you I've seen it all before," the doctor said, smiling a little. "This is my job, and not something that gives me that sort of pleasure. I enjoy bringing babies into the world, but that's it. I promise I won't do anything inappropriate, and you can remain here with your wife during the visit."

Raina trembled and I nodded for the doctor to step into the hall. I kissed Raina's cheek and told her I'd return in a moment. When I left the room, I pulled the door shut behind me. "Dr. Gray, what do you know of my wife?" I asked.

"Her chart says it's her first visit, and she believes she's about five to six weeks along."

I lowered my voice and stepped closer, not wanting everyone to hear Raina's story. And I'd only tell the man what I thought he needed to know, in order for him to understand her hesitance over him touching her, even in a clinical way. "A man purchased Raina when she was barely five years old. While she was still a child, he let men rape her as payment for his debts. Her reluctance over having a male doctor doesn't have anything to do with you personally. She fears men, and having someone other than me touching her, or seeing intimate parts of her body, could trigger a panic attack. Do you understand?"

Sympathy filled his eyes, as well as a few tears. "I see. I'm so very sorry she went through something so awful. Of course, I understand why she'd want a female doctor. If you'd still like to be seen today, I may have another option for you. My sister is a midwife. There are times, like this instance, when Dr. Pierce and I agree to let my sister visit a patient. My sister is down the hall."

"Get her," I said. "And thank you."

I went back into the room to give Raina the news. She'd paled and worried at her lip until it started to bleed. I held her to me, murmuring to her softly until she calmed. "You'll see a midwife today, and we'll set another appointment with Dr. Pierce."

"Thank you, Feliks. I'm sorry I'm so broken that I can't handle even seeing a doctor."

"Hush," I said, smoothing her hair back from her face. Her curls sprang wildly, and I smiled, remembering how much I'd loved them the first time I'd set eyes on her. I still loved her hair.

A knock sounded and the woman I assumed to be the midwife hustled into the room. "I'm Mary Gray. My brother let me know I could be of some assistance today." She smiled warmly at Raina. "I don't have a medical degree like my brother or Dr. Pierce, but with the help of one of the technicians, I think we can still do a rather thorough exam today."

"Thank you, Ms. Gray," I said, stepping to the side and releasing Raina.

I remained close as she asked Raina questions and introduced her to the technician who would be assisting during the visit. We were able to hear the baby's heartbeat, and my heart felt like it swelled three sizes. I'd never realized I could love a person I'd never seen. Not until then. Knowing Raina was pregnant and having solid proof were two different things. It made the baby seem more real to me.

By the time the visit ended, and we'd set a new appointment, I had so many emotions trying to burst free. I'd always thought myself to be cold. Unfeeling. A monster. It seemed Raina was humanizing me. With her, I became a husband. A father. An everyday man who had the same desires as everyone else. The blood on my hands vanished in those moments, and it felt as if we lived in our own little world.

Until my phone rang, and Viktor's name flashed on the screen.

"I'm still with Raina. We're just leaving the doctor," I said, hoping he hadn't called to assign me a job.

"We have a small problem."

"How small?" I asked.

Viktor cleared his throat. "About the size of a five-year-old. I need you to come to the house. Now."

Well, fuck. "Can I take Raina home first?"

"*Nyet*. Bring her. She can visit with Cerys. Besides, you'll need her for this one."

The call dropped and I stared at my phone. A five-year-old problem and it required Raina? What the hell was going on?

I helped Raina into the car and headed toward Viktor's house. I filled her in on the call, and pressed the pedal a little harder, wanting to get this -- whatever it was -- out of the way. At the house, I led Raina inside.

"Viktor, is this necessary today of all days?" I

asked. "I'd planned to take Raina to lunch in celebration of hearing our baby's heartbeat."

Viktor stepped to the side, leaving Cerys in view... Along with a five-year-old little girl. I stared and nearly staggered back a step. It couldn't be. I looked from the child to Raina and back.

"*Lastachka*, you said Leeds always made men use protection, yes?"

"Of course," she said, frowning. "I mean... He didn't at first. Not until I got really sick. He said it was because someone had been careless. After that, he changed the rules for the men who came to the house."

My throat started to close as I looked at the small girl. There was no doubt in my mind. The child belonged to Raina. How did she not realize she'd had a baby? Exactly how young had she been? I did the math quickly. According to Aleksi, Raina was nineteen. He'd tracked down her birth records in Tahiti and arranged for the proper documentation. My woman would have been fourteen when she gave birth to the child, which meant it was possible she'd been thirteen when she conceived. If Leeds weren't already dead, I'd have murdered him with my bare hands right then and there.

"*Lastachka*, during that illness... did your stomach get bigger? Were you sick in the mornings? Do you remember pain later?" I asked.

"I... I..." She swayed, and I put my arm around her waist. "Are you saying... Is that... She's..."

"Yes, Raina. I believe you were pregnant, and that's your daughter. *Our* daughter." I faced her, putting myself between her and everyone else. Pressing my forehead to hers, I hoped I could calm her. How could she have had a child and not known? I wouldn't have put it past Leeds to have drugged her.

"I'm sorry you went through that, Raina. You must have been terrified. Confused. Alone. But you have me now, and we can take care of her together."

Viktor approached, and I glanced down, seeing the little girl being towed in his wake. She stared up at me with wide, brown eyes, so much like her mother's. Her skin was a bit lighter, and her hair held hints of blonde. Wondering about her sperm donor would only drive me crazy. It was best if we never found out.

Kneeling, I smiled at her. "What's your name?"

Her eyes widened and she trembled. My heart ached at the knowledge she'd likely been hurt for speaking. She didn't even feel safe answering a direct question.

I stood and held Viktor's gaze. "Where did you find her?"

"Remember the errand Maksim went on?" I nodded. "He found her in the basement. Chained inside a cage. Cerys cleaned her up and got new clothes for her. We weren't sure if we should call you or not, but the girl needs her family."

I felt Raina move closer, and I reached out to take her hand. She leaned into me and whispered in my ear, "Gary kept me in a cage until I bled the first time. Then he moved me to a room upstairs. Since he kept me chained, I never went downstairs again. Was she there the entire time?"

I held her hand tighter. It was possible. No, probable. Telling her that wouldn't change anything. I merely kissed her forehead and hoped she'd let the matter go. I didn't want her to blame herself for this. Together, we kneeled in front of the girl.

"I'm Raina," my woman said. "And this is Feliks. I... I think I might be... your mom."

Tears gathered in the little girl's eyes. "Momma's

dead."

I growled softly and cut it off the moment I saw fear in the child's eyes. "*Nyet*. They lied to you. I'd bet all my money your mother is right here, kneeling beside me. And since you're her daughter, and she's about to become my wife, it makes you my daughter, too."

"Gary Leeds was an evil man," Raina said. "He hurt me. Let other men break me. But he's gone, and you're safe. Did he... did he touch you?"

"Only when it was bath day," the little girl said, her voice a near whisper. "He washed me in cold water. Said he had to scrub me good to get me clean."

Bile rose in my throat, and I saw Raina was close to losing control of her emotions. We didn't need to scare the child. She'd been traumatized enough already.

"And your father?" Raina asked.

"He hasn't come to see me in a long time," the little girl said. "He was mean, and I didn't like him."

I looked up at Viktor and knew he was every bit as heartbroken and furious as I was. All these years. Raina had a child, someone she could have loved who would have loved her in return, and they'd been locked up separately in that house. If I'd had any idea the day I'd removed her from Leeds' home, I would have taken the little girl with me. "Your mom is going to have another baby," I said. "Taking care of them will be a big job. I'm not sure she and I will be able to handle it on our own. Do you think you'd want to come live with us and help care for your brother or sister?"

She glanced from me to Raina and back, a spark of hope in her eyes. God. It gutted me, reminding me so much of Raina when I'd first made her think she'd be safe. Wanted.

"And you'll be my new daddy?" she asked.

I nodded. "I will. And I can promise, no more cold baths. You can either wash yourself, or your mother can help. You will be protected. Loved. Your mother and I would be honored to have you live with us."

"I don't have a name," she said. "They just called me Girl."

"Your mother is from an island. It's why you and she have such beautiful golden skin. My country is far from here, and much different. Would you like a name to honor your mother's people, or mine? Or perhaps you want an American name since you were born here?" I asked.

"Can I have two names?" she asked. "Can you both give me one?"

I nodded. "We can do that. But first, let's go home. You can pick your room and tell me your favorite colors. We'll have it decorated before bedtime tonight."

Raina slowly reached for the girl, her hand shaking. My heart broke for my *lastachka*. My mind spun from this revelation, and I could only imagine how much worse it was for her, to have given birth and not even realized it had happened.

The little girl threw herself into Raina's arms, and I watched as they hugged and cried. Unable to hold back, I wrapped them both in an embrace, and vowed to keep them safe at all costs.

When I looked up, Viktor and Cerys were gone, and we'd been left alone in the front entry. I led my girls to the car and wondered what other surprises would come our way. For all our sakes, I hoped we had an uneventful few weeks.

* * *

Raina

A daughter. How the hell had I given birth to a daughter and never known? I tried to think back. I remembered being sick. Getting fatter. Although, I hadn't gained anywhere near as much weight as other women seemed to. My belly had gotten slightly bigger, but I'd never looked like the pregnant women I'd seen on TV since Feliks saved me. It hadn't been enough to make me think anything was wrong other than being ill.

Gary had monitored what I could and couldn't see. I hadn't had any idea what a pregnancy looked or felt like. I'd been little more than a chained pet since the age of five.

I remembered intense pain one day, and... nothing. I'd been sore between my legs for weeks after. Considering how often the men liked hurting me there, I'd assumed Gary had knocked me out and let men use me while I'd been unconscious. It wouldn't have been the first time.

Had they drugged me? Was that why I didn't remember giving birth? If they had, would it have harmed my child?

Feliks had given her the name Vera, and after researching Tahitian names, I'd chosen Heimana. Vera Heimana Sobol. Our daughter had shone as bright as the biggest star once she'd received her name.

I watched her from the doorway of her bedroom. Feliks had the walls painted lavender, after discovering Vera loved all things purple. Any shade of the color made her happy. He'd filled the room with toys of all sorts. Art supplies, dolls, stuffed animals, games... He'd given her a small table and chairs, with a tea set.

At the moment, she was having a party with her favorite doll and stuffed lion.

I felt the heat of Feliks' body behind me right before his arm snaked around my waist. It had been a week since we'd brought Vera home. As often as I stood here watching her, I caught him doing the same thing. In the middle of the night, I'd wake and find myself alone in bed. Every single time, Feliks would be hovering outside our daughter's door, watching her sleep.

"She's beautiful, like her mother," he murmured.

"And resilient. It's like nothing bad ever happened."

He tightened his hold on me. "She remembers. But children adapt better than most adults. She can tell we love her and trusts us to protect her. That's enough for now. Perhaps one day, the memories of her past will fade."

"Do you wish you knew who her father was?" I asked.

"I'm her father. The only one she'll ever have, or need."

I smiled and leaned into him. "Still want that big wedding? Between the baby growing inside me, and getting to know our daughter, I'm not sure I have the energy for anything else right now. But I want to be your wife, Feliks. I want it more than anything."

"The Vor is in town still. I'll call Viktor and have him set something up. How about a small ceremony in our backyard? It's a sunny day. I'm sure Viktor could bribe enough people to have a priest marry us today."

"Please. That's all I want or need. Any of the outfits you've bought me will be fine. I don't need fancy things, Feliks."

"I know." He kissed my neck. "As you've often

said, you only need me."

I nodded. He was right. Well, partially. I now knew I needed our daughter and the baby we'd created as well. Family. That's what I needed and wanted. *Our* family.

"Get Vera ready. Tell her the big news, and then my two girls need to dress in their fanciest attire. I'll ask the cook to prepare something, as soon as I've spoken with Viktor. Would you like me to have someone come to the house and help with your hair? Paint your nails?"

"I think Vera would enjoy that," I said.

"I'll handle it." He kissed me again and walked off, pulling out his phone to start making calls.

I went into Vera's room, drawing her attention away from her tea party. She smiled widely and shot up out of the chair. Running to me, she threw her arms around my legs and hugged me. "Momma!"

"I have something to tell you. We're going to have a party later. A wedding." I tipped up her chin. "Want to come get pretty with me? Daddy said to put on our best clothes, and he's going to ask someone to fix our hair. Sound like fun?"

She nodded eagerly and took my hand. I flipped through the dresses in her closet and selected the nicest one, then led her to my bedroom. I draped her dress across the back of a chair while I studied my own wardrobe. I still had several dresses with tags on them. One in particular caught my attention. Cream silk. The dress itself was a simple design, but I thought it would be perfect for a wedding dress. Especially for a backyard event. I set it out, along with some matching shoes.

The next hour passed in a blur. True to his word, Feliks paid someone to come help us feel beautiful. The woman pulled my hair up but left some curls loose. The makeup she'd put on me was light and accented my looks. She even put a little pink lip gloss on Vera, who kept twirling and calling herself a princess.

A knock sounded at the door, and Aleksi entered the room. "Raina, it's time."

I pressed my hands to my stomach and smiled. "I'm ready. Come along, Vera."

Aleksi held out his arm to me. "I'd be honored if I could escort you. I know you don't have family here. Permit me to walk you down the aisle?"

"Thank you, Aleksi." I kissed his cheek.

We descended the stairs and went out into the backyard. I gasped when I saw how it had been transformed. Someone had brought in a gazebo and strung twinkling lights around the top, then twined white and pink roses around the bottom. Feliks waited inside with the priest. His heated gaze warmed my cheeks and made me eager to celebrate our marriage later, after everyone had left and Vera had gone to bed.

With Vera's hand in mine, and me clutching Aleksi's arm, we walked to Feliks. Vera held tight throughout the ceremony, and I realized she needed this as much as I did. I may have given birth to her, but she wanted to be a part of this special day, to feel as if she belonged. I knew the fear she felt, and I'd do anything to ease it.

Feliks and I said our vows, had our first kiss as husband and wife, and then he did something that nearly took me to my knees. He kneeled down and held up a small gold ring for Vera.

"Vera, you're the daughter of my heart, and I hope I can be the dad you deserve. Would you wear this ring as a token of how much I love you? I vow to always protect you, to dry your tears, kiss all your booboos, and chase away all the boys." He grinned. "Even the ones you don't want me to run off. Because you're my little girl and no one will ever be good enough for you."

Vera had tears slipping down her cheeks as she hugged Feliks. I didn't hear what she whispered in his ear, but the look on his face told me enough. He held her, told her he loved her, then slipped the little ring onto her finger.

"Come! We'll eat, dance, and celebrate the greatest day in my life… because today, I officially gain a beautiful wife and the smartest, bravest daughter in the world."

Someone raised a champagne flute. I thought it might the man they called the Vor. "To the Sobol family! May you live long and have many happy memories together."

Everyone cheered and I leaned into Feliks. "I love you, Feliks."

"I love you too. More than you'll ever know." He kissed my temple. "You tamed the monster, *lastachka*. Showed me exactly what I'd been missing in my life and have given me the greatest gift of all. I can never repay you, but I look forward to loving you every day for the rest of my life."

Vera ran off with some other children, and they squealed and played nearby while the adults drank, ate, and danced the hours away. I'd never had the opportunity to dance. While I'd thought I would feel awkward, being in Feliks' arms made all the difference. We swayed to a slow song, and I heard the click of a camera. It wasn't the first time someone had taken our picture at the wedding.

"Mr. Sobol, I'd like to get a shot of you and your family," a man said.

I turned and Feliks called Vera over. We posed in front of the gazebo and had no less than a dozen pictures taken in different poses. My feet began to ache, and fatigue pulled at me.

"Sit," Feliks said, leading me back to our table. "Not much longer. I'll send our guests home soon, but it would be rude to toss them out too early. While I'd intended to pay for our wedding, the Vor, Viktor, and Maksim said it was their gift to us. The man taking pictures is Aleksi's present. And Ilya decided his gift was better suited for Vera."

"What gift?" I asked. Feliks pointed and I turned in time to see Vera and a little white puppy running through the yard. "He gave her a dog?"

"Not just any dog. When it's old enough, it will be trained to protect Vera. It's her own personal guard dog. Or will be. We'll have to make sure she doesn't spoil it too much."

"I never dreamed I'd have this life," I said. "If you hadn't come to Gary's that day… if he hadn't offered me to you…"

"I like to think Fate would have brought us together another way, but it's hard to say. What I do know is I was wrong that day. I'd thought of you as an unwanted complication. A problem I needed to resolve so I could carry through with my plans." He cupped my cheek. "But you're very much wanted, Raina. And you don't complicate my life at all. In fact, you're the reason I get up in the morning. I'm sorry I ever thought of you as anything other than essential."

"We have a lifetime for you to make it up to me." I smiled. "I think an eternity of your love should be a good enough price."

"And you have it. My love. My heart. My everything…"

He kissed me soft and slow. I didn't know what our future would bring, or if we'd run into more trouble along the way, but I'd never been happier than I was in that moment. A husband. A daughter. And a baby on the way. Life couldn't have possibly gotten better. I had everything I could ever want or need, and the love of a man people called a monster. But he was *my* monster, and I knew he'd do anything to protect me. Even bathe the town in the blood of our enemies.

For some women, that might be terrifying. For me… it meant everything.

Epilogue

Feliks

My hair stood on end from running my hands through it. If Raina screamed one more time, I might very well kill the doctor. I thanked every god in the known universe I'd left Vera in the waiting room with Viktor, Cerys, and their daughter, Alina. If she'd seen her mother like this, it might have scarred her for life.

"Push, Mrs. Sobol," Dr. Pierce said.

"I…" *Pant. Pant.* "Am…" *Pant.* "Pushing!"

She squeezed my hand and I worried she might break the bones, but I'd let her. I'd fracture every bone in my body if it would take away her pain. I hated the way she suffered through this delivery, but we'd arrived too late for them to give her much for the pain. Her contractions had gone from six minutes apart to two minutes far too fast. I'd half expected to deliver my son on the side of the road. Instead, he'd stubbornly remained inside Raina for several more hours.

"You can do it, *lastachka*."

Her gaze held mine, and then she screamed long and loud. One more big push and our son entered the world. My sweet Raina collapsed back on the bed and looked seconds away from sleep. I couldn't blame her. The delivery had been far from easy on her, and I knew she hadn't been sleeping well the past few nights.

"You did so well, *lastachka*. Our son is beautiful, like his mother." I kissed her brow. "Rest a moment."

The nurses carried our boy away. He returned, clean and wrapped in a blanket. The hair on his head wasn't quite as dark as Raina's, and I wondered if it might be the color of mine as he got older. But his skin was the same beautiful gold as his sister's.

"Ivan Sobol," I said as I took him in my arms for the first time. "Would you like to see your mother?"

I carried him to Raina and helped her sit up to hold him. A nurse remained, to walk Raina through the first nursing, and our boy latched on right away. He drank greedily, until his eyes began to droop.

"He's so small, Feliks," Raina said. "So defenseless."

"That's why he has me." I kissed her, then our son's head. "I'll keep the monsters away, until he's old enough to take care of not only himself, but his mother and sister too."

"Have you told everyone?" she asked, glancing at the door.

"*Nyet.* I wanted another moment with the two of you, but I'll get Vera. I'll ask the others to wait at least fifteen minutes before coming back to see Ivan. They won't stay long. Everyone knows you're exhausted."

I stopped in the doorway, admiring Raina and Ivan. Discreetly, I took out my phone and snapped a picture. With a smile, I saved it and went to get our daughter and inform my friends and colleagues my son had been born.

In the waiting room, everyone stood the moment they saw me.

"Ivan has arrived and is currently nursing." I grinned. "But he'd very much like to meet his big sister. Vera, are you ready to see your mother?"

She bounced on her toes and ran to me. I lifted her into my arms.

"Does he look like me?" she asked.

"A little. I think you'll like him. And he's going to need you. You'll have to teach him all sorts of things."

"Feliks, tell Raina congratulations," Cerys said.

"We'll wait here to give the four of you a little time to bond. Just send a nurse to get us when Raina is ready for visitors."

"Thank you." I looked around the room. "All of you. We're glad you could be here with us."

Carrying Vera down the hall, she gasped when she first saw her brother, then squirmed to get down. She went running for the bed and I had to catch her, placing my hand on her shoulder.

"Be gentle, Vera. Your momma still hurts, and you might startle Ivan if you move too quickly."

She nodded, eyes wide as she stared at the baby. "He's so cute. He's really my brother?"

"Of course." I ran my hand over her curls. "Let me help you up beside your momma, but be still once you're on the bed."

She lifted her arms and I picked up her, placing her beside Raina. My wife put her arm around Vera, tugging her closer, as they both peered down at Ivan. I took another picture, and knew I'd frame it for my office.

I'd thought I needed power. Money. To be feared.

What I'd really needed was in this room with me. A family. Love. And a wife who accepted me, darkness and all.

"I love you," I said. "All of you."

Raina smiled at me, looking tired, yet radiant.

"We love you too, Daddy," Vera said, not even taking her eyes off the baby.

I'd been a heartless, soulless man. I'd had nothing to lose except my pride.

Now I had *everything* to lose… and God help anyone who tried to take my family from me, because I'd rain down hell and bury them all.

Harley Wylde

Harley Wylde is the International Bestselling Author of the Dixie Reapers MC, Devil's Boneyard MC, and Hades Abyss MC series. When Harley's writing, her motto is the hotter the better -- off-the-charts sex, commanding men, and the women who can't deny them. If you want men who talk dirty, are sexy as hell, and take what they want, then you've come to the right place. She doesn't shy away from the dangers and nastiness in the world, bringing those realities to the pages of her books, but always gives her characters a happily-ever-after and makes sure the bad guys get what they deserve.

The times Harley isn't writing, she's thinking up naughty things to do to her husband, drinking copious amounts of Starbucks, and reading. She loves to read and devours a book a day, sometimes more. She's also fond of TV shows and movies from the 1980s, as well as paranormal shows from the 1990s to today, even though she'd much rather be reading or writing. You can find out more about Harley or enter her monthly giveaway on her website. Be sure to join her newsletter while you're there to learn more about discounts, signing events, and other goodies!

Harley at Changeling: changelingpress.com/harley-wylde-a-196

Paige Warren

Paige Warren is a contemporary romance author who believes in happy-ever-after for everyone. Sexy, steamy stories about mobsters, cowboys, inked bad boys, and interracial couples… sometimes with a bit of kink. If you like alpha heroes and strong heroines, then you're in the right place! No matter the odds, in a Paige Warren book, true love conquers all.

When her husband, children, and furbabies aren't demanding her attention, she's typically either writing or reading. Paige enjoys reading a variety of genres from young adult books, to general fiction, and of course, romances! But when it comes to movies, she's a big-time horror fan -- especially the '80s slasher flicks. That being said, ghostly movies are her favorites regardless of when they were made, like Rose Red or The Amityville Horror.

Paige at Changeling: changelingpress.com/paige-warren-a-202

Changeling Press E-Books
More Sci-Fi, Fantasy, Paranormal, and BDSM adventures available in e-book format for immediate download at ChangelingPress.com -- Werewolves, Vampires, Dragons, Shapeshifters and more -- Erotic Tales from the edge of your imagination.

What are E-Books?
E-books, or electronic books, are books designed to be read in digital format -- on your desktop or laptop computer, notebook, tablet, Smart Phone, or any electronic e-book reader.

Where can I get Changeling Press E-Books?
Changeling Press e-books are available at ChangelingPress.com, Amazon, Apple Books, Barnes & Noble, and Kobo/Walmart.

ChangelingPress.com